PENANCE

DEBRA DUNBAR

debra dunbar

FIENDISHLY FUN FICTION

CHAPTER 1

$\mathcal{A}$wakening was like the reverse of a white light at the end of a tunnel. I was moving into the darkness instead of away from it. Everything felt heavy and thick. I was suddenly solid, slow, dim. And something smelled really, really bad.

"Looks like she's breathing after all. I'm glad she's not dead." A voice swam into my mind—a woman's voice, tobacco-raw and full of sarcasm.

There was a soft laugh in response. "Me too. I wasn't looking forward to being locked in with a ripening corpse."

I forced my eyes open, wondering if someone had glued them shut as I'd slept. A blurred form came into focus inches from my face—wavy black hair coming loose from a messy pony tail, and exotic, dark eyes in a brown angular face. For a brief second I saw beyond her skin to a soul that was battered and tired, but bright with an inner glow of strength. Then the glow fell away and all I saw was a young woman—little more than a girl—with worried eyes far older than the face they adorned.

"*Smells* like she's dead."

It was *me* that stank? Although as I inhaled, I realized I wasn't the only one with significant body odor.

"Gah. Damn, did they find her sleeping in the sewer? Neck deep in animal carcasses? How the hell can someone smell that bad and still be alive?"

The voice came from my right—the sarcastic smoker voice. I tried to turn my head to see the speaker, but couldn't. My neck was making alarming popping noises with the effort, as if I'd lain in this position for weeks and everything had locked tight.

"Knock it off, Sugar," the woman in front of me said. "We all stink. And we'll probably stink a whole lot worse before we get out of here."

Where was 'here'? My head was killing me. My mouth tasted like someone had filled it with salt and cotton balls. My limbs were beginning to twitch with a life of their own. I wasn't sure if that was preferable to the frozen sensation I'd had a few moments ago or not. My sense of smell came fully on-line and I immediately wished it hadn't. The air reeked of unwashed, sweaty bodies and diarrhea. And yes, I was one of those unwashed, sweaty bodies. When was the last time I'd bathed?

"She's a junkie," another voice said. "Scoring the next fix takes priority over personal hygiene, and it's not like flophouses have running water and hotel-sized bottles of shampoo."

Junkie? Flophouse? That didn't sound right, or maybe it did. Blurred memories surfaced briefly then vanished—a favorite childhood movie, a book read a few months back, the rich sweetness of Boston cream pie, the warmth of a soft blanket. I frowned and tried to think of something more specific about my junkie-self, but came up with only these shadows. *Was* I a junkie? I couldn't seem to remember. In fact, the last thing I remembered was...

Nothing.

Panic shot through my chest as I struggled to sit. I had nothing but vague emotions and fleeting impressions, not what I'd done the day before or the week before. Not the details of my childhood. Not my parents. Not anything about where I lived, the car I drove, or even what I looked like. Who was I? And *where* was I?

"Easy, easy." Warm hands grabbed my arms, steadying me as the woman with the exotic dark eyes peered at me with concern. "You're safe. No one here is going to hurt you."

"Except for the guys. They'll probably hurt you," Sugar added.

Who? Hurt me? Something in my midsection twisted and I tasted bile.

"If you've got to puke, do it in the corner. And try to do it quietly. I don't wanna hear that shit."

Sugar again. I was beginning to sense the irony of her name, and couldn't help feeling a twinge of amusement. But I *did* have to puke. Somehow through my gagging I was dragged into a corner where I dry heaved over a pile of very wet excrement. How long had we been in here that everyone had taken to relieving themselves in a corner? Had I been peeing in my pants, or had I arrived here after the rest of them? And where exactly were we?

Gentle hands held my hair, and the woman who'd helped me whispered reassurances in a soft voice. She'd help me. She'd keep me safe. The woman was just as dirty and smelly as the rest of us, but I appreciated that she'd assumed the role of my protector. I was so weak, so sick, confused and out of place in this body that felt like it was trying to turn itself inside out.

When I was finished throwing up, at least for the moment, I scooted away from the poop pile and propped my back against the wall. That's when I started to shake.

"It's gonna be rough for a while," the dark-eyed woman warned me. "It's cold-turkey, hon. Ain't gonna be easy, but I'll do what I can to help you."

I reached out to grip her hand, holding tight as if she were my lifeline, my guardian angel. The feel of her skin against mine, the pressure of her fingers, the way her nails with their chipped polish dug into my palm…it grounded me.

"I changed my mind. Think I'd rather be locked in with a corpse than a junkie," Sugar muttered.

"Shut it, Sugar," my savior shot back. "I seem to remember doin' the same for you a few times."

"I was hung over, not coming down off a years-long heroin bender," Sugar retorted.

Heroin. I looked down at my trembling arms, seeing the tell-tale track marks. No wonder I felt so sick. I might not know where I was or who I was, but clearly I *was* a heroin user, which meant the headache and dry heaves were going to be the least of my problems during the next few days.

"You'll feel worse. Gets real bad around day three or four, but it'll be better after that. Just hang in there." I felt the woman's other hand smooth my hair and leaned against her, my teeth chattering so hard I feared they might break apart.

"This is going to suck," Sugar complained. "If they were going to grab a junkie, they should have brought some drugs as well—for us if not for her."

"Well, they didn't and I doubt they're going to pull over to juice her up." The dark-eyed woman commented. "Poor thing."

Pull over? For the first time I recognized the swaying, the frequent jolt of what I'd assumed was a very small window-less room. We were in a vehicle in motion—one with very poor shocks. There were ventilation slats up near the top that let in a tiny bit of light, and an even tinier bit of fresh air judging by the hot, close stench of our surroundings. The rear of the truck trailer had a roll-up door that looked to be tightly locked down, and up front on the side away from the poop pile, was a much smaller access door—no doubt equally locked down.

The door seemed to swell from the middle, like the metal had suddenly become a balloon. I stared hard at it, convinced that if I focused I could break it open and set us all free—or at the very least get some much-needed fresh air in here.

"Crap, she's burning up." I felt a hand on my forehead. "She shouldn't be running a fever this soon."

We don't have any medication for her. No cold towels, or even water.

Was that the dark-eyed woman's thoughts I had heard? She was concerned I might die, worried that she couldn't protect me as she'd promised. She had to help me. I was weak. She'd been weak once too, and there'd been people who helped her. Pay it back. And hope that in her time of need, someone would be there once again to protect her.

Heaven above, I *must* be running a heck of a fever if I was hallucinating and imagining myself reading other people's minds.

"She's gonna die, you know. I say we strangle her and do us all a favor." Sugar crossed her arms, her gaze unemotional as it swept me. "Probably do her a favor too."

The chorus of voices berating Sugar were drowned out by my resumed retching. I crawled back toward the poop pile, not sure if it was motion sickness, the odor of human waste and unwashed bodies, or the lack of drugs in my system causing my stomach to revolt in this fashion. It was all I could do to remain on my knees and to keep from falling into the wet excrement. No matter how horrible I felt, I knew my agony would be worse if I face-planted into the toilet space.

"Water," I croaked between dry heaves.

"Hon, if we had any water, I'd give you some."

The woman's voice was so kind that I couldn't help crying. Now I was puking acid out of the depths of my digestive system, and bawling my eyes out. Every inch of me hurt, and I couldn't stop trembling. When I'd finally stopped vomiting bile, arms held me tight and rocked me as I shook and muttered half-coherent words in a strange language.

"What the hell is she saying?" Sugar's voice seemed closer than it had been before. "Thought she was American. Don't tell me we've got another foreigner here who don't speak English."

"It's just the fever." The woman's hand was cool on my forehead and cheeks. "You sleep now, hon. Just sleep it all off. I'll be here, right by your side, okay?"

I replied and it came out that weird language, as if I were speaking in tongues. Then I fell silent, and slept, dreaming of a world where I flew on wings of crimson and gold, a world filled with anger and sorrow and grief, a world I wasn't sure I ever wanted to return to.

* * *

I'D BEEN AWAKENED by the truck coming to a stop. We'd sat, listening for something, anything to tell us what was going on. Sugar and the dark-eyed woman exchanged a silent, tense glance, then scooted closer to the side door while the other girls huddled together near the back of the truck. Doors slammed. There was a muffled, deep-voiced conversation, then a laugh that faded as if the drivers were walking away.

"Pit stop," a girl in the back with spiky blue hair whispered.

Why didn't we scream for help? Try to get the attention of someone parked nearby? I opened my mouth, only to snap it shut as the dark-eyed woman shot me a warning look. "Don't. They park us way out away from the other cars, and if we make noise, we don't get food or water."

"And they hit us," an accented voice added. It was dark in the truck, but I could see the girl who spoke was holding her arm at an odd angle. I was pretty sure the dark marks on her face were not just from dirt, either. "Last time…last time I scream and they take me out of truck to woods and hit me. And…what is the word?" The girl said something in a foreign language. Russian? It sounded Slavic, but I couldn't recognize it.

Something buzzed in the back of my head. There was a time when I knew this language. There was a time when I knew a great many languages, but that knowledge was locked behind some wall, as inaccessible as all the memories of my past.

"They fucked you, and not with their dicks either," Sugar said coarsely. "Probably got splinters all up in that thing."

I winced. The girl really didn't look well. She needed a doctor. That arm. The bruises. The way she sat angled against another girl up on one hip. She *needed* a doctor. Did these men not care if we lived or died? Did they not care that this poor girl was in obvious pain?

"Shhh." The dark-eyed woman put a finger to her lips and inclined her head toward the side of the truck. Once more we heard muffled conversation, then the clank of something metal.

A few seconds later, we were blinded by daylight as the access door opened and a man tossed in a plastic jug of murky water and a loaf of white sandwich bread. The jug thudded to its side, the bread narrowly missing our bathroom pile. Everyone sat as if they were frozen as the man peeked in at us, obviously counting. The moment he closed the door, everyone sprang forward, frantically trying to be first to the bottle of water.

"Share," the dark-eyed woman commanded. "Little sips, everyone. Pass it around and make sure everyone gets some. Tasha, too."

I looked over at the girl with the broken arm, still huddled safely away from the others where she wouldn't be jostled. The girl with the blue spiky hair took a swig from the bottle, then brought it over to Tasha, helping her to drink, handing it to me afterwards.

I sipped from the half-empty bottle. The liquid soothed my chapped lips, as I dribbled it into my mouth and down my parched throat. The water smelled like sulfur and iron, but nothing had ever tasted so sweet. I felt more stable than I had earlier, my stomach quiet in spite of the gnawing emptiness.

"Here." The dark-eyed woman handed me a few slices of crushed, dirt-smudged bread. The other girls were cramming pieces into their mouths, unconcerned about the lack of any sort of hygiene. I stared down at the soft bread and frowned. Hungry people didn't care about dirt. Starving people didn't think about bacteria or disease. Food and water. The bottom slab of the hierarchy of human needs. For some reason it all felt foreign, as if these needs didn't really apply to me.

"You gonna eat that?" A girl with a softly rounded face and a Spanish accent asked me, eyeing the bread.

I wasn't hungry, but I knew this body needed food. Still, I handed her one of the slices, forcing myself to take a bite of the other. It was artificially soft with preservatives, becoming a mushy glutinous lump on contact with my saliva. Something inside me rebelled at the thought of eating this bread. I ignored it and took another bite, wondering if I'd be puking this all up in another hour or so.

"You're detoxing really fast. Guess you weren't as much of a junkie as I thought." It was grudging praise from Sugar. And it gave me some hope that the bread and water I'd just consumed wouldn't be coming back up.

Her words made me realize that I *did* feel better than I had earlier. I sipped the water, taking little bites of the soft tasteless bread and closed my eyes, feeling something bright deep down that seared through my flesh, easing the desperate cravings and the horrible flu-like symptoms. I still radiated heat, but it was as if the drugs and addiction were being burned from my body rather than sickness. Cleansed by fire. Only in my case it was more like cleansed by fever.

By the time I'd finished with the bread, my shaking had subsided and I felt less like I was going to vomit my insides out. Straightening my legs, I looked around and wondered how long we'd be parked here before the men started up the truck again. It must have been close to noon and sunny out, because the light coming through the slats was stronger than it had been earlier. The space we were in seemed to be the back of a box truck by the size and shape. There was nothing inside except the eight other women. No straps, seats, mattresses—only the smelly pile in the left corner and the faint light that filtered through the open slats near the roof. I wondered not only how long we'd been rattling along in this truck, but why we were in here at all.

What had I been doing before I got here? I searched my memory and came up empty. No, not quite empty. There was a very clear knowledge of things like what music I liked, how warm pavement smelled after a rain, that real bread tasted far superior to this mushy stuff they'd given us. But beyond that, I only remembered vague shadowy impressions of what my life had been before today. I closed my eyes briefly and tried to concentrate and got only guilt. I'd done something wrong. No—I'd not done something I should have done. I'd been weak and others had suffered because of it. And now I needed to suffer as well.

Great. I was a woman with a martyr complex, with no idea who I was, or the circumstances that led me to be locked in a truck with eight unkempt women. The likely scenario was that I'd been shooting up and passed out somewhere when they grabbed me and put me in with these others. But why? If this was a drug intervention, it was definitely not like the sort I'd ever seen on TV.

"Where......where are we?" I asked.

I was a bit embarrassed about my strange amnesia, but it was time to swallow whatever pride I had and figure out what was going on. Remembering the marks on the inside of my arms, I figured whatever pride I'd once made claim to was long gone anyway.

"Whoa, she speaks. And she speaks English." Sugar took a bite of her bread. "We're in a truck, girlfriend. Thought that much was obvious."

"But where are we going? How long have we been in here? What's happening?" I looked around at the other women. "I don't remember much of anything."

Understatement of the year.

"I'm not sure how fast we're traveling, but we left New York City almost two days ago," the woman with short, spiky blue hair told me.

"They tossed you in here with us early this morning," the dark-eyed woman told me. "What town were you in when you last shot up? Might give us an idea of where we're headed."

I closed my eyes and tried to think of something, anything that might trigger a memory. Shooting up. Could I at least remember that?

Nope.

"I don't know. I don't remember," I confessed.

The dark-eyed woman shrugged. "You were so out of it we thought you were dead. Must have been one hell of a bender you were on if you don't remember what town you were in. Runaway?" She peered at me. "I thought maybe you were Kitten's age, but you look older now that the light is better."

"Junkies all look old," Sugar announced. "She's probably twelve. A couple more months on heroin and stores would have been offering her senior citizens' discounts."

"Her face doesn't look like a junkie's," the girl with the Spanish accent said. "Her skin is beautiful. It glows."

I blinked at her in surprise then looked down at my arms. The track marks were gone. All that remained was creamy-white, smooth flesh. And it did glow, as if I'd coated myself in some iridescent powder.

"You all came from New York?" I asked, my voice raspy, as if I were reviving long dead vocal cords.

"Yeah. They kept us chained in an old warehouse for a day or so before they loaded us up. One night some guy came through, herded us onto this truck, and off we went." Sugar shrugged. "Mess's and my pimp is probably raging around Soho, thinking we ran off on him."

The dark-eyed woman laughed. "Like hell he is. Who do you think sold us to these guys? Probably for a twenty and some smack."

Sugar spat into a corner of the truck. "Dick. I hope he ODs. It would serve him right."

New York City. I closed my eyes and clenched my teeth, trying to force some kind of memory into my mind. An apartment, a boyfriend, a job, some flophouse—anything. But nothing concrete prior to my waking up sick in this truck existed in my mind.

Nothing except the overpowering need to suffer, to atone for my sins. I'd done something horrible in my life—something that had nothing to do with the vanished track marks on my arms. I'd been weak, and made a horrible choice, and that choice was eating my insides worse than the stomach acids and bile.

"What's your name, hon?"

I looked up at the dark-eyed woman, having no idea what my name was. Thinking too hard about it only brought on a pounding headache.

She ran a hand over my shoulder. "That's okay. Two of us don't speak any English, and Sugar and I don't exactly go by the names on our Social Security cards anyway. Keep your secrets, bury your past. We're all in the same boat here."

We weren't. I would have gladly given her my name if I'd only known what it was. The throbbing grew in my temples, spreading down into the base of my skull as I contemplated the blank pages that told the story of my life.

"I'm Mess," she added, "as in One Hot Mess. That's Sugar, 'cause she's so sweet. Over there is Pistol, Kitten, Tasha, and Lacy. And that's Pillow, and Baa."

They were all semi-indistinct figures in the dim light of the truck, but one thing was clear—they were all young. Most looked to either be in high-school or barely out of it. All were dirty, with filthy clothing and wary eyes. Sugar had shoulder-length platinum blonde hair and was wearing a tattered and stained little black dress. Mess appeared to be a mix of African-American and Asian heritage, with an angular brown face and long, wavy hair. Kitten looked like a preteen with soft golden-brown curls spilling down past her shoulders, and Pistol was the one with the spiked blue hair. Tasha, Pillow, Lacy, and Baa were clustered near the front of the truck—Tasha cradling her broken arm. They all had dark hair, but I couldn't make out much of their features except for the fact that Pillow and Baa were curvier in build than the other two girls.

I nodded at each in turn, trying to appear friendly. I was vulnerable, a woman without a past on a truck bound to who-knows-where. I needed them. My life, my future depended on their assistance.

"What shall we call her?" Sugar asked, the usual cynical note in her voice. "Junkie? Red? New Girl?"

"She looks like that mermaid."

That statement came from the one introduced as Kitten. She stepped closer, and I caught my breath at how very young she appeared—I'd thought teenager, but she seemed barely that with her soft curls and a heart-shaped face.

"Mermaid?" Everyone looked at my legs, encased in a pair of torn, dirty blue jeans, not ending in a fin.

Kitten smiled at me, looking sweet and innocent. "Yes. The Disney one. Ariel."

Now everyone looked at my hair for some reason.

"Yeah, Ariel. That's what we'll call her," Pistol said with a laugh.

Sugar snorted. "I'm not calling her a Disney name. Red. Her name's Red."

Sounded good to me. It was better than Jane Doe in my book. "So why are you all on this truck?" I asked, more wondering why *I* was on this truck.

Mess scooted closer beside me. "Sugar and I were working girls who got on the wrong side of our pimp and found ourselves 'traded.' I don't know everyone's story. The foreign ones were probably lured over with the promise of jobs. The other girls are likely runaways."

"I'm not a runaway," Kitten's voice wobbled.

"Me either," Pistol added. "And it doesn't matter how we got here. All that matters is how we're going to escape, to get out."

"In a body bag, that's how we're gonna get out," Sugar replied. "Do you wanna end up like the Russian girl? Or worse? We shut up. We do as we're told. Hopefully once we fuck enough guys, we'll be allowed a little freedom. That's how these things work."

One of the curvy girls from the back edged forward, the one named Pillow. "Maybe we'll get arrested," she said in a soft, Spanish-accented voice. "Screw enough johns and one of them is bound to be an undercover cop. Then we can ask the police for help."

Mess shook her head. "Oh, girl, the cops won't believe one word you say. They'll lock you up for the night, then your pimp will come and spring you. Then he'll beat your ass for causing him the inconvenience."

"But most of us aren't even eighteen," Pillow protested. "I'm just sixteen. If I tell them—"

"If you tell them, they won't do shit," Sugar interrupted. "They'll say you're lying about your age so you don't have to be in jail. They'll call you a dirty whore. And when your pimp comes to get you, they'll think you probably deserve the beating you're gonna get. Girl, cops are not your friend. Getting arrested isn't gonna be your salvation."

"We just need to stick together," Mess told her. "Look out for each other. Try to protect each other as best as we can. It's not so bad. As long as we help each other out, we'll be okay."

"Not so bad?" Sugar laughed. "Standing on a corner and picking up five or six guys a night isn't so bad. Being stuck in a room and spreading 'em for twenty to forty a day is the meaning of bad. We'll be lucky if we can walk by the time they're done with us."

Kitten caught her breath and Mess tried to shush Sugar.

"What?" The blonde girl scowled. "I'm just telling it like it is."

I frowned in confusion. "So they're going to prostitute us out? We're going to be in some kind of sex ring?"

Sugar nodded. "Damn right. They'll stick us in a room and advertise us on a few internet sites. On the street, we did maybe five guys a night. We had a quota, but it was mostly just a money quota, not a guy quota. You could pick and choose who you wanted and what you'd do. Some girls went all basic and they'd need to do more to make the quota. Others would do kink and not have to screw as many guys to earn out."

"Most pimps take a cut, but there's a minimum you have to give them each night," Mess told me. "The more you pay, the less chance you've got of getting beat."

"These sex rings are worse," Sugar added. "Like I said, get ready for twenty to forty guys a day. You don't get to keep no money. You don't get to pick and choose who you screw or what you let them do to you. We're all whores now—the worst kind of whores."

"I'm not a prostitute," Pistol argued, the sharp edge of panic in her voice. "This is a mistake. I'm in college. I have a family, and friends. I'm not a prostitute. I won't do it. I'll just refuse and fight them. They can't make me have sex with a bunch of random guys."

Sugar laughed. "They *can* make you. Beat you enough, starve you enough, and you'll be happy to have sex with random guys. Look at Tasha back there. You think she wouldn't blow some nasty-ass guy to keep from having her arm broke, her face beat, and some stick shoved up her again? A few bruises and you'll fall in line and do as they say. We all will."

Pistol glared at her. "Guys won't want to have sex with a beat-up woman, or a starved one. I'll refuse. I'll fight. I'm not going to be a prostitute, no matter what happens."

Mess eyed her sadly. "Hon, the kind of guys who we'll be servicing don't care if you're bruised or got your ribs showing. They just want to screw a girl, and some of them might want to add a bruise or two to your collection. Fight all you want, but in the end same thing will happen. It'll just hurt worse."

I caught my breath, trying to comprehend what Sugar and Mess were saying about our future—about *my* future. Grabbed by a prostitution ring. Runaways, girls-on-the-corner, girls lured from their country with the promise of a job... With the exception of Pistol, they all seemed to be high-risk. I guess I was high-risk too, as an addict. I didn't want to imagine what kind of bottom-barrel prostitution ring this was that they scooped an ODing junkie off the street to sell. "Why me?" I asked, half to myself.

"Why'd *you* get nabbed?" Sugar snorted. "Damned if I know why they'd want a junkie. Well, actually I do know. You're gorgeous, even with the weird hair you've got going on. Your face...your skin...you're beautiful under all the vomit and track marks. That's probably the only reason they'd take a chance on buying a girl who might die before we got wherever we're going."

I looked back down at the smooth, clear, flawless skin, glowing with a pearlescent sheen. Rotating my arm, I didn't see any sign of the track marks. I didn't see a freckle, a mole, a scar, or anything beyond smooth flesh and a dusting of fine hair so pale that it blended in with the skin.

"You *are* beautiful," Kitten said, shyly reaching out to touch my hair. "Like a mermaid. Like an angel. So beautiful."

"Don't go getting all lezzy on us," Sugar told her. "It's gross enough in here without having to watch a bunch of carpet munchers go at it. Save that shit for later."

"How'd you get your hair that color?" Pistol asked, eyeing me curiously. "I need to freshen mine every week to keep it blue like this, and red is even harder—especially that color of red. You look like a cardinal, a red bird, turned into a human. All you need is a set of wings to go with that red hair."

I reached up to touch the knotted mess that was pulled back into a low, disordered bun and wished I had a mirror. Realizing how long the tresses were in their elastic, I yanked a lock free and pulled it in front of my face.

It was red. Red as in not-seen-in-nature red. Well, not-seen-on-a-human-head nature anyway. As Pistol had said, my hair was the color of a cardinal's wing. Bright, bright red.

I'd clearly dyed it at some point, and recently if what Pistol said was true. What color was under the dye? I wondered why I'd chosen this particular shade of red. Given the color of the hair on my arm, I assumed that I was a natural blonde. Maybe I'd felt too monochrome with that hair color. Maybe I'd wanted something shocking to stand out in a life where I felt I'd never been noticed.

Maybe it had been on sale at the drugstore and I'd figured what the heck?

"Where do you think we're going?" I asked, my voice still raspy from the vomiting and dehydration, and lack of use.

"Doesn't matter," Sugar told me. "When the truck stops, we'll be herded out, cleaned up, chained to a bed, and sold like a piece of meat until we're not worth paying to screw anymore. If we're lucky, they'll drug us to make it all bearable."

Kitten choked back a sob and turned her head, her shoulders shaking.

"Cut it out. You made your point earlier. No need to keep harping on it, scaring all the girls." Mess made a *tsk* noise and glared at Sugar as she put an arm around the other girl.

Sugar shrugged. "There's one reason girls like us get grabbed up, and that's to make a bunch of money for someone as sex slaves. Those foreign girls won't know how to escape, and the rest of us, except for the blue-haired college princess there, won't have anything to escape to.

When this truck stops, we're just gonna have to spread our legs and survive as best as we can."

"Stop it." Mess pulled Kitten into her arms, hugging her tight. "Just stop."

"There's no escape for us," Sugar continued. "None."

"No," Pillow protested, the word rolling with her Spanish accent. "We *can* escape. We can always escape. It's better on the streets on our own than living with someone who…" Her voice trailed off and my heart lurched as I mentally completed the rest of her sentence.

"We don't *know* what's going to happen," Pistol said, eyeing the other girls huddled in the back of the truck. "We don't know. There's no reason to go scaring everyone and panicking ourselves here. Because we don't know."

The look on her face said she *did* know what was going to happen, and her vision of her future was the same as Sugar's.

As for me, I doubted we'd be carted around in the back of a box truck for the rest of our lives. There had to be something planned for us, and I was pretty sure it would be unsavory. I might not remember anything beyond yesterday, but some time in my life I'd clearly read enough news to know a human trafficking operation when I saw one. I looked down at where the scars on my arms had once been. I didn't feel any incredible cravings, only grief and guilt, but I'd seen those scars when I'd first woken. And I knew in my heart why, if not how, I'd woken up here. Penance. I needed to repent, to make amends for a past I couldn't remember.

No matter who I'd been or what I'd done, I needed to atone. And I had a feeling that here, with these eight women, was where I was going to make amends. Here, with them, was my chance for redemption.

CHAPTER 2

The truck eventually rumbled to life. We braced as it bumped through whatever remote parking area we'd been in and sped up onto a main road. The light inside the truck faded as day slid into night, and we slept fitfully to the swaying, bumping motion. When dawn came we were still moving, our filthy water and loaf of bread long gone. By the time it started to become uncomfortably hot, the truck slowed, bounced over what were either speed bumps or some serious potholes, then jerked to a stop. We sat, sweltering in the heat, inhaling the wafting odor of our excrement and sweat as we waited. When our captors finally rolled open the back of the truck bed, we were blinded by the unfamiliar bright light.

When my vision adjusted, I saw we'd driven into a huge distribution-warehouse sort of building. It was one cavernous, open space with what looked like a stage against one wall, racks of folded metal chairs next to it. Along another wall were doors and shuttered windows—offices perhaps. The other wall was just one huge block of cement, a soda machine humming in the corner. I wasn't about to turn around and see what was behind me, but I envisioned a row of bay doors.

Three men stood outside the truck next to the two drivers who'd tossed the water and bread in to us. None of us so much as twitched. We were like rabbits, holding very very still in hopes the wolves at the door didn't notice us.

"Damn, Serge. You testing our ability to make diamonds from coal or something?" A man took a step closer. He was short and built like an elongated triangle with broad shoulders and narrow hips. Acne scars divoted his cheeks like pockmarks. His face twisted as he got a whiff of the inside of the truck.

"They're just dirty," one of the drivers said. "They'll clean up nice. King picked 'em out himself. Look, we even got a really young one. I'll bet she's a virgin too."

Mess moved to stand protectively in front of Kitten. I heard Pillow inhale sharply.

"Well, let's get them out of this truck and see what we've got." Pockmarks stepped back and rubbed his palms together. The small door near the front of the truck opened and we were trapped, the two drivers herding us forward with broom-handle sticks. There were no steps to climb out of the truck, so we each knelt and hopped down unaided, stumbling and falling as the three guys laughed.

None of us had eaten more than a few pieces of bread, and we were all seriously dehydrated and shaky. One of the women who'd been huddled up front the entire ride, a tiny Asian girl who didn't look a day over fifteen, tripped climbing out of the truck and fell. Her skirt slid up around her waist, and as she stood tugging it down, blood ran from a cut on her knee.

The heat was oppressive—dry as the hard cement we stood on. Pillow swayed next to me, and I put out a hand to steady her, even though I could barely stay upright myself.

The three men looked us over while behind us I heard the drivers closing up the truck.

"Yeah, they'll do," Pockmarks said to Serge as the drivers rejoined them. "They all under eighteen?"

"King said two are over eighteen," Sergio pointed to Mess and Baa. "And the blue-haired one is eighteen. She and the hookers are real pretty though, and the Oriental chick doesn't look anywhere near legal. We've took her ID and she don't speak no English, so we'll sell her as fresh meat and no one will know the difference. Her and the curly-haired one will bring in some serious money. Everyone wants them under sixteen nowadays."

"What about the redhead?"

Serge shrugged. "King said she's a bonus. We picked her up in Philly. Look at that skin. Someone is gonna pay top dollar to put their marks on that."

"Miller's gonna love that." Pockmarks's gaze slid from me to Pistol. "Maybe he'll take two. Or three. Red, white, and blue."

One of the other guys laughed. "Miller can be patriotic."

We stood there like a row of mannequins as they started to evaluate our various assets. I learned that King had originally only wanted to buy Mess from her pimp, but the man had offered Sugar as an extra in a deal that supposedly was too good to be refused. They moved down the line of us, making fun of Lacy and Baa for their lack of English, then laughing as the drivers recounted their tale of punishing Tasha in the woods, claiming she'd give them no trouble at all after what they'd done to her.

And I believed them. The girl followed their conversation with wide eyes, cradling her arm. Her face was misshapen and discolored with swelling and bruises, making it impossible to tell what the girl really looked like. One of the drivers reached out to touch her face and she flinched, whimpering as he stroked her cheek.

"See? She's a good girl now, aren't you?"

Tasha nodded, choking back a cry as the man pinched her bruised face before moving on to the next girl. Pistol. One of the guards turned her around, squeezing her ass and kicking her legs apart to slide a hand between her thighs.

"I might try this one out tonight. Ass or pussy though? Or maybe both."

With a strangled "no," Pistol jerked away from the man and made a run for it, shoving past a surprised Serge and running around the side of the truck. Two of the guys snapped to attention, grabbing the broom poles and keeping the rest of us grouped together as Pockmarks, Serge, and the other driver ran after Pistol. Footsteps echoed off the walls, as did loud laughter, and Pistol's shrieks. I heard a scuffle, and winced at the sound of fists hitting flesh.

We moved closer together, huddling to either hide or gain collective comfort, I wasn't sure which. Kitten began to quietly cry, resting her head on Mess's shoulder. Pillow began to do the same, like a chain reaction. I couldn't help but look at the two women who didn't speak English—Baa and Lacy. Both had that stoic wariness of people who needed to be constantly vigilant. Tasha looked like she was going into shock. Sugar and Mess appeared…resigned. And oh so very tired. For some reason, it was for them I felt the biggest surge of sympathy.

Serge and Pockmarks dragged Pistol back around the truck toward us, then kicked her as they shoved her on the ground in front of our feet, the other two guys holding us in a cluster with the broom poles. She curled up in a fetal posi-tion, clutching her stomach. Blood coated her face from a slash above one of her eyebrows, and her nose was crooked. Mess walked forward to go to the girl, and was shoved back with a sharp rap across her chest from Sergio's broom handle.

"We've got an extra," Pockmarks announced. "We're supposed to have eight, and we've got nine. One dead still keeps us at quota. Keep that in mind, girls, when you start thinking about running away from us."

We were frozen in fear, huddled together with the truck at our back and guys with wooden poles holding us in place. Any spark of unity we'd begun to feel on the truck had fractured with Pistol's beating. At this moment, every single one of us only wanted to survive, and survival depended on being very quiet, very still, and very obedient.

A lone memory broke through and surfaced—there were rules. I'd been all about following the rules, setting rules, organizing appropriate corrections for those who didn't follow the rules. But I'd fallen in love and realized that some rules were better broken. I tried to remember the one I'd loved, but his image swam away from my awareness, almost as though he'd been without shape and form. He'd changed me. He'd made me a better person. He'd opened me to a whole world that had previously been unseen to my eyes. But when the critical moment came, I fell back on the old me. I went back to the rules that should never be broken, to the intractable self I'd thought had broken free from her chains.

It seems some chains never completely loosened.

I'd complied, fallen in line with the rules once before. And I was paying for it now. The part of me that wanted order and obedience and adherence to the rules fought against the knife-sharp memory of pain and shame and loss and guilt. The rules-me cracked and I ran forward to Pistol, dodging the guards to bend over her. One hit me on the ass with a pole. I sucked in a breath, but held position, shielding Pistol with my body.

"You okay?" I wiped the blood from her face. She looked

up at me, her mouth a tight line, her eyes blurred with tears. I wanted to gather her up in my arms, to hold her and rock her as if she were my child, but from the way she was clutching her stomach, I feared such a move on my part would only cause her additional pain.

"Can you stand?" I knew these guards would want to move us soon. It would be easier for her if she had someone to help her as opposed to trying to stand and walk on her own.

She took a shallow breath and nodded. I helped her to her feet and back to the group, remembering what she'd said in the truck. She had a family, was in college. People would be looking for her, missing her. Maybe, just maybe that would be what saved us, because I was pretty sure there wasn't anyone looking for the rest of us.

Especially not me. No one would miss me. The certainty of it nearly drove me to my knees. Additional memories trickled like tiny droplets of water through my mind. Parents who had given up on their wayward addict daughter. Years on the streets, trying to earn or steal enough money to score a daily hit. A craving so strong it eclipsed every other emotion. It was all like watching a movie or the life of a stranger. This wasn't me, it was somebody else. But that was the past that sprung up in tiny flashes like a silent movie.

There was another past, overlying those faint memories like a thin blanket. A terrible choice. Loss. Guilt. Self-recrimination. In a way those memories were worse than the faded junkie ones. They weren't truly memories, but echoes of painful emotions. But far off in the distance of guilt and loss, there was a light. If I could just find my way to the light, I'd be forgiven. I knew this deep inside, and the thought was a lifeline that I clung to in my despair. There was something I needed to do, and I believed it had something to do with the fate of these eight women.

"Get them cleaned up," Pockmarks said to one of the other men. "And we'll see what they look like under the dirt. I hope King sent us some good product. We've only got five days until the sale."

We were herded through the main building then through a door at the end of the row of offices that led into something that looked like it used to be the cafeteria. There were cot mattresses lined up along one side and cabinets with a brown countertop along the other. A gaping hole was in a corner where a fridge or vending machine must have once stood, but the sink fixtures were still there. Sheets and a blanket sat on the end of each cot. I was relieved to see they looked relatively new and clean.

It was terrible how a few days in a filthy truck with stale air made someone appreciate the relative luxury of clean sheets and a cot bed.

"You're the big money girls," one of the guards commented. I caught a whiff of his breath and grimaced at the overwhelming aroma of onions. "New beds and the works. Can't have the product arriving at the sale covered in lice and stinking of old sweat, can we?"

None of us answered him. We continued through another door to a windowless room in the rear that reminded me of a school gym bathroom. There was an open large stall with four shower heads and benches, two sinks with mirrors and plastic tubs on the floor that held towels and washcloths, and two stalls that housed the toilets. The two men stood guard, broomsticks in hand and instructed us to shower.

Everyone hesitated. None of us wanted to get naked in front of these guys, but the lure of cleaning the filth from our skin beckoned with an irresistible call.

"Screw it." Mess yanked her grimy tank top over her head and dropped it on the floor to unsnap her bra. We all followed suit, Mess helping Tasha disrobe without jostling her broken arm, and me assisting Pistol. Each of us grabbed a wash cloth and towel, and headed into the open-air shower spot, trying to ignore the guards who took in every bit of our nakedness as we walked past them.

Hot water and soap never felt so good. The water ran brown off our skin, washing away any shame of being naked in front of our captors as well as the collected dirt and grime. There were metal dispensers on the tile walls, and we were liberal in our use of soap, shampoo and conditioner, Mess again helping Tasha to shampoo and rinse her hair.

I felt better just being clean—stronger, clear in mind and even more determined to get us out of here. Glancing at Pistol's face, I could see she felt the same. They'd hurt Tasha. They'd hurt Pistol. But we couldn't just stay here and let them turn us into living sex toys, to profit from and to use until we died or were of no more value. They'd beaten Pistol, but now that she was upright and rinsing the grime from her body, I saw the resolve, the fire, return to her eyes. They'd beaten but not broken her. She'd risk another beating, or even worse, to get out of here, and I knew right then and there that I'd support her all the way. If Pistol could be strong, then so could I.

She was smart, sensible, as were Mess and Sugar. The four of us were the eldest. Kitten was terrified. Pillow looked equally scared as did the three others. Whatever plan we made, whatever we decided to do, it would be up to Pistol, Sugar, Mess, and me to lead the way, I thought as I rinsed the conditioner from my hair.

I had no idea where the heck we were—what state, if we were in an industrial complex in a big city or some old warehouse out in the middle of nowhere. If we escaped from here, we might need to hike for hours through the woods or fields or swamps to get to some sort of town or a road busy enough to flag someone down. Remaining undetected and getting help would be easier if we were in a big city, but we would still be at a disadvantage there—in an unfamiliar area that our captors probably knew well.

Could we steal the truck or some other vehicle? Did any of us know how to hotwire a car? Could we overpower these guards and get out, or manage to sneak away as they slept? Or should we wait and make a run for it when, or if, they tried to move us? Surely they couldn't mean to prostitute us out of here. They'd mentioned a sale, and that would mean they'd need to transport us again to deliver us to a buyer. That might give us our chance to escape, as long as they didn't divide us up before then.

The thought sent a bolt of panic through me. I needed to save these girls. If I saved them, then maybe I could forgive myself for whatever sin I'd committed in my past. But I couldn't save them if these men split us all up.

The showers turned off and the guard who reeked of onions motioned us to get our towels. None of them had made a move to grope, pinch, or slap any of us, although their eyes had done quite a lot of roving, and one had made lurid remarks under his breath to the amusement of the other. As we got our towels, catcall-guy pulled out a trash bag and began stuffing our clothing into it. I eyed it nervously, getting the impression that they weren't going to be laundering our outfits and returning them.

"We'll wear what they tell us to wear," Mess muttered. "If they let us wear anything at all, that is."

"Might be fun to keep you girls naked," Onions said. "Make it easier when we want to spend some quality time with you. Sampling the goods, you know?"

"Also make it harder for you girls to hide anything you might decide to use as a weapon," Catcalls added.

"They could still stick a shiv in their asses." Onions grinned.

"I'd rather stick something else in their asses." Catcalls laughed.

They continued to comment on all the other orifices they'd like to stick things in as we dried off. The towels were warm and soft. We all tied them around our bodies, then headed over to the sinks to brush our teeth. I noticed little baskets with combs and feminine hygiene products in addition to the toothbrush, toothpaste, and mouthwash. It was weird. Somebody cared enough to make sure we had clean sheets, soft towels, all the toiletries we might need. I was pretty sure that someone wasn't any of these guards.

Onions waved one of the broom handles at us. "Hurry it up. Time for the demon to take a look at you all."

Demon? Did he mean Pockmarks, or was there someone else who needed to see us naked and clean? I didn't like the idea of anyone who had the nickname of "demon" looking us over.

We hurriedly brushed our teeth, then walked out clad in only towels. I looked around, already searching for possible means of escape. The guards must have sensed the change in our attitudes, because they suddenly became more assertive with their broom handles, poking us, and lifting the back of our towels to leer at our backsides, shoving the end of the broom handles suggestively between our legs.

I wasn't too surprised when we were told to drop the towels and stand naked in front of the three men as if we were auditioning for a porno. Correction—three men and a woman.

Pockmarks was in the former-kitchen-now-bedroom standing next to a very elegant woman. She was stunning— Asian with long, straight black hair that hung like a glossy, silken sheet down to her hips. Her face was a perfect oval, her lips full and pink, her eyes dark and sultry. She was tiny —short and slight but evenly proportioned with an easy confidence that belied her small stature. Her tight forest-green dress barely covered her crotch and clung to her small breasts and narrow waist. She exuded sex appeal like a tangible thing. It washed over my skin, warmer than the water from the shower I'd just taken. Longing sparked through me, and I clamped my legs together trying to keep them from trembling.

"Towels off, now," Pockmarks snarled, taking a menacing step toward us.

We complied and the woman looked us over, her gaze stopping on Tasha and Pistol. "They have been here less than half an hour and you've already taken your fists to two of them?" Her voice was soft with a lilting accent, and a core of steel.

Onions and Catcall shifted, turning their heads. Pockmarks tensed. "The drivers had to teach a lesson to the Russian girl about trying to escape, and the other bitch tried to make a run for it in the warehouse. What did you expect us to do, pat them on the head and give them a cookie?"

"I expected you not to beat the crap out of them, especially their faces." The woman scowled. "I understand how difficult it is for you Neanderthals to keep your hands to yourselves, but try not to damage the merchandise."

Pockmarks shrugged. "Doesn't matter. You can fix whatever bruises or broken bones they happen to get."

Her eyes narrowed. "Every repair I do increases the risks of them dying early. Not all of our buyers are like Miller. Most of them would like their purchases to live longer than a few weeks."

There was a bit of a staring match between the two as the other guards carefully looked elsewhere. "Understood," Pockmarks snapped. "But if any more of them tries to make a run for it, or proves to be uncooperative, then you'll be fixing more than bruises and broken bones." Then he turned to the other guards. "If you need to hurt them, hurt them. Fuck 'em. Beat 'em. The demon can fix them up before the sale."

I felt a rush of fear and panic at his words. The price for an escape attempt would be steep, and from what they'd said, we'd be expected to willingly service these guys until the auction. The nightmare didn't begin in five days, it started now. But who was this woman, and how was she expected to fix any of our injuries in the short time before we were sold? Was she a doctor? She'd have to be a pretty good doctor to have bruises and cuts vanish in less than a week.

The woman waved her hand. "So tell me what you would like me to do here with these women, besides repair the injuries you fools have inflicted on them."

Pockmarks walked down the line of us, commenting about each individual's assets and flaws as the woman watched. The other two guys kept their eyes on us. I took the opportunity to look around at the block and drywall for anything that might be used as a weapon—or an avenue for escape.

The joints in the concrete appeared to be tightly mortared—nothing crumbling or gaps that could be enlarged with a spoon or stick. Who knows what was on the other side of the drywall, but I doubted the Sheetrock was the only barrier between us and the outside. Besides the mattresses and the old kitchen cabinets, the room was completely bare. The cement floor had a coating of shiny gray epoxy on it— the stuff used to coat garage floors. There wasn't even a pebble within sight.

So that left the bathroom. I hadn't examined the toilets, but I figured the tank parts might prove useful. The arm attached to the float ball would hopefully be metal and not plastic, and the lift chain was usually copper. Tank lids were heavy. Whacking one of the guards upside the head with one would at the very least knock him out. Other than that, I could think of nothing there usable. We hadn't been provided with razors, but I was assuming they'd eventually want us to shave. There wasn't a big market in the US for women with furry legs and armpit hair. I'd need to see if there was an opportunity to slip the blade from one if they ever provided them.

How the heck did I know all this stuff? I frowned as the headache returned and I tried to remember if I'd needed to escape from somewhere before, if I'd needed to defend myself with toilet parts anytime in my past. There must have been a time before I'd become a drug addict when I was a scrappy survivor, but there was nothing in my memories to confirm this—nothing but a blur.

"What did you do to your hair?"

The voice as well as the jab of a broom handle brought me from my thoughts. "I…I dyed it?"

"At least it's not green or blue," Pockmarks commented. "That other girl's is horrible, and it's short. I don't like women with short hair." He turned to the woman. "Can you fix that? Grow her hair longer and make her and the redhead into blondes?"

The woman's lips narrowed and her eyes flashed, then suddenly she became sultry and demure once more, hiding that powerful aura I'd sensed. "I suggest we use dye and hair extensions before we consider more extreme measures. I wouldn't want to do so many modifications that they die on the auction block."

Pockmarks scowled. "None of the other girls you fixed up died before the sale. This is cosmetic stuff. It's not like we're telling you to make them six inches taller or anything."

The woman pouted, and every eye in the room turned toward her. She'd been beautiful, irresistibly sexy, before but suddenly she was like a magnet. Catcalls took a step toward her, transfixed. Then in a blink it was gone, and everyone took a collective breath. Pockmarks shook his head and glared.

"You do that again, and I'll call the boss. He'll have you in a bottle for centuries. Forget ever seeing Hel again."

The woman lowered her head and her eyes, but I saw the quick glance of hatred she shot toward Pockmarks. "Box dye first, and then, if you are unsatisfied with the results, I will correct them myself. How long do you want the blue-haired one's hair to be?"

Pockmarks looked over at Pistol, eyes narrowed. "Past her shoulders at least. Go ahead and make her and the redhead into blondes. We've got too many brown-skinned, black-haired girls in this group. I want more blondes."

"It's going to be difficult to bleach that red and blue to platinum," the woman complained. "Let me dye that curly-haired girl's a dark gold. Red can be a medium copper, and Blue will end up a dark ash-blonde."

He turned a glare on her. "Did I say blonde? I think I said blonde. I don't give a shit how you do it. I want four blondes and four brunettes. Got it?"

"Why can't one of them be a redhead. I like red," Onions complained, scratching the stubble on his chin. "Yeah, I like redheads, just not *that* color red."

Catcalls made a few lewd comments about the supposed prowess of redheads in the sack. Pockmarks quelled them all with a glance. "Well *I* don't like redheads, and the boss don't care as long as they bring in the bucks. Blondes and brunettes only. Preferably blondes. They sell better."

Guess I was about to become a blonde. Although judging from my skin tone and the faint hair on my arms, I'd been a blonde for most of my life. It made me wonder. I'd been the kind of girl that dyed my blonde hair a bright, unnatural shade of red. I'd been someone who'd turned to heroin for......whatever. I was someone who was a good choice to grab out of an alley or flophouse. Was I a runaway? Had my family thrown me out, disowned me because of the drugs and the crimes the need for them ultimately brought? I looked down at the backs of my hands, to see if they would give me any clues to my past.

Unlined, creamy skin with not a sunspot or freckle in sight. My gaze moved upward. The faint blonde hair on my arms was gone. Nada. Now that I thought about it, I'd been surprisingly hair-free during my shower. Had I subjected myself to all-over body waxing? Did I have some disease that was making all of my hair fall out except what was on my head? Had I gone overboard with the laser hair removal treatments? I couldn't be one of those people with alopecia, or someone would have commented on my lack of eyebrows and eyelashes. And I wouldn't have long, bright red hair either.

"Nice bunch, huh?" Onions asked the demon. "King did a good job this time. Got us some real beauties. Shouldn't be too much for you to fix beyond the hair and some boobs here and there."

"No, not too much as long as you all can restrain yourselves from beating the crap out of them," she snapped back.

I glanced around and realized that Onions was right. Cleaned up it was very apparent that we were a bunch of very attractive girls. Very different, but each of us beautiful in our own way.

Pockmarks looked us over again with a critical eye. "They're pretty enough, but they won't draw top dollar without some work."

"That's why the demon is here," Onions laughed.

Pockmarks smiled. "Exactly. Five days with her and these girls will be red-carpet worthy."

"Silk sheets worthy," Catcalls added.

What a bunch of comedians. They were all laughing now,

but they'd underestimated us—underestimated me. I might not be able to remember who I was, but I was determined that five days would see the nine of us free.

I swore it. Right then and there I swore on all I felt holy that I would save these girls—every last one of them.

34

CHAPTER 3

They left, the sound of the lock being turned on the door loud as a gunshot. We all looked at each other and gathered up the towels that seemed to be our only clothing option right now. I found an extra one and between Mess and me, we managed to put together a makeshift sling for Tasha's arm. Pistol wasn't as bad off—mostly just the broken nose and bruising on her face as well as across her ribs and stomach, but I worried about the other girl. If only we had a way to immobilize her arm and some painkillers, I think she would have been okay, but being jostled around the back of a truck, filthy and dehydrated, hadn't helped her one bit.

"What did they mean she was going to fix us?" Pillow plopped down on the cot beside Tasha's and hugged her knees to her chest. "It didn't sound like it was just beautician stuff."

"Do you think she's a doctor?" Kitten asked. "Doctors fix people. Maybe she could fix Tasha's arm."

"And give us boob jobs on the side?" Sugar laughed. "Get

ready for butt implants and puffy duck lips, girls. They're gonna silicone us up before they pimp us out."

Mess sat down beside Pillow. "They were probably just trying to scare us. They said five days—that's not long enough to be doing plastic surgery on us."

"I don't want bigger boobs," Pillow whispered. "Actually I *do* want bigger boobs. I just don't want hatchet-job boobs done in a warehouse by someone I'm thinking isn't a real doctor."

Sugar snorted. "I hear you on that. I don't want that woman anywhere near me with a scalpel. Actually I don't want her near me at all. She gives me the creeps."

Really? I'd thought she was powerful and gorgeous. Intimidating, yes, but not creepy.

"Do you think we have any chance of getting out of here?" Kitten's voice wavered. "I don't want a boob job. And I don't want to be a prostitute."

"I'm all about us getting out of here." Pistol went over to the cabinets and started going through them. "Let's see what we've got here. Maybe there's something we can use as a weapon."

"Girl, ain't you been beat enough?" Mess eyed the other woman's face, which was swollen and sporting some colorful bruising.

"I'm not just going to lay down and accept that my future involves me being a sex slave." Each cabinet door the girl opened showed empty, except for the last one which looked like it was full of blankets. "No weapons," she turned with a sigh.

"Maybe we can smother them with the blankets," Sugar drawled. "Or snap them with a wet towel."

"Are they going to feed us?"?" Kitten eyed the door nervously. "I'm so hungry."

"Probably not," Sugar replied. "If you're thirsty, you'll need to drink water from the bathroom sink."

"Why wouldn't they feed us?" Pillow asked. "Don't they want us alive and healthy for this sale of theirs?"

Mess glared at Sugar. "They'll feed us. They want to keep us weak so we don't run away or fight, but I don't think they want us to starve."

"Clearly they're not going to tonight." Sugar hung her towel on the end of a cot and sprawled across the mattress, wrapping herself in the clean sheets and blanket. "Might as well get some sleep. Not like any of us got more than a few winks in that nasty truck the last few days."

It was a good idea. The rest of us made our way over to the beds, each picking one. I ended up smack in the middle, between Pistol and Kitten. Sugar and Mess were closest to the bathroom, Pillow, Baa, and Tasha at the other end. Lacy hesitated a moment, then took the last bed between Kitten and Sugar. I couldn't imagine how scared she must be, not understanding one word of what everyone was saying, trying to watch everyone else and anticipate what was expected of her. I could tell she was consciously trying to make herself small and invisible, to just survive this any way she could. But weren't we all?

Settling back on the cot, I sighed at the wonderful feeling of soft and clean sheets. After being in that hot smelly truck, these simple things felt downright decadent. I was clean. I had a bed to sleep in, a toilet, soap and shampoo and towels. Kitten's stomach growled loud enough for me to hear and my brief moment of contentment faded. None of us had eaten more than a few slices of bread since we'd been put in that truck. Mess's assurances aside, I worried that they meant for us to go hungry for the next five days. But hadn't they said we were supposed to bring in top dollar? That this woman was supposed to fix us up for the sale? I couldn't imagine anyone would pay top dollar for a girl who was so weak with hunger she could barely stand.

"Do you think maybe that woman would help us?" Kitten asked. "She didn't like those guards either. Maybe she can help us get away."

Mess laughed. "Honey, she's working for them. They all work for this boss of theirs. She might not like the guards, but she's probably getting some of the profits. Forget about her helping us. We don't need her help anyway. We got each other. We don't need her."

"Did you see the look in her eyes when the one guard said he'd tell the boss on her? I agree with Sugar. She's creepy. She scares me. I don't think she's a nice woman." Pillow shivered and added a few words in Spanish.

Baa replied in the same language, and Pillow tensed, her face pale. The two exchanged words, then Baa made the sign of the cross and huddled on her bed, rocking as she clutched her blanket to her chest.

"What did she say?" Sugar demanded.

"She said that woman with the guards is a demon. She's going to take our souls. She'll kill us and take our souls and torture us for all eternity." Pillow's voice was unsteady.

Sugar let out a curse. "I'm stuck here with a bunch of Catholic school girls. Idiots. Just because they call her a demon doesn't mean she's an actual demon. There is no such thing. She's just a bitch. That's why the call her a demon."

"She's going to fix us, to make Pistol's hair grow longer and other stuff," Kitten said, her voice rising and cracking. "I think Baa is right. She's a real demon. She's going to do all sorts of horrible things to us, then they'll sell us to someone and when we're dead, she'll take our souls."

Sugar rolled her eyes. "There is no such thing as a demon. She's some kind of beautician maybe. She's just going slap a bunch of makeup on us, put us in push-up bras, and put some extensions in Pistol's hair. She's not going to take our souls."

"Maybe she *is* a plastic surgeon," Pistol said. "That's how she's going to fix us if one the guards cuts or bruises us. She's going to stitch us up and do some kind of doctor-thing for the bruises."

"And make us look like supermodels in five days?" Pillow scoffed. "Baa says she knows a demon when she sees one. She's got the sight, and she's seen them before."

"Catholics," Sugar muttered, flinging herself down on the bed and burying her face in a pillow.

I sat up and turned to Mess who'd been unusually silent throughout the exchange. She was staring at Baa, an alarmed expression on her face. "What do you think?" I asked her, feeling foolish for even entertaining the idea that Baa might be right.

"I…I don't know. My mom used to tell me demons were real, but she was crazy. I never met a demon before to know. At least I don't think I have."

"Seriously?" Sugar popped her head up out of the pillow. "Trust me. Tomorrow she's going to show up with boxes of hair dye and some extensions for Pistol, and you'll all see that there's no such thing as demons."

"Let's talk about something else," Kitten begged. "Anything else."

"Like what?" Sugar rolled her eyes. "The weather? Sports? Politics? Whether we like it on top or missionary style?"

"Stop," I told her. "Don't be mean. She's just a kid, and she's hungry and scared. We're all hungry and scared."

I wasn't. I was scared, but I wasn't hungry. It was a bit of a shock to realize that. Maybe junkies didn't get hungry. I would have happily downed a plate full of nachos right now, but I didn't feel like my stomach was ready to turn itself inside out. Mine wasn't growling like the others. And I didn't feel particularly weak either.

"I'm less scared when we talk," Kitten admitted.

"Whatever." Sugar flopped face down on her cot. "Talk quietly though. I'm going to try to get some sleep."

I sat up and motioned for Kitten to join me on my cot, then pivoted to face Pillow. "You go first. Where are you from?"

"Cleveland. Although I also lived in Dallas and Denver growing up. But that's not what you're asking, right?" Her eyebrows shot up. "My parents came from Columbia. Mom ran off when I was two. When I was fourteen, Dad got in some trouble and wound up in jail, which put me in foster care. I bounced around homes for two years, but the last one, the guy was a little too friendly with me, if you know what I mean, so I took off. I was doing okay in Cleveland on my own, but I met a guy and we took a bus to New York for some job he was supposed to get. Next thing I know, he's gone and I'm chained to a bed in a warehouse with half a dozen other women."

I winced.

"I live in Ohio too," Kitten confided. "Cincinnati. It's just me and my parents and my little sister. She's such a pain in the butt, but I miss her. And my dog. She's a labradoodle. Her name is Autumn." The girl's mouth trembled and her shoulders shook. "I love my family. I miss them all. I want to go back. I want to go home."

I put my arm around her. "How old are you?"

"Thirteen." She took a deep breath. "I met a boy online and went to New York to spend a week with him. A woman met me at the station, saying she was his mother, but instead of taking me to Cade's house, she took me to the warehouse with the other girls. I'm supposed to be at a band camp. I'm supposed to be coming home tomorrow. My mom...she's going to panic. My dad too. They're not going to ever know what happened to me. I'm going to be raped and killed, and they'll never know what happened to me. I'll never see them again. I'll never see my sister again. Or Autumn. I just want to go home. I want to go home."

The last word ended on a wail and she collapsed in my arms. It didn't matter that we were naked aside from a towel, that we hadn't known each other more than a few days. She was just a girl, just a child, and she was so scared. I looked up at Pillow, then over to Pistol with her bruised face, Baa still rocking on her cot, Tasha trying to find a position that didn't jostle her arm, Lacy trying to sink as far into her sheets as possible, Sugar faking sleep, and Mess with that tired, resigned expression on her face. We needed to get out of here. I needed to get them out of here. It didn't matter if I got beaten like Pistol and Tasha, I needed to get these girls out of here.

Tasha turned on her cot, wincing as she moved. "My parents do worry as well. I came here to work for summertime. I was to call them. I never have chance to call before men take me. I know they worry." She shook her head. "There is not much they can do from Ukraine to help me. I will not call, not come home after summer, and they will hurt for me."

Pillow turned and pointed to Baa who was whispering something that sounded like a frantic prayer for help. "She's in the same boat. She's from Guatemala and was supposed to be here for a job."

"What about Lacy?" I asked. The girl still sat rigid on her bed as if she wanted to blend in with the pillows and sheets.

Pillow shrugged. "No idea. She doesn't speak any English at all, or Spanish. I think she's probably Chinese or something."

Kitten's crying softened and she lifted her head, wiping her eyes on the corner of her towel.

"You tired?" I asked, my arm still around her.

She nodded. *I'm afraid to sleep alone. Autumn always slept in my bed with me, although she wasn't supposed to. And sometimes when Casey was scared, she'd come climb into my bed as well.*

I had a clear picture in my mind of a fluffy dog with tawny curls, snoozing at the end of a bed with a bright blue comforter. The door cracked open, and a face peered in—an eight-year-old girl with hair a few shades lighter than Kitten's and huge blue eyes. She smiled, then ran forward to scurry under the covers. The two giggled, staying awake far longer than they should have.

"Pull your cot over here against mine," I told the girl. "It will be like a sleep over. You can pretend I'm your older sister."

Older sisters keep their younger sisters safe. I could use a big sister right now.

I leaned over and kissed the top of Kitten's head. "I'll keep you safe. I promise I'll keep you safe."

And I would. No matter what happened to me, I'd make sure Kitten was okay. Thirteen. So young, and so scared. I had to get her out of here and back home to her family. I had to get them all out of here.

And somehow, I needed to keep them all safe.

CHAPTER 4

The next morning the doors opened up and the guards came in—guards and the Asian woman. She shouldered past the men with a confidence completely at odds with her fragile, doll-like appearance and came to a stop in front of us.

"Today is a spa day ladies," she announced with false cheerfulness. Setting two bags on the floor, she pulled out a box and tossed it at Pistol. "You shall go first. We'll need to pre-bleach that hair to strip the blue. Go get started while I work on the others."

Pistol rose and adjusted her towel with a nervous glance at the guards. Then she headed to the bath area, reading the back of the box.

The woman pulled another two boxes out and tossed one to Pillow and one to me. "You two as well. Go dye some hair."

Pillow and I both stood, Pillow's towel slipping a bit to reveal more than she probably wanted. I guess Sugar had been right. The woman wasn't a plastic surgeon, or a real demon, whatever that meant. Hair dye, nail polish, and some padded bras would thankfully be the extent of our "improve ments." It was a relief. Trying to figure out how to get the nine of us past the three guards and out of the warehouse to safety was enough of a problem without worrying about some mythical creature trying to take our souls.

"Those two need bigger boobs," Pockmarks said, pointing to Tasha and Lacy. "And bigger boobs for the blue -haired one as well."

I lingered, adjusting my towel. Push-up bra. With padding. That's what he meant. That had to be what he meant, because the alternative was ridiculous. They couldn't do plastic surgery right here in the middle of nowhere in a warehouse. How the heck would we be expected to heal from that within five days? No, there were probably a whole bunch of padded bras in those plastic bags.

"And when you're done, clear up that one's complexion, and do something about that one's ass. I don't know, make it more perky or something," Pockmarks continued, pointing to Sugar and Baa.

Bras, some acne cream, and one of those lift-and-enhance pairs of undies. Still, I lingered and saw something flicker in the woman's ebony eyes at Pockmark's words. Anger. Then resignation. "Anything else?"

"The usual. Cheekbones. Eyes. They need to be top-rate. This auction needs to draw the big spenders."

Make-up. Bras and acne cream. Fancy foundational garments. I continued to stall, watching the woman for her response. Her gaze flickered to me, then narrowed. I made a bit more haste heading to the bathroom door, fiddling with the box of dye as I walked.

"I can fix the mild acne and the other minor cosmetic flaws" she said. "But there's no need to do anything extensive. You got a good batch this time. They are beautiful. I don't want to mar their natural beauty, and the boss doesn't want to have a group of porn-star looking girls on the auction block." She waved a dismissive hand and turned to approach Sugar who was watching her with a wary gaze.

Pockmarks put his hand on the woman's arm. His fingers tightened enough to dent her flesh. I stopped and held my breath. She was tiny and he looked like he could snap her in two, but I got the feeling if they came to blows, Pockmarks wouldn't be walking away from the fight.

"I'm taking pictures for the sale ads in three hours and these girls need to be ready. Auction's in less than five days and they have to look perfect. Bigger boobs. Lift that one's ass. And you *will* do any cosmetic stuff you need to do to make them worth a million bucks. Cheekbones, jaw angles, longer legs, nose jobs. Everything."

I saw the woman's mouth thin, the muscle in her jaw twitch. "There are repercussions. It's not like high-end cosmetics or plastic surgery. I do these things and...and people eventually die."

I heard Kitten choke back a frightened sob.

"You're better than plastic surgery. Faster too. And they're going to die anyway. They'll probably die before anything you do causes any problems. Boss says do it, so do it." Pockmark and the others turned to leave. "Three hours." The men filed out the door. I heard the lock slide home.

Were they putting on a show to scare us? Because we really didn't need any more to be terrified. Bras and make-up and hair dye. That was all they were going to do. All this people-dying talk was just to keep us on edge and make sure we didn't try to get out of line. Well, they were wrong. We were strong, determined woman, and together we were going to escape, to survive. They could try all they wanted to scare us, but a cornered animal was even more vicious and desperate. Frighten us, make us feel like we had nothing left to lose, and just see what we could do.

The woman turned, her eyes meeting mine. There was

more than suppressed anger in her gaze, there was regret and…sympathy. Then in an instant it was gone, and the woman seemed harder than a slab of granite. "Go dye your hair. Now. The next time I see you, you had better be a blonde."

I scurried through the door and into the shower area while the woman barked instructions to the others. Inside, Pistol had already mixed up the bleach solution in a plastic bottle and was beginning to apply it. Pillow was staring at her box, a resigned expression on her face.

"Do you know how much money I paid to get my hair this shade of blue?" Pistol lowered the bottle, looked at herself in the mirror, gently touching a finger to the dark bruise on her cheekbone. With a sigh she continued squirting the white liquid on her head. "More than a hundred bucks. And I like it short. If they wanted a bunch of blondes, why didn't they just take girls who were already blonde? There were plenty of women in New York City to choose from."

"I've never dyed my hair," Pillow jabbed a finger at the box. "I'm going to look like a cheap two-bit tramp as a blonde. They should do Kitten instead. At least her natural hair color is closer to this."

I looked at my box and saw that the demon woman had picked a strawberry blonde color for me, no doubt worrying the red would be too difficult to completely strip out. I was surprised she didn't have me pre-bleaching like Pistol.

"Come on. Let's start dyeing before she comes in here and beats us or something." I'd been joking, but as soon as I said the words I heard a scream of pain from the room and the sound of someone crying. We all froze and turned to stare at the door.

Bras and make-up. Bras and make-up. I remembered the guards beating Pistol and shivered. Pillow shot me a nervous glance, and tore open her box with shaking hands. We hurriedly mixed the solution and slathered it on our hair, stuffing the gloves and empty bottles back into the boxes.

None of us had watches or phones and there wasn't a clock anywhere to be seen, so we sat on our towels on the cold tile floor and took turns counting. We hadn't eaten last night or this morning, and I could tell the girls were starting to feel light-headed. After more than twenty-four hours without even bread, they were weak. If they didn't feed us soon, one or more of us was going to be passing out.

But not me. I felt…fine. Strong. Almost as though I didn't even need food. It must have been some lingering effects of the heroin, I figured. Which meant whenever those effects wore off I'd be in the same boat as the rest of these girls. We had to get out of here. Now. Before we were too weak to help ourselves. Before whatever I was on wore off and I was too weak to help them.

There was another scream. Pillow lost count and turned to me, her eyes huge. "What is she doing to them?"

"I'm guessing that she's making their boobs bigger," Pistol commented dryly. "Be glad you've got a big rack. I'm probably next as soon as I'm done with my hair."

She probably was, from what that guard had said. I looked down at my chest, wondering why no one had insisted I get an augmentation. I wasn't much bigger than Pistol.

"She's just got bras and make-up and stuff in those bags," I said with faltering confidence.

"Then why are they screaming?" Pillow asked.

"She's…she's probably hitting them because they're not cooperating."

"No, they'd cooperate." Pillow echoed my doubts. "Everyone is so scared right now that no one is going to sass back or try anything."

"Then she just likes hurting people." I was really grasping at straws now. "Or she's trying to scare and intimidate us, like the guards are. They'll make us think they're going to kill us, or hurt us real bad. They'll make us think that woman is some kind of supernatural creature, a mythical monster, just so we don't try to escape. They beat Pistol, broke Tasha's arm and did other things to her. They're trying to beat us down, to make us so scared that we'll do anything they want."

"Well, it's working," Pillow said. "I'd rather screw twenty guys a day than have them work me over with those sticks, or worse."

"Not me." Pistol glared at the door. "Yeah, I'm scared. I don't want to be beat again. I don't want to be raped, or sliced up, or have my bones broken, but I'm not going to give in. We're getting out of here. Even if they break every bone in my body, I'll still fight them. I'll still try to escape if I have the chance."

"Good. You do that." There was another scream and Pillow huddled in on herself, her shoulders trembling.

"Okay, change of subject." Pistol scooted to lean her back against the wall. "I graduated high school a year early, and started college last fall. My birthday's in August, so I'll be nineteen going into my sophomore year. I can't wait to go back. I love living in a dorm, all the classes. I love it."

It worked. Pillow raised her head, eyeing Pistol with interest. "College. You must be smart. And rich."

The other girl shook her head. "Not so rich. My mom teaches school. My dad is an electrician. We've got a small house, but I had my own bedroom with posters all over the walls. It helps being the only girl. My two brothers had to share a bedroom. Mine is barely big enough for a twin-sized bed and a little dresser, but it was all mine."

A smile trembled at the edge of Pillow's lips. "Wow. White picket fence and all."

Pistol nodded. "Pretty much. Every weekend we'd go for a family hike. When I was little I loved it. I'd find all these cool rocks along the path and make my dad carry half of them for me. Mom would bring a nature book and we'd look up birds and flowers that we saw along the trails. My brothers would run off and sword fight with sticks." She laughed. "Half the time they'd come back with poison ivy. When I got older, I never wanted to go. I wanted to hang with my friends instead, or just sit in my room on my phone, but Mom and Dad always insisted. They said we were all growing up too fast, that soon we'd be gone and there would be no more family hikes." Pistol paused, her voice growing soft and misty. "I'd give anything to go on a stupid hike with them again, to pick up rocks and look up flowers in the book, and watch my brothers be total weirdos. I'd give anything to do that just one more time."

Images flickered through my mind—her memories, not mine. Pot roast with potatoes and little carrots on a big oak table set with colorful plates. A tiny, cookie-cutter split level house on a postage-stamp-sized lawn. A woman's warm voice pointing out Mountain Bluets while boys shouted gleefully in the distance.

"Tell us about college." I urged, trying to break the painful nostalgia and feeling of loss and bring the conversation back to a more light-hearted tone.

She smiled. "College is amazing. It was like I was finally a grown-up. I loved my classes. I made new friends. I was in a big city with all this glitz and glamour, so far from my little home town. It felt like a fairy tale."

"But it's summer," Pillow interjected. "Why were you still in New York and not home with your parents? Isn't that what college people do? Go home for the summers?"

The girl's smile faded. "Yeah. If I'd been home, I guess this wouldn't have happened to me. But I stayed in New York for the summer. The work-study job I had during the school year offered to keep me on, so I stayed. I love the city. It's so different than home, so alive. There's something surprising around every corner—little out-of-the-way curio shops, unusual ethnic groceries. Even the graffiti looks like works of art."

"Are we talking about the same New York, here?" Pillow teased. "You do realize there are probably drug deals going down in that cute curio shop, and the graffiti are gang tags showing their territory?"

Pistol shook her head with a sad smile. "I know. Naïve college kid from the sticks, looking at the big city through rose-colored glasses. I wanted to get my degree in social work, and I was full of blind optimism about how I was going to save the world, how I would pat some gangbanger on the back and suddenly he'd give up his lawless and violent ways. I should have been scared to death to go to some of the places my friends and I partied at. I thought I was safe, like a saint in holy armor walking through the slums and blessing the poor."

"Saints get killed." Pistol shot the other girl an ironic glance, her arched eyebrow making her look far older than sixteen. "That's how they get to be saints, you know. Somebody kills them."

"Yeah." Pistol laughed. "If someone had told me a week ago that I'd be in a warehouse in God-knows-where, beaten, forced to dye my hair, and about to be sold into sex slavery, I would have laughed my head off."

"When I first saw you, I thought maybe you were a runaway like me." Pillow said, shooting the door a nervous glance as we heard another scream.

Pistol shook her head. "My family in Swansboro is frantically looking for me right now. Friends at college probably have flyers up everywhere. There will be missing person's reports, rewards, and everything. If I could just get out of here and get to a phone, my folks would have the cavalry riding in to rescue us in under an hour. All of us." She turned to Pillow with a smile. "If you don't have anywhere to go, you can stay with me at my folks' house. You can stay for the summer until I go back to school. Have my room, and I'll take the couch."

"Go on weekend hikes with your family?" Pillow grinned. "That sounds fun. I'd miss the city, though. I'm not sure how much I'd like living the white-picket-fence life."

Pistol's background was so different than the other girls'. Tasha and Baa had been lured to the country with the promise of jobs. Sugar and Mess were already prostitutes, Pillow a runaway, me an addict, and Kitten caught up in an internet scam. If Pistol was right, her family might be the ones that got us found. Although I wasn't sure they'd be in time to save us all. They might not even be in time to save their own daughter.

"So, how *did* you end up here?" I asked her. "I mean, why you? You seem too high-risk a target for human traffickers to grab."

She shrugged. "Honestly? I think it was a mistake. There's this seedy club that some friends and I wanted to go to. Last thing I remember I was sipping a margarita and feeling insanely, fall-down drunk even though I only had two drinks. Next thing I know, I wake up in a warehouse chained to a bed. I guess they thought with the blue hair, and me being in that club, that I was someone who wouldn't be missed."

"Then there *is* hope...." Pillow's voice trailed off and she smiled at the two of us. I knew what she was thinking. Pistol's family was the middle-class American stereotype. If they went to the police, they'd be believed. Maybe they'd track her down and save us all. I didn't want to burst her hopes with the reality that they'd need to do it fast if we were going to be sold in five days and split up all over the place to our "owners."

"Yeah," Pistol patted the girl's shoulder, but I could see the shadow of doubt in her eyes. "There's hope. I know my family is looking for me."

Pillow shook her head. "I don't have anyone looking for me. At least, I hope I don't. I doubt if that foster family they stuck me with ever reported me missing. They're probably still getting checks for me."

"Your mom ran off?" Pistol asked. "And……you said your dad was in jail?" She winced as she said the last bit.

"Mom ran off when I was little. I was born here, in Dallas. Dad says after I was born, Mom had a real hard time of things. She cried a lot and one day when I was about two he came home and she was just gone. We never heard from her again. I don't know if she's even alive or not." Pillow looked down at her hands. "I don't have anything of hers. Dad threw it all away when she left. I don't even know what she looked like, or what her name is."

Or if she ever thinks of me. Does she ever think of me? Does she ever wonder what happened to the daughter she left behind?

The words slid into my mind and I turned to look at Pillow. I saw her father, loving but overworked and clueless about how to care for a child. I saw her climbing up on the counters at age two to put bread in the toaster for her breakfast because her father had already left for work. She'd be locked in all day, but he always left her with food and she'd felt safe. There had been warm blankets and stuffed animals, and coloring books, and when he came home after work they'd snuggle on the couch together and watch television. A neighbor found out and called social services. Pillow had hidden under the bed, terrified while they banged on the door. After that, an old woman stayed with her during the day, sleeping as Pillow colored and got her own meals.

"Dad's in jail," she continued, unaware that I'd been sensing her most personal memories. "He wrote to me a few times. I think he gets out in a couple of years."

He just hadn't come home one night. She'd gone everywhere—even to check at the hospital—then found out from one of his friends that he'd gotten caught in a drug bust. There was no money for bail, and with him in jail there was no money for rent or food. In two months she was out on the streets. There she had lived for a few weeks until she got picked up and put into foster care.

With all that, the thing that saddened her the most was that she had nothing from her childhood. All their belongings had been put out on the curb. She'd shoved a stuffed bear in a bag with some clothes when she'd been evicted. It was all she'd had, the only thing tying her to those nights on the couch with her father, those imaginary tea parties during the day when she'd been all alone. The guy who'd come to New York with her, the one who supposedly loved her, had taken her bag and she hadn't seen it since. They'd probably thrown it away.

I drew a ragged breath, struggling to keep the tears down. It hurt. I couldn't block Pillow's memories, her emotions, and they tore through me like a wildfire. The girl sat on the floor, her hair wet with dye, telling her story with complete composure, even nonchalance, but I felt the fear and loss that boiled underneath.

"What about you?" I turned in surprise at Pistol's question.

"I don't remember anything. Not my name, or where I'm from, or anything about my family." I closed my eyes and fought through the instant headache. "There are snatches of memories, but they're wispy and brief, and they don't make sense. Some of them feel like they belong to someone else—like I borrowed them."

I popped open my eyes and saw the two girls watching me expectantly. "Those memories…they're crumbling and fading—the ones of me shooting up, of living on the streets. Other memories are growing stronger, but those are the ones that don't make sense. I think…I think I did something bad. I think I hurt someone I loved—several people I loved."

Pillow's eyes were huge. "Did you shoot them?"

It was a valid question. I shut my eyes again and probed the recesses of my mind further. "No, I…I turned my back on them. I had a chance to help them, but I was a coward and too weak to stand up for what I knew was right. I walked away from them and I'll never see them again."

I felt a hand grip mine. "If we get out of here, I'm going back to Cleveland to see my dad. I'll find a way to make things work in foster care. I'll wait for him to get out of jail, and we'll make a life together. Maybe you can go back to your family, too. Go back and tell them you're sorry."

Tears spilled down my cheeks and I squeezed my eyes tight. "I think it's too late."

"Families are more forgiving than you think," Pistol told me. "Tell them you regret what happened, that you want a chance to make it right. Even if they don't accept you back, at least you've made an attempt. That's the first step toward healing—making the attempt to bridge a rift and right old wrongs."

"They're dead." The words were torn ragged from my depths. "It was my fault. I turned away from them, and they died. I need to suffer for that, to pay for not being brave enough to stand for what I knew was right. I will never be forgiven and I'll spend the rest of my life in penance for my sins."

Arms came around me and I felt both girls hug me close.

"Killing yourself with heroin isn't going to make any of that right," Pistol said.

I wasn't trying to kill myself with heroin. I wasn't trying to do anything with heroin. That drug addict was someone else, not me. Although maybe the girl who had been shooting up, the girl whose memories were like old tattered albums in the attic, was me after all. We both had made terrible choices in our past. We'd both lost people we loved. The only difference was she'd wanted to numb herself, to push the agony away, and shed life itself. I didn't want to be numb. I didn't want to die. I wanted to feel the pain, to let it suffuse every pore, to hold it in my heart. There was a peace to be had through suffering. I knew this, I just didn't know how. There wasn't a light at the end of the tunnel, but I believed that that there was a light somewhere, and if I suffered enough I'd find it.

"God will forgive you," Pillow whispered. "The souls of your family will forgive you. Confession and penance isn't about suffering, it's about knowing that you were weak and making the right choice the next time. It's about redemption through action, not misery."

Maybe. But right now, that light of redemption seemed forever hidden to me. I took a deep breath and forced back the tears, trying to bring us back to what I faced right now, in the present. We all carried pain. Mine wasn't any worse than these other girls'. What mattered was that I get us all out of here, bring these girls to safety My suffering, my penance, would need to wait for that.

CHAPTER 5

"Is it time to rinse this off?" Pillow asked Pistol. We got up and went into the shower area, each of us peeking at the others to see how the whole process had turned out. Pillow's hair was a bit on the brassy side, but it was within the realm of dark golden-blonde. It was pretty and flattered her skin tone and coffee-colored eyes. Pistol's hair had turned a pale blue that, although very pretty, was probably not what the demon woman had wanted. I rinsed the conditioner from my hair while the other two stared. Pistol snorted, causing me to drag a strand forward to see what was so funny.

It was red—cardinal's wing red. "Was something wrong with that stuff?"

"Did you follow the directions?" Pistol asked with a laugh. "Maybe you forgot to squeeze the tube of developer into the bottle? You know, the stuff with a big number 'two' on it?"

"I followed the directions." Padding across the floor, I picked up the empty box and stared at the picture. I should have reddish-gold hair like the model, or at the very least goldish-red hair. It was as if the dye had washed right off without the slightest effect.

The door opened and the demon woman breezed in, all business until she caught sight of my still-red hair.

"What…you were supposed to dye it." There was a hint of anger behind the astonishment.

I held up the box. "I did. Must have been some kind of manufacturer defect or something. Do you have another box? I'll do it again." And again, and again because I got the feeling I didn't want this woman pissed at me.

She stared at the box then slowly walked forward to take it from my hands and give it a closer look.

"I guess they put something else in the developer bottle by mistake?" Anything to keep her from thinking I'd done something wrong here.

"That's…strange." She tossed the box into the garbage can and reached out to rub a lock of my hair between her fingers. "It doesn't seem damaged. We will try another box and hopefully it won't fry the hair right off your head."

She left and I thought about how much money I'd bring at an auction bald until she returned with another box. This was the super, ultra pre-bleach stuff that she'd given Pistol, and I winced thinking that it probably *was* going to fry the hair right off my head.

"Use this. Her blue is light enough that we won't need a second round." Then she turned to Pistol and tossed her another box, this one featuring a smiling model with light ash-blonde hair. "If this doesn't work, we'll go with a slightly darker color."

"Not worried about frying the hair right off my head, are you?" Pistol's voice was sardonic and bold, but she didn't quite meet the demon woman's eyes, and cringed slightly after the question.

The woman's dark eyes were cold and impersonal, but in

their depths I saw a flicker of humor. "No, not particularly. I'm going to have to grow it out anyway. Creating a whole head of hair from scratch won't be any more difficult."

She went over to examine Pillow's hair while Pistol and I got to work. By the time we'd piled newly dyed hair on top of our heads, the demon woman and Pillow were out with the others, leaving Pistol and me to count, and hope that we hadn't messed up putting the second round of dye on still-damp hair.

"It's going to hurt," Pistol told me. "She's going to do something to me to make my hair longer and boobs bigger and it's going to hurt. You heard the screams."

"Push-up bras and make-up. And extensions," I assured her. Although at this point, I was beginning to doubt that was true.

"No. And you know that as well as I do. There's something weird about that woman. I'm not one-hundred-percent buying that she's a demon or anything, but I think there's something a whole lot more painful going on out there than push-up bras and make-up."

I gave up trying to convince her, or myself. "Probably. I can't imagine what, though."

"I didn't want to frighten Pillow any more than she already was, but I'm scared. My nose hurts from where they hit me. I've got a line of bruises across my ribs from that stupid broom pole. I don't know what she's going to do to me, but I'm thinking it's going to hurt far more than getting beat up by those guys. I'm scared."

The girl was on the edge of panic, so I did what anyone would do and tried to talk her down. "From what they said, there have been other groups of girls through here. She's done this before. It's probably just a quick pain, then it's over. Whatever she's doing."

"And then we'll be sold at an auction and sent where the

pain will be anything but quick. We'll be raped over and over again. You heard Mess and Sugar, most girls in these sex rings have to service twenty to forty guys a day. A *day*. I haven't been with that many guys in my entire life. I haven't been with half that many guys. And then we'll die. And we'll probably spend weeks or months wishing we'd hurry up and die. My parents won't find me in time. The police won't find us in time. We're all going to die. And before that, we're going to suffer so much pain and degradation that we'll wish they would just kill us."

"Well, that hasn't happened yet," I told her, trying to be as confident as I could. "We need to keep our hopes up, and not sit around waiting for your parents or the police to find us. Let's instead think about how we might be able to get out of here."

She laughed. "Nine of us, naked, half-starved women, two of whom don't speak any English, against a bunch of guys and a woman so terrible they call her a demon. I want to escape. I'm determined to escape no matter what, but hope and optimism isn't going to improve our odds."

"Nine of us," I emphasized. "We've got numbers on our side, and that woman isn't here all the time. The guards don't have guns that I can see. If we act fast, before we're any weaker from lack of food, and before they move us to wherever this auction is going to be, we can overpower them and escape."

"I want to escape. I'm totally with you on this. I want to get out of here as much as you do, but we need to be smart about it. We're wearing towels, in case you haven't noticed. What do we do when we get out of here, run through the streets like we've all escaped from a sauna at the gym?"

I was glad to see Pistol hadn't lost her quick wit, even though nine women running through the streets of wherever dressed only in towels wasn't our most pressing problem.

"Let's work on getting out of here first. There has got to be something around we can use to defend ourselves. We can see if anything is loose on the beds that we can unscrew and use as a weapon, and I'll bet the parts inside the toilet tank are metal."

"What are you, MacGyver?" she teased. "I'm voting for picking the lock and sneaking out instead. You can't seriously think we'd be able to take down three guards with metal screws and parts to a toilet, all while wearing towels?"

"Yes, I do. We'll surprise them."

"And get the crap beat out of us with a broom handle," she replied. "And what are we going to do if we *do* manage to get one over on these guards? Wander around what I suspect is a deserted industrial complex in the middle of the night until they come after us? We don't know where we are. We'll have more time to get our bearings if we sneak out when they're asleep."

"Sneak out or knock them out and make a run for it. We'll figure it out. Maybe if we steal one of their cell phones, we can call for help." I threw my hands up. "I don't know. I just want to do something rather than sit here, while everyone gets weaker and weaker from hunger, waiting for this sale."

Pistol slumped back against the wall. "You're right. Once this woman is gone, let's talk to the group. At the very least, let's see if we can come up with some sort of weapons—something we can use to defend ourselves if the guards get too handsy, or start beating on us again."

"And we need to think about timing," I added. "Do we try to get out now, or when they move us? Because when they get us to that sale, we're going to be out of options." We'd be sold, and I truly believed our best chances of getting out of this alive were as a group. One woman alone, captive in some guy's fallout shelter or cabin in the woods didn't have the advantages of nine working together to escape.

"Agreed." Pistol stood. "I'm going to wash this stuff off and hopefully not see all my hair go down the drain. You ready?"

We went through the shower ritual once more and I saw that Pistol's hair had stayed in her head and was actually a really attractive color for her. She took one look at me and burst out laughing.

"I'm sorry. I shouldn't… I mean, that woman is probably going to be pissed, but it's so funny. I don't know what hair color you used Red, but if we ever get out of here, you need to tell me the brand."

My heart sank as I pulled a strand forward. Red. The exact same red as it had been before. I could see one defective box of hair color, but couldn't imagine there being two, especially when it seemed to work on the other girls. My dismay was immediately followed by a shiver of fear.

"Guess you're not the only one who's going to get the special demon spa treatment." My voice shook a little and I tried for a cocky grin to counteract it. "My hair color and your extensions."

"Don't forget the boob job," Pistol said with a grimace. "You probably won't need one. You've got an amazing rack."

I looked down, feeling somewhat ambivalent about the boobs, about my entire body. Sometimes it felt like a shell, strange and alien.

The door swung open and the both of us jumped. It was the woman again. I swallowed hard, knowing what was to come.

She stopped, her jaw dropping as she stared at me. "What is going on with your hair?" she hissed.

"I saw her dye it," Pistol spoke up in my defense.

I flinched as a hand reached out and grabbed my arm. She wasn't gentle as she yanked me over, pawing through the locks to examine my scalp and the ends. "I will get some more dye tomorrow and make one of the others a blonde. Maybe if we go dark instead of trying to strip this red out, it will work."

I exhaled, realizing that I'd been holding my breath. She wasn't going to use whatever special skills she had to change my hair color? I was grateful, but knew Pistol wouldn't get such a reprieve. I slid a worried glance her way and saw the girl braced and ready.

The woman left me and examined Pistol's hair, making approving noises. Digging her hands into the short locks, she yanked. There was a silvery light and the hair grew as the demon woman pulled, like one of those gimmicky dolls. Pistol screamed.

It wasn't a clip-in extension. By all that was holy, the woman was using some sort of magic to grow Pistol's hair. It wasn't extensions and push-up bras and make-up, it was magic—demon magic. And whatever it was, it was clearly excruciating for the recipient.

My breath came fast and hard. I'm ashamed to admit that I retreated, not stopping until my bare back hit the cold tile of the wall. And there I shook, terrified and fighting the urge to vomit as Pistol's screams went on and on. When the demon woman let go, Pistol's hair was to her shoulders, a silvery ash-blonde. Her nose was straight, the cut on her head gone along with her bruises. The girl trembled and begged in between sobs for the other woman to stop, to not do anything else to her.

I now knew why they called her demon woman, and it wasn't just that she'd grown ten inches of hair from some-one's head. Her eyes were cold and hard. She didn't revel in Pistol's pain and fear; she just didn't care. No, that wasn't right. She was irritated. Annoyed. I got the impression she wanted to slap the girl.

Or maybe it was someone else she wanted to slap.

"I don't understand why they want your breasts bigger." The woman reached out and took one in her hand as Pistol flinched. "They look fine to me. Why do men want such huge breasts on women? They should go have sex with cows if they want big udders."

"Please don't. Please don't. Please don't," Pistol chanted.

I worked up my courage to take a few steps forward. "Just leave her alone. Don't hurt her anymore. Leave her alone."

The demon woman hesitated, shooting me a quick puzzled glance. "I've got my orders. Blondes. Bigger breasts. Firmer buttocks. Then in a few weeks a new batch of girls will come through here and I'll do it all again."

There was a kind of tired regret in her voice, and I seized on it. "Her breasts aren't much smaller than mine. I'll bet those idiot guards can't tell the difference anyway. Let her be, and lie to them. Just lie to them."

"Lie?" Something sparked up in the woman, and for a second I thought she would be on our side, be an ally we could rely on. Then whatever it was vanished, and all that was left was that flat, cold, resignation.

The silvery light came from her hands again and Pistol screamed.

Before I realized what I was doing I was across the room, grabbing a fistful of the demon woman's long black hair. Twisting it, I yanked her head around. Then with my other hand I slapped her across the face as hard as I could. "I said, leave her alone!" I shouted.

I was stronger than I'd thought because my slap sent the demon woman sprawling across the floor. Her hair had pulled free of my hand, leaving a few of the silky strands behind. I moved to stand in front of Pistol and wait for whatever violent punishment was coming my way.

The demon woman raised a hand to the side of her face and stared at me in amazement. "You hit me!"

"Stop hurting her. Leave us all alone," I commanded. "Do not harm mine…my friends."

I'd actually meant to say "mine," which was a weird thing to say about a bunch of girls I'd known only a few days. They weren't mine. I didn't own them. They weren't my possessions. Yet somehow they *were* mine. An odd sensation bloomed up inside of me with the word, shoving out through my skin like a shockwave.

The demon woman recoiled, as if I'd hit her again, then the surprise of what I'd done must have dissipated because her eyes grew cold and hard once more. She stood, brushing herself off, and tried to stare me down. I held her gaze, wondering how long I could fight her off before she got the best of me.

Pistol put a hand on my shoulder. "Don't. There's no sense in getting yourself beat up on my behalf. We'll just both end up hurt that way."

And then neither of us would be strong enough to fight when we needed to fight, was the subtext. I lowered my eyes and stepped aside, my hands balled into fists at my side. When I peeked up from under my lashes, I saw the demon woman still watching me, a strange expression on her face. With a sigh she turned to Pistol and once more put her hands on the girl's breasts.

I held my breath, waiting and listening to Pistol's ragged breathing.

"Forget it. They're big enough. I'm not going to make you into some ridiculous caricature to satisfy those Neanderthals," she snarled, stepping away from Pistol. Then she spun around and left, slamming the bathroom door on her way out.

CHAPTER 6

Miracle of all miracles, we were finally brought food. The guard who reeked of onions brought it in, grumbling about how he would have rather just let us go hungry. It wasn't anything special, but a tray of sandwiches, a few bags of chips, and some sodas seemed like a four-star dinner to us.

None of us made a move until the guard had left, then Mess took charge of ensuring everyone got an adequate portion. It was finger food, which didn't even give us the opportunity of pocketing a few dull knives or spoons to use as weapons. Once everyone got their food, the only sounds were people eating.

Four of us were hurting. Pistol sat dead-eyed on her bed, hunched over as she picked at her sandwich and chips. Sugar's complexion was now perfectly clear, and she chewed slowly and carefully, wincing with every bite. Baa couldn't even sit, her rounded, lifted rear so painful that she ate while lying on her stomach. Tasha was also hunched over, whimpering as she supported her larger breasts with one arm and ate with the other.

Yeah. Tasha's arm was no longer broken, and hers as well as Pistol's injuries were all gone. As uncomfortable as Tasha clearly was, it was clear she felt far better than she had before the demon had laid hands on her. I know the woman had fixed Tasha's arm to get her ready for the sale, but for some strange reason, it made me feel a bit grateful—as if the demon woman had healed Tasha, fixed her arm out of the goodness of her heart. It was a stupid, naive thought, but looking over at the girl that feeling of gratitude persisted. I'd been worried about our ability to escape with Tasha so injured. Now, our chances seemed just a tiny bit better.

I knew there could be no escape attempt tonight. Tasha, Pistol, and Baa wouldn't be able to run if they tried, and I wouldn't leave them behind. Hopefully they would be in less pain tomorrow and feel good enough to possibly try to get away. Until then, we needed to eat and regain our strength—and try to determine what sort of weaponry we might have at hand.

I stood and went over to where the guard had haphazardly set the food. The sandwiches were on a plastic platter that wouldn't serve as a shield, although possibly we could launch it like a Frisbee to distract them if we could find a way to hide it between the mattresses. The bags that held the chips, the plastic soda bottles and plastic cups were useless, as were the flimsy napkins.

"We could break the cups and use the jagged edges?" Pistol asked. "I cut myself once on a cracked red Solo cup. Bled like a pig."

Her words got everyone's attention. Sugar grabbed a few cups and shoved them under her pillow. Mess and Pillow got up and started examining the undersides of their cots, wiggling the legs and yanking on loose springs.

"Got one," Pillow surfaced holding a twisted thick wire.

"Think I can sharpen it a bit on the wall if I work on it tonight?"

"Probably." Mess stood and showed us the three screws she'd slotted between her fingers. She closed her fist and swung at the air. "Think this could do some damage as long as I get close enough to hit one of them."

Lacy watched us wide-eyed, then stood to look under her bed, shaking her head as she stood up. I motioned for her to follow me and we went into the bathroom.

Here was a dilemma. If we took the parts out of the toilet tanks, they would no longer work and we'd soon be found out. I motioned to the one at the far end, deciding that we'd need to restrict ourselves to using the front toilet. Lacy followed me and watched as I pulled the heavy ceramic tank lid off and carefully put it aside. We both peered into the tank. She said something, then reached in and touched the wire and the chain. I nodded, thinking that like Pillow, she could sharpen the end of the thick wire. The chain wasn't long enough, nor probably strong enough to use as a weapon, but having it at hand couldn't hurt.

Back outside we all sat on Mess's and Sugar's cots and talked.

"We were on the road for days," Mess said. "I wish we knew where we picked Red up because that would give us a good idea of overall distance travelled and narrow down where we are."

"The guard said Philly when they were all talking yesterday," Pillow chimed in. "So we were headed south, at least for a while."

"I felt the truck shifting downward to climb," Kitten said. "West of the Rockies, maybe?"

Sugar shook her head. "No, 'cause the truck going up and down the mountains happened right after we picked up Red.

We wouldn't have gotten that far in two days, not at the speed we were going."

Pillow nodded. "I used to live in Denver a while back. The truck wasn't climbing long enough to be going up mountains of that size. I'm thinking that we might have been going over the Blue Ridge mountains, maybe in Virginia or somewhere around Tennessee or North Carolina?"

Mess chewed the tip of her finger. "That first day from New York to Philly to pick up Red, then onward to cross the mountains south and west?"

"The driver would have taken it slow, obeyed all the traffic rules and taken state roads and more rural routes when possible," Pistol speculated. "I'm not sure we're past Texas. Actually, we might be east of Texas."

"So, Alabama? Oklahoma?" I asked. We'd stopped a few times where the truck sat for hours on end. Yeah, the guys could have been in getting something to eat, but every time they would have parked at a rest stop or shopping center lot, they would have run the risk someone would have heard us in the truck bed.

"Or Oklahoma," Pillow replied. "There were two guys to share the driving and in case things went wrong. We didn't drive straight through, we stopped a few times for hours at a stretch. It would have been easy for them to park the truck way in the back of someplace like a Walmart lot to sleep. I know from being on the street that lots of homeless with cars sleep there. Those big box stores are really tolerant of people overnighting it way in the back of their lots, and no one who is camped there for the night in their beat-up Dodge Neon is going to say squat about noise coming from a truck."

"We weren't exactly beating on the sides and screaming for help either," Pistol said with a grimace. "We were afraid all that would get us was raped and killed, especially after what they did to Tasha."

"So where are we thinking?" I asked.

Sugar lifted her shoulders. "Who knows? And does it really matter whether we're in Oklahoma or Alabama or Tennessee? All that matters is how close we are to a major road or a police station. I'm thinking we're probably outside of some podunk town. Someplace where most of the businesses have left and there's a bunch of old, abandoned commercial buildings that no one gives a rat's ass about."

"Yeah, but even podunk towns have police. And we may be in a remote area, but it can't be more than three or four miles from *somewhere*." Pistol's voice radiated hope.

"I can run three or four miles," Kitten chimed in. "Even barefoot, I'm sure I can do that."

Everyone looked down at their feet. Sugar laughed. "Actually I think that's going to be our biggest problem right there. Even if we escape, running on rocky ground or down through fields barefoot wearing towels...yeah, we better make sure those guards are either dead or tied up, or they'll catch us before we're ten feet away."

"I wish I knew how close we were to a populated area or a busy road." Pillow shook her head. "Doesn't help that they drove the truck right inside and let us out without being able to see anything to give us a clue about where we are."

Pistol scooted forward on the bed. "But they had that huge bay door open to get the truck in. Did anyone smell anything? Close your eyes and think, what did you smell when they opened the back of the truck to let us out?"

We did as she asked.

Sugar snorted. "Air that didn't smell like nine unwashed bodies and a pile of poop."

"Diesel fuel and exhaust," Kitten said. "Although that might have been from the truck we were in."

"A plasticky smell."

"Hot rubber."

"Something sharp and hot."

So we were in an industrial area? Or were all of those smells from the truck as well? Or the warehouse we were currently living in? I squeezed my eyes tighter and tried to remember the moments before we'd arrived. The truck had slowed quite a bit and was going over uneven ground—off road or potholes in well-worn streets? I'd heard a car honk, faint and filtered through the noise and the metal sides of our truck. A tire lifted on one corner as if we'd run over a curb. There was a jangle noise of rattling chains, the squawk of a gate opening, the rattle of corrugated metal as a bay door lifted. Then the noise of our truck intensified, echoing off the warehouse walls as we'd pulled in. My eyes popped open.

"We all agree that we're probably in an industrial area. I remember hearing some traffic, so it's either close to a road or not too isolated from other buildings or a residential section, or even the highway. We could be in a city, or we could be on the outskirts with other warehouses or businesses nearby—businesses that have traffic after hours."

"At least we won't have to go hiking miles through the desert if we escape," Pillow said.

"No, we'll just have to keep from getting raped as we dash through glass-strewn ghetto alleyways dressed in only a towel," Sugar drawled.

"That's if we *can* escape." Kitten chewed her lip. "Three guys against nine women in towels armed with broken plastic cups and rusted screws."

"Yeah, what could go wrong with that?" Sugar laughed and adjusted her towel. "I've been eying the guards, thinking that maybe we could distract them with offers of sexual favors, although I'm sure we're not the only girls through here that have tried that."

Mess shook her head. "Even if they do decide to have a little party, they would probably do it one at a time. If we managed to take down the guy with his dick out, we'd still have two guys with their pants on to deal with. No, I think our best bet is to wait until night when they're taking shifts sleeping and surprise them."

"But the door is locked," Pistol said, glancing that way. "We'll either need to jump them when they bring us food, or use some ploy to get them to come in, like say we're sick or something."

"They'd know something was up if we pulled that," Sugar told her.

I was getting an idea. "Those toilet lids are really heavy. We ambush the guy who brings us lunch tomorrow, hitting him with the toilet lid and knocking him out, then we sneak out the door and make our escape."

"That might kill him." Kitten's eyes were wide at the thought. "Are we okay with that?"

"I am most definitely okay with that," Sugar replied. The other girls nodded, and I decided that I didn't mind the thought of possibly killing one of our captors. I wasn't going to hold back and risk us all just to make sure the guy didn't have a brain hemorrhage. Go to bed with the devil, expect to get burned…or killed by a blow from a toilet tank lid.

"What about the demon woman?" Pistol asked. "What if her magic is more than just making hair grow and boob jobs?"

I remembered how my slap sent the woman across the room, the look on her face as she touched her reddened cheek.

"Hopefully we'll be able to make a move when she's not here," I said. "And if not…don't worry about the demon woman. Leave her to me."

* * *

WE'D BARELY FINISHED CHECKING our cots for additional loose wires and screws when the guards came back, one of them holding his cell phone and the other two with the usual broomsticks. The demon woman was with them, somehow managing to look both bored and annoyed at the same time.

"Why does that one girl still have the stupid red hair?" Pockmarks demanded.

The demon woman held up her hands. "We dyed it twice and neither time made any difference. I can run out and get some more dye and try to make it brown if you like, but I don't think anything we do is going to make her blonde."

Pockmarks glared at her. "You're a damned demon. Demon her hair blonde if the dye doesn't work."

The woman's eyebrows lowered. "These are high-dollar girls. I'm not going to mess with them more than I have to. You've got three blondes. If you really want, one more can dye her hair blonde, and I'll get a box of brown for the redhead."

Pockmarks scowled as he looked each of us over. "Fine. Do it tomorrow. Let's go ahead and get pictures of them, and we can update those two girls later if we need to. I want to get their profiles up in time to generate some hype for the sale. Buyers are already asking to see what we've got to offer."

The demon woman nodded and walked forward grabbing the arm of the closest girl, which happened to be Kitten, and leading her over to stand a few feet away from the wall. The girl trembled, her mouth clamped tight to keep from crying out as the demon woman removed her towel and positioned her.

Thirteen. She was only thirteen. My hands curled into fists, and I desperately wanted to launch myself at the guards and rip them apart with my bare hands. The demon woman stood back, out of the frame. Kitten whimpered, tears running down her cheeks as Pockmarks took pictures of her from several angles. They had her turn around and he took more from the rear.

The demon woman stepped forward with the towel outstretched in one hand, then as if she'd suddenly changed her mind, she wrapped it gently around Kitten, tucking the loose end in the top to hold it snug. "There. We're all done with you, child. Go back to your bed."

If was the first real glimmer of humanity I'd seen in her. She'd held back on further enhancements to Pistol's breasts but I hadn't been sure whether she'd done that out of sympathy for us, or just as a passive act of rebellion against the guards. But this tenderness toward a young girl…it made me wonder.

Pillow was next. One at a time we were each led over to the wall and made to stand naked for our pictures. The demon woman posed each of us—head tilted this way or that. No one cried aside from Kitten, although Baa looked as though she were about to explode when the guards began to admire the demon woman's work on her rear end. I was last for some reason. And I was surprised by the light, almost tentative grip the demon woman had on my arm as she led me over.

I dropped the towel, unwilling to let her undress me, and heard a soft gasp.

"Oh." The demon woman ran a finger down my arm. My reaction to her touch was downright embarrassing. My breath hitched. My skin flushed. And something deep inside me leapt at the feel of her skin against mine.

"I don't think I can get that on camera," Pockmarks said as he snapped pictures of me with his cell phone. I wasn't sure what he was talking about until I glanced down.

My skin was smooth and creamy, without visible pores, without hair, as if I were made of warm-tinted marble. It glowed with an iridescence, like it was covered with some kind of pearl dust.

"List her as one of those sparkly vampires," Onions joked. "Or a Tinkerbell or something. All the weirdos are gonna want her with that skin."

I want her. There's nothing that says I cannot sample the merchandise as these men so crudely do. Maybe I will this time….

The words flowed into my mind, and I shot the demon woman a sharp glance. Was I meant to hear that? Probably not judging from the bland, expressionless look on her face. I'd been occasionally hearing the other girls' thoughts since I'd woken up in the back of that truck. I guess it wasn't too far a stretch for me to hear this woman's as well.

Oddly enough, the idea of her having her way with me wasn't nearly as unnerving as the thought of the guards doing the same. Again I remembered her reaction as I slapped her in the bathroom. It made me think that any interaction between us, including sex, wouldn't be so very uneven as far as power and control went. Slapping one of the guards would get me beaten within an inch of my life. Slapping her had somehow put us on an even playing field, reminded her that I wasn't just a thing to be used and tossed away.

Weird. I felt an equal to a powerful demon that could alter women's bodies with a touch of her hands, but I was afraid of three human men with broomsticks.

"Miller is gonna want her with that skin," Pockmarks announced. "Do you know how much he'll pay to take a knife to that? There'll be a bidding war between him and the other sickos. Our share is gonna be huge for this girl."

Just like that, I snapped back to reality. The demon woman might somewhat respect me, but these guys sure didn't, and they were calling the shots. I really didn't like the idea of me, or anyone else, being sold off to this Miller guy.

The demon woman's hand on my shoulder was gentle as she turned me around. "Yes. She'll bring in a lot. Probably as much as the young one."

She didn't sound particularly excited about it. Maybe demons didn't care about money. Her fingers caressed down my arm as she stepped back for Pockmarks to take the picture.

I wish I could buy her for my own. I wish I could buy them all.

My head jerked around in astonishment. Had she said that out loud? Had I heard that thought, or imagined it? Pockmarks cursed. "Hold still." I complied, then turned again when I felt the woman touch my shoulder once more.

"Make sure they get something else to eat tonight," she said. "And bring in the T-shirts and sweatpants from the front office. There's no sense in keeping them naked now that we've evaluated them and taken their pictures."

"But I like 'em naked," Catcalls protested. "It'll make it easier later when take them for a test drive."

The woman's fingers tightened on my shoulder and she pushed me in front of her toward the cots. "You're not going to be trying all nine in one night. And it takes all of five seconds for them to take off sweatpants and a T-shirt."

"We can make them strip for us," Onions chimed in. "Then take turns fucking them. I get to go first."

"You can go first tonight, then someone else gets to pick," Pockmarks said. "One girl a night, that way we don't need to keep track of two of them. The boss will have our asses if any of them escape."

"I want the black chick," Catcalls announced. Mess stiffened at the comment, remaining silent as she lifted her chin.

"No, me first." Onions looked us all over, hesitating on

Pillow, then sliding over to me. "Red. I like redheads, and she's got that pretty skin."

The demon woman sighed, turning me back around. "Can you try not to bruise and cut the pretty skin too terribly much?"

"Yeah," Pockmarks agreed. "She and the young one are going to be the headliners of the sale. Screw all you want, but nothing that's gonna scar or that the demon can't easily fix." Onions went to protest, only to shut his mouth under Pockmarks's glare. "Don't do anything that jeopardizes our profits, or you're out of the group. And out of the group means you're dead in a back alley. Got it?"

Onions nodded. "Okay, fine. But if she tries to scratch me or kick me in the nuts, I'm gonna hit her."

Pockmarks rolled his eyes. "Tie her up then, idiot. And hit her all you want. Just don't beat her to death like that girl two months ago."

They beat a girl to death? My heart rate kicked up. They beat a girl to *death*?

"That wasn't me," Onions turned to glare at Catcalls. "Slapping around is one thing. I'm not the one who gets off on screwing some half-dead chick."

Catcalls shrugged. "She had it coming. Besides, we had an extra."

Pockmarks pointed a warning finger at the guard. "You're damned lucky we had an extra, otherwise the boss would have cut your nuts off for that one."

Catcalls licked his lips and eyed me. "Got an extra this time too."

"No." Pockmarks's command was sharp. "Only what the demon can fix. You get carried away again, and it's your body we'll be dumping in a back alley. Got it?"

Catcalls glared sullenly at the floor. "Yeah. Got it."

"Her." Onions grinned at me. "Now. Me first, then one of

you can take a turn with her. Then maybe I'll take a couple more before we bring her back."

The demon woman pushed me forward and Onions reached out to grab my wrist. The feel of his calloused fingers digging into my skin made me want to vomit. He pulled me along, and the other guards and the woman fell in behind him. At the door I glanced back to see the other girls staring at me—scared and relieved it wasn't them. Onions yanked me hard enough that I felt the muscles pull in my shoulder. Then the door closed and I found myself out in the main part of the warehouse with three men and a demon.

CHAPTER 7

 tried to yank my arm free, struggling as Onions half dragged me across the warehouse. The towel slipped and fell, and the others hooted and cheered Onions on as he yanked me forward, smacking me hard on my ass when I continued to resist. He was taking me to where the line of offices stood, and I knew very well what was going to happen to me once he got me inside.

Bile rose to burn my throat at the thought of what this man intended to do to me. I thrashed around but his fingers were like a handcuff around my wrist. If I could just get free, I could run for it—outrun the three men, evade the broomsticks, escape this room and race straight to someone who could call the police and rescue the others. In the back of my mind, I knew I couldn't outrun these guys. They'd be on me before I could get the warehouse door open. And if they didn't stop me before I got out, the demon would.

And if she didn't, I'd be running barefoot and naked through who-knows-where. They'd catch me before I got help. And when they caught me, it would be ten times worse.

What the drivers did to Tasha would look gentle in comparison.

They had an extra. And they'd killed one before. They could easily do so again and hide my body where it would never be found.

"Stop fighting, bitch." Onions twisted and pulled on my arm, nearly yanking it from the socket. The others laughed. Desperate, I dropped to the floor, a dead weight. Still he retained a hold on my wrist, tightening his fingers painfully. With a string of curses he went to pull me across the floor and stopped, looking over at Pockmarks. "See what I mean? Let me take a stick to her a few times so she'll come willing."

"What, you can't handle a little thing like that without a stick?" Pockmarks scoffed. "Open hand. And if she doesn't get the idea, you can use your fist."

I kicked and pulled, desperately trying to get free as Onions dragged me across the floor. With a grunt, he tossed me through an open door into one of the offices, then closed and locked it behind him. I scrambled to my feet, my arm and shoulder aching, finger marks red and swollen around my wrist. In the seconds it took the guard to lock the door, I looked for a window, another door, or something to use as a weapon. There was nothing. The only way in and out was through the door Onions stood in front of. There was nothing in the room besides a bed, a small refrigerator, a few empty pizza boxes, and a coil of rope. Nowhere to run. Nowhere to escape.

A hand gripped my hair so tight tears sprang to my eyes. I jabbed an elbow backwards and felt it connect. Onions let out a curse and hit me hard in the lower back. Everything blurred as pain bloomed deep into my back muscles and down my legs. I dropped to my knees, my head arched backward as he retained a hold on my hair. Then his palm hit the side of my head so hard everything went white. I tasted blood. He hit me again.

And again. After the third time, I felt myself lifted upward and slammed onto the bed. My arms were yanked up over my head, tied with rough rope and looped around one of the headboard posts. I spat and kicked, struggling in vain to get free. When he was done with my hands, he put a knee on my stomach, resting his weight on me as he yanked one of my legs over to the side and began to tie it to a footboard bedpost. I gave up trying to get free and struggled to breathe, his weight restricting my air intake. One leg secure, he lifted himself from me and grabbed the other leg, pulling it wide to tie to the other footboard post.

"Wildcat bitch. Embarrass me in front of the others, will you? I'm gonna screw you so hard you can't see straight. Then I'm gonna carve my initials into that glowy skin of yours, maybe take a stick to you a few times before I let the other guys have a turn."

I inhaled, going cold with fear. My shoulder ached. The rope was chafing my bruised, swollen wrist. He had my legs spread so far apart that I was getting a cramp in my hip. My towel was long gone, and I was naked with my breasts thrust outward, and my arms stretched tight above my head. The guard unzipped his fly, the sound abnormally loud. Everything sounded abnormally loud—my breathing, the grunt he made as he stroked himself, the squeak of the bed as he climbed on top of me. I shut my eyes tight, tensed, and bit back a cry as he drove himself into me.

I just needed to survive this, I thought as he pressed his hips down. Just survive this man with his overpowering onion smell, his ragged foul breath against my face, his weight pressing the breath out of me. Just survive the pain of him inside me, of his hand twisting my breast. Survive him, then the next guy, then the next, then all of them again as many times as they wanted to take me throughout the night. Survive the beatings, the cutting of my skin. Just survive until morning when they untied me and shoved me, bruised and filthy back into the other room where I could spend the day huddled under a hot shower trying to wash the feel of this man and the others from my skin.

They'd pick someone else tomorrow. One of the other girls would need to endure this. One of the other girls would be tied down to this bed and repeatedly raped until they'd had their fill. They'd be hurt, their arms twisted, their legs spread to their limits. They'd smell the horrible fetid odor of this man, hear his raspy breath, feel him spill into them as he came, shuddering and grunting like a pig.

Something fierce and bright bloomed up inside me. I was more than this body. There were parts of me these men could never touch, never soil. Do what they will, they wouldn't see me broken and humiliated.

But my girls… They were *mine*. They were my girls, and these filthy swine couldn't have them.

My skin burned, like I was too close to a sudden burst of flame. The guard slumped on top of me, his weight crushing the breath from my lungs. I was wet, and not just between my legs either. Had someone thrown a bucket of warm, slimy water on us?

And why did the bucket of water smell like copper pennies?

I blinked my eyes open to a haze of red mist. When it cleared I found that I was splattered with blood. The guard's body was heavy on my chest, his legs sprawled, his dick still inside me. I shifted as much as I could manage, to try to get him to roll off me enough to breathe. He slid slightly to the side, his head lolling off my shoulder. Inhaling, I gagged at the smell of blood and burned flesh.

Had he cut me, carved his initials into me as he'd promised to do? Burned me? I hadn't felt it, but he must have nicked me during sex—and nicked me good if all this blood was any indication.

"Get off," I hissed, bucking my hips and wincing at the sharp pain the movement brought. Wiggling, I managed to get him to move enough that I could take a deep breath. Idiot. Was he drunk? He hadn't smelled drunk, just of onions. Maybe he passed out after he came. I had a sudden vision of a fainting goat, and bit back a horribly inappropriate laugh. Then I turned my head, realizing as I did so that I hadn't smelled the oniony-aroma of his breath since I'd opened my eyes.

One look at his face and I started shrieking. He was covered in blood, as if it had come out of his very pores, and where his eyes used to be were smoking black holes. His mouth was open in a silent scream. My screams were not so silent.

No one came running to my aid. They probably thought Onions was doing something horrible to me. So instead of screaming, I started yelling for help. Then I realized that probably wouldn't bring them either, so I started yelling "he's dead" over and over as I twisted as much as I could, trying to get this dead, blood-soaked body off me.

That finally brought them, but they couldn't get in because the idiot had locked the door from the inside. I had visions of me trapped in here forever with a decomposing corpse while they banged on the door, asking if Onions was okay, and telling him to come unlock the door so Catcalls could have a turn. There was some muffled cursing and then silence. I managed to get Onions off me, the top half of him dangling from the side of the bed, his lower half still draped across me. At least my efforts had removed his dick from inside me.

Was that weird? I was covered in blood, tied naked to a bed with a corpse half on top of me, and my biggest worry was getting his dick out as soon as possible. I shuddered, more revolted by the way it had slid wet and limp from between my legs than this cadaver lying on me. His blood was far more acceptable than his ejaculation. It was *that* I wanted to shower off, not the blood.

The door handle jiggled and turned. It opened, and Catcalls stood in the opening, his hand over his mouth.

"Get out of the way, you idiot." Pockmarks pushed by him, only to stop and mimic Catcalls's motion. "Fuck! What did you do?"

I stared at him in astonishment. "You think I did this? I'm tied to the bed in case you didn't notice."

"There's no one else in here," Catcalls choked as he said the words. "No windows or closets or other doors. This one was locked from the inside. How did he... How did he..." The man turned and started to retch.

Pockmarks strode into the room and turned Onions over. The dead man fell completely off me onto the floor, face up.

"His eyes. What happened to his eyes?' Catcalls babbled, on the edge of panic. "It's like some kind of internal combustion or something. Like he blew up inside and burned out his eyes."

"Go get the demon." Pockmarks's voice was hard and cold, but I heard the sharp edge of fear in his words. Catcalls vanished, reappearing a few minutes later with the woman. She breezed through the door, tiny and elegant with enough presence to bend an army to her will, but even she stopped abruptly and clasped a hand to her mouth when she saw Onions.

"I didn't do it. I'm tied up," I babbled. "He was......he did... and my eyes were closed because he was gross and it hurt, then I felt something wet and his weight and when I opened my eyes..."

They ignored me. Pockmarks pointed to the dead body. "Did you do that?"

He wasn't asking me; he was asking the demon woman.

She tilted her head still looking down at the dead body. "Did I do what?"

"Kill him? He was behind a locked door, fucking a tied-up, naked girl. No other way in. No other way out. No one else in here."

"I don't teleport. It's not one of my skills." She finally looked up at him, her face impassive. "And I was with you in the other office the whole time. What are you suggesting? That I cloned myself and snuck under the door crack as a wisp of smoke?"

"Well, he certainly wasn't killed by a human. Look at him. He wasn't shot or stabbed or beat to death. Looks like… I don't know what it looks like, but it ain't natural."

She lifted her hands. "Why? Why would I kill him? He stank, and wasn't particularly smart as humans go, but he wasn't worth the effort to kill. And in case you've forgotten, I *can't* kill any of you. Can't kill you. Can't injure you. Can't seduce you and take your energy or your souls. It. Was. Not. Me." She looked me in the eyes. "And clearly it wasn't her, either."

Pockmarks snorted. "I know it wasn't her. One of your demon buddies, maybe? Did someone track you down and decide to free you?"

"Well then, my demon buddy killed the wrong human." She folded her arms across her chest. "This dead man does me no good."

Pockmarks stared down at the corpse for a moment, then headed for the door. "I'm calling the boss."

The other two followed and Catcalls closed the door behind him, leaving me alone with a dead body, blood cooling and congealing on my skin along with sweat and other bodily fluids I was even more grossed out about. I heard Pockmarks on the phone, heard their footsteps as they walked away.

I drifted in and out of sleep, completely losing track of time. My arms were going numb, which meant my wrist wasn't throbbing as painfully as it had been. The cramp in my hip had faded, but I was pretty sure it would come roaring back once I was untied and was able to actually move my legs. They'd left the light on in the room, which meant I could see the cold, sticky blood on my body as well as the corpse on the floor next to me. The shock was beginning to fade. I was cold, desperate for a shower, and even though I didn't seem to feel hunger, I knew that I needed to eat. The other girls might have gotten dinner, but I hadn't. That mini fridge was tempting me from the corner of the room, making me imagine all the leftovers it might hold. Pork fried rice? Pizza? A wedge of smoked gouda? A six pack of Bud Light?

Finally, the door opened, and I wasn't sure whether to be relieved or scared. I decided on relieved, figuring no guy could possibly want sex enough to screw me next to a corpse while I was covered with blood.

It was the demon woman. She walked in, closing the door quietly behind her. I kept my mouth shut, wanting her to untie me, but worried that she might have something else in mind. If she really was a demon, she might not mind about the blood or the corpse.

She didn't untie me. She didn't even look at me. Instead she crouched down next to the body, her hands emitting a silvery glow as she ran them over Onions' face. After a few seconds, she sat back on her haunches and stared down at the dead guard.

"Dar?" she whispered. "Ni-Ni? Ni-Ni? Ni-Ni, is it you? Did you finally come for me? If so, then I hate to say you've killed the wrong human. He's not the one who summoned me."

She fell silent. I held my breath, not wanting her to notice me. Who had she been talking to? Had Pockmarks been right? Was there another demon, one who had snuck in and killed Onions while he was raping me? If so, why hadn't the demon killed me as well? Or better yet, rescued me?

The woman sighed and stood. As she turned to leave, I overcame my fear and spoke.

"Ma'am? Lady? Can you untie me? Please?"

She stopped and turned slowly around, seemingly surprised to see me still tied to the bed.

"Please?" I begged.

She looked over her shoulder at the door.

"Will you get in trouble?" I asked. "I know they think you might have had something to do with this guy's death. Are you worried they'll beat you if you let me go?"

Her eyes flashed. "They wouldn't dare."

I hid a smile and tried to look wide-eyed and innocent like Kitten. "Please?"

She sighed and walked over, undoing my arms first. My circulation returned with a vengeance and I held back a cry as the pain screamed along my nerve endings. My legs were worse, and I sat on the end of the bed, worried I wouldn't be able to stand. I felt her fingers brush the hair from my face. Something sparked in the air, and I leaned into her hand, turning so my lips brushed her palm.

"How badly did he hurt you?" Her voice was gentle as her fingers stroked my cheek.

Surprisingly I felt fine. My face where Onions had hit me didn't hurt. My arms and legs were as if I'd never been tied to a bed for hours. Looking down at my wrist, I saw nothing but unblemished, creamy skin—no rope burns, no bruising from being dragged across the warehouse floor. Had she healed me? Fixed my injuries as she had Tasha's and Pistol's? If so, then why hadn't I felt the horrible pain the others had when she'd "magicked" them?

"He hurt me, but I'm okay now," I told her, wondering if I should thank her or not. Probably not. It was her job after all, to make sure that we were perfect for the sale. It wasn't like she was doing me any favors.

"Good." Her fingers continued to stroke my face, lighting up all sorts of feelings throughout my body. Here I was sticky with blood and ejaculation and I felt turned on. How sick was that?

"Help us. Help us escape." I looked up at her as her fingers stilled their motion. Such dark eyes. So very beautiful. "Come with us."

Come with me was what I meant. What was she doing to me? Was this some seductive demon magic? If so, I didn't really care.

"I can't." Her hand left my face and the sensual atmosphere vanished abruptly. "I can't help you escape, and I can't come with you." She stood. "You're beautiful. I'd love to make you mine, but I can't, at least not for more than a night or two. Just like all the other girls, you'll be sold and go off to be a slave to whoever buys you." Her hand reached to my face again, hastily withdrawn. "I hope it isn't Miller. I hope whoever buys you doesn't kill you."

"I hope whoever buys me does kill me," I told her. "It would be better than night after night like this, being beaten, tied to a bed and raped. There are things worse than death."

"I can't." She took my arm and helped me stand, walking me through the warehouse, and unlocking the door to the room I shared with the other girls. Inside, they were all quiet lumps on their cots, completely unaware of what had happened outside this door. It hurt that none of them had stayed up worrying about me. Did anyone care whether I was bleeding, tied to that bed? Did anyone care whether I was the one dead on the floor?

"Shower. Get some sleep," the woman whispered. "I'll make sure they bring you breakfast in the morning."

"Will you be here in the morning?" I asked.

She eyed me sharply. "I can't help you. Don't ask me again. And know that if I see you trying to escape, I'll stop you. I will find you and bring you back. I am not your salvation."

The door closed behind me, separating the captors from the captives. For a long time I stood there, watching the other girls sleep, thinking about the demon's words.

I am not your salvation, she'd said. But deep in my heart, I suspected she was.

CHAPTER 8

I went straight to the showers and took an inordinately long time under the hot water. No matter how I scrubbed, I couldn't seem to get clean, so I ended up sitting on the tile floor, letting the water cascade down on me as I hugged my knees.

"You okay?" Mess peeked through the door, then tiptoed over when I didn't answer. I realized she was wearing a pair of yoga pants and a T-shirt. We were being fed, and now had clothes. It was the little things that counted right now, and I got the uneasy feeling that was step one of accepting that this was our lot in life.

"I'm fine. Go back to sleep." I couldn't keep the bitterness from my voice. I'd been the one taken, beaten, raped. And as that was happening to me, they'd put on clothes, ate their dinner, and slept.

"I wasn't sleeping, and neither were half those girls out there. The others finally dozed off after they couldn't keep their eyes open any longer." She padded barefoot into the shower area. "I saw the demon woman bring you back, but you needed a few moments by yourself before we jumped all over you. I know. I've been there."

Tears stung my eyes. When I'd been tied to the bed, I'd been glad it was me and not the other girls. I still felt that way, but to come back and find them sleeping, seemingly indifferent to my plight…it hurt far worse than anything Onions had done to me.

"Hey, hey," her voice was soft. She came close enough that the water was splashing up on her sweatpants, making little dots of dark fabric in the light gray. "We were all scared—scared of what they were doing to you, scared that you might not come back at all, scared that we'd be next. We were worried they'd take us one at a time, separate us. Because every girl in that room knows that separate, we're weak. It's only together that we'll get through this, that we'll survive and get back to whatever shitty lives we had before."

I'd been scared too. An extra girl. And although Pockmarks seemed annoyed that Catcalls had killed a girl before, he didn't seem all that bothered other than the loss of profit.

Mess knelt down, peering at my face, her dark eyes full of concern. "We need you, Red. If they'd killed you, if they'd broken you, we'd all be lost. We're family now, and you're our salvation."

"No, you're the leader. You're the one who takes care of the girls. You're our salvation," I told her.

"I take care of them, soothe them, try my best to protect them, but I'm not like you, Red. They see you as someone strong and darn near invincible, as someone who can stand up to these guys, who can take what they dish out, give as good as she gets, and *survive*. Maybe even win. Pistol told us about you slapping that demon woman. We could hear you fighting even through the closed door when that man dragged you out of here. But you came back. And you're not bruised or cut up with your arm broken like Tasha either.

You walked in with your head high, defiant, like you didn't have a scratch on you. I know what they did to you out there, but they didn't break you. Damn girl, I don't even think they *touched* you, at least not inside where it counts. *You* are our salvation. You."

I'm not your salvation. It was what the demon had told me. It was what I felt like saying to Mess. How could I be anyone's salvation? I was weak. When it came time to be brave, I crumbled and fell back on what everyone else expected of me, I hid behind rules while those I loved—the truly brave ones—risked their lives and died for what they believed in.

No. I wasn't weak. Not anymore. I was willing to suffer, to die so that these girls could be saved. And that meant I needed to get up out of this shower, dry off, and be the strong leader they needed.

But first, I needed to stop crying.

Mess sat down next to me, her butt just out of reach of the water. "I was eight the first time. The neighbor kids took turns while one held me down. Wasn't like I could tell my mom about it. Wasn't like she, or anyone else, would have cared. Happened every week or so for six months until we got evicted. Never thought homelessness would be such a blessing."

I felt the water beat against my skin as traces of her memories lit up inside my mind, making me realize that there were girls every day going through what had just happened to me, and worse.

"You'd think I'd be used to it by now, but I'm not. Every time some john climbs on top of me, I have to pretend I'm someone else, that I'm acting in a movie or something. It's easier when I'm on top, but the corners my pimp used to put me on didn't bring the sort of guys who want a woman on top."

We sat in silence for a moment before she spoke up again. "Wanna hear something funny? I'm not a runaway. It's my mom that ran away, not me. She's crazy—not crazy enough to get locked up, but crazy enough that she can't seem to keep a job. We'd been living on the streets for about a year when I came back one day to find her gone. She'd picked up all of our stuff and left. Guess she forgot about me."

My head came up. "You were nine?"

Mess nodded. "There was a group of us living under the bridge there. The others took care of me for a while, but they had their own problems and taking on a little girl full-time wasn't something any of them could do, you know? I stole some. Begged some. Wound up being a lookout for a corner dealer for a while. At ten I was turning tricks, because it was good, reliable money, and at least I had a roof over my head. That first pimp wasn't so bad. People pay a lot to screw a ten-year-old girl."

I felt a sudden urge to kill people who would pay to have sex with a ten-year-old-girl, as well as the pimp that would profit from such a horrible thing. There was some satisfaction in imagining myself shooting them, slicing their throats, hitting them repeatedly with something large and hard.

"Sugar ran away from home at thirteen, but in a way she's had it worse. A couple close calls with some sickos, a few pimps that would rather beat on her than put her on a corner. She had a boyfriend a few years back that was supposed to take her away from all this, but he ended up just wanting her regular-like for free. Expected her to keep working and giving him a share of her percentage." Mess shrugged. "One good thing out of this whole situation? Had a bunch of burn scars on my leg where mom used to put her cigarettes out on me when she was off her rocker. That demon woman fixed 'em. Hurt like hell, but they're gone now." She pulled up a pants leg and showed me a shapely leg with smooth, unmarked, mocha skin.

Too bad the demon woman couldn't take away the other scars, the ones below the skin. But maybe we needed those scars. We couldn't undo the horrible experiences of our pasts, but perhaps they allowed us to have compassion for others.

"He's dead," I told Mess. It felt like I was lancing an infected wound. "The guy that smelled like onions all the time? He beat me, then tied me to the bed and raped me. Then he died."

She stared. "Like stroked out or had a heart attack while screwing you?"

"No. It was like spontaneous human combustion. He was finishing off, all hot and smelly and gross on top of me, then bam. Blood all over me, and black smoking craters where his eyes used to be."

Mess recoiled in shock, staring at me wide-eyed. Then suddenly the pair of us began to laugh. It started light, like a tickle, like we were barely able to process the amusement of it all, then cascaded into deep belly laughs that took our breath away and had us rolling on the floor in tears.

"Oh, the times I wanted some guy to spontaneously combust on top of me," Mess said, wiping her eyes with the edge of her T-shirt. "How'd you do that? Let me know your secret, so I can kill off a few of these assholes myself. You got Jedi mind tricks, or something?"

The amusement faded and I frowned. "It wasn't me. He had me tied to the bed. I had my eyes closed, was trying not to think about what he was doing, and suddenly he was dead on top of me. Pockmarks thought it was the demon woman, but there was no one else in the room with us. The demon woman believes it was one of her buddies come to get her, but when she snuck back in and called to them, no one came."

"It was you." Mess reached out and touched my wet shoulder. "I think you've got a guardian angel looking over you. Can you let me borrow him? Sure could use one of my own."

I got to my feet and turned off the water, feeling so much better. It helped to know I wasn't in this alone. We'd stick together. We'd help each other. We'd survive as long as we didn't turn our backs on one another. And I'd be strong for these girls. I'd never be weak again. They needed me, and I'd do everything in my power not to let them down. As for a guardian angel…

"I'm not sure you want to borrow him." I took the towel Mess handed me and started to dry myself off, noting again with surprise that I'd come through the evening's activities without a single bruise on my skin. "I mean, what kind of guardian angel shows up *after* you've been raped? And then leaves you tied spread-eagle to a bed with a dead guy on top of you?"

Mess chuckled, putting her arm around me as we headed for our cots. "Hey, at least he showed up. Better late than never, huh?"

* * *

THE OTHERS WERE awake and sitting on their cots when we came out. Everyone eyed me silently, not sure what to say to someone who'd been dragged across the warehouse floor, beaten and raped.

"I'm okay." I told them.

Pistol reached under her bed and pulled out a napkin, handing it to me. Inside was half of a sandwich and some chips. "I saved this for you. And there's some clothes over there for you to put on."

Pillow hopped off her cot and hugged me. "You sure you're okay? I mean, of course you're not okay. I know what those guys did to you. But…"

"The arm is not broken," Tasha added with a wry smile. "That is a good thing."

"More than that, one of the guards is dead," Mess announced triumphantly. "Wrath of God stuff too. Blood everywhere. Eyes burned out of his skull. Red slaps demons in the face and makes rapists explode on the inside."

There was a moment of shocked silence, then Sugar laughed. "No way. So I'm assuming only the one guy raped you or we'd all be strolling out the door right now. Wonder if they'll put a warning label on you for the sale. 'Caution. Girl slaps demons and explodes anyone who fucks her.' No one is gonna mess with you, Red."

Okay, it *was* kind of funny. Not when I'd just been raped and had a bloody dead guy on top of me with his dick still inside, but here, freshly showered and surrounded by my girls, it was funny. And it made me seem far more badass than I really was.

"I didn't kill him," I told the girls as I wiggled into the clothing at the end of my cot. "He had me tied to a bed. He was…you know. And then suddenly he was dead."

"Sounds like you killed him to me." Sugar's grin was downright maniacal. "Wasn't there some creepy-ass story about a woman who had knives or sharp teeth or something in her vajayjay, and when a guy would screw her, she'd shred his dick to bits. Red's like that only on steroids. She doesn't just shred a guy's dick, she blows him up inside."

"And how would I have done that *tied to a bed*?" I didn't want these girls thinking I had magical powers. I was going to do all I could to get us out of here, to ensure their safety, but I couldn't go exploding guards to do it.

"Then who did it?" Kitten curled up on the edge of her cot, hugging her knees. "Someone killed him. People don't just spontaneously combust, you know."

"Maybe one of the other guards poisoned him," Pistol volunteered. "Maybe the demon woman poisoned him."

That was a whole lot more believable than the other theories.

"The demon woman didn't do it," I told them. "She thought maybe it was one of her demon friends come to rescue her."

"I think Red has a guardian angel," Mess announced. "She hit that demon woman and didn't get killed. The guy raping her dies a gruesome death. He beat her, but she doesn't have a mark on her."

I opened my mouth to tell them the demon woman had healed me, only to snap it shut. Had she healed me? It hadn't hurt like it had when she'd healed the others. And my track marks… They'd vanished within hours of waking up in that truck. Maybe the healing was me. Maybe I'd acquired super-powers somehow—been bitten by a radioactive spider or something. Or maybe I did have a guardian angel, one who wasn't smart enough to get us the heck out of here, one who left me in a room, tied and naked with a dead body on top of me. What sort of lousy guardian angel would do that?

"Well, if it's a guardian angel, he needs to get with the program and help us escape," I told the girls. "Now, let's all try to get some sleep. Tomorrow we're going to get out of here, and we need to be well rested."

I slept fitfully, hearing the other women as they turned on their cots, hearing their soft moans of discomfort as they tried to find a position that wouldn't put weight on wherever they'd had 'work' done. I should have been doing that too.

With the beating I'd taken, with my arms and legs tied to bed posts for hours, I should have been aching and sore. But I felt fine. It was as if nothing had happened, as if my body had been healed of all wounds. Too bad my soul hadn't the same abilities.

It wasn't just the discomfort of the others that kept me awake, it was the film reel of the night's events that kept looping through my mind. His smell. His feel. The heaviness of his body on mine. His hand bruising my flesh. The way he'd shoved himself inside me. How he'd slipped wet and limp from me as his body slid off to the side. The shock of seeing the black smoking holes where his eyes had been. The sticky feel of blood and semen on my skin, between my legs, dripping down my thighs once the demon woman had untied me and I'd tried to stand.

But he was dead, and I wasn't. And out of all the girls here, better me to go through that than any of them. I closed my eyes, feeling them on either side of me. My girls. Mine. Every last one of them. We were a family, just like Mess had said. A family.

In the morning we were all bleary eyed, splashing water on our faces and taking turns peeing in the one toilet we hadn't cannibalized for parts. Catcalls came in with breakfast, and we descended on the trays of food like a pack of piranhas, ignoring the fact that he was eyeing us, stroking the broomstick as if it were his dick. At one point he made a move to grab Mess's butt, and I pushed myself between them, staring the man down.

"You offering something, Red?" he sneered. "Didn't get enough last night? I gotta warn you, I hit harder than the other guys. Might not want to offer yourself up so readily."

"I hit back," I told him. "Ask that demon woman how hard I hit. And don't forget what happened to the last guy who raped me."

He laughed. "You were tied to the bed, screaming your head off. Don't go acting like you had anything to do with that. He probably ate some bad shellfish or something."

Yeah, because shellfish often result in blood bursting from your pores and your eyes burning out of their sockets. But I couldn't counter his other statement. I was tied to the bed. And I had been screaming my head off, completely freaked out by Onions's death right on top of my naked body. I might not be able to scare this guy, but I could try to distract him from the other girls. I got the feeling that Catcalls was all about making a girl pay for what she'd done. The more a woman pissed him off, the more he wanted to take it out of her hide. I'd just have to make sure I was top of his list, because tonight was his night to pick one of us. If we couldn't manage to get ourselves out of here, I wanted to make sure it was me he was beating on and not someone else.

I could take it. I'd survive. If he hurt me, I'd heal. And if I were really lucky, maybe he'd wind up dead as well.

After a few more lewd comments, Catcalls left, and we sat on our cots, trying to smear cream cheese on bagels with our fingers, and sipping from little containers of yogurt drink. "Think you can run for it later today?" I asked Tasha. After what happened to me last night, I was more determined than ever to get us out of here. We only had two more days until the sale. Better to go now than wait for a better opportunity that might never come.

Tasha touched her breasts gingerly and nodded. "Yes. They are not so bad today."

Pistol turned and said something to Baa, waiting for the girl's reply. "I think we can do it. I was worried about Baa since she's the one who got her butt lifted and enhanced, but she says she's ready whenever we are."

I looked over at the Guatemalan girl, who was most definitely still moving gingerly. She set her mouth in a grim line and gave me a thumbs-up sign. I hadn't paid much attention to the two women who didn't speak English, but now I did. Baa looked determined, ready to take on anything. Lacy's eyes darted to each of us, her body tense and aware. I felt the most sorry for her. The other at least had Pillow to translate.

How horribly alone and afraid Lacy must feel, not knowing a word of what we were saying, worried that if we made a move she'd be unprepared, or even left behind. I walked over to her and made a circular motion with my finger. Then I pointed to the door, and pantomimed a fight, then jogged in pace.

She nodded. The girl might not know the details of what we were about to do, but she was watching carefully, and I knew she'd take her cues from us when the time came. One thing was very clear from her anxious, alert gaze—Lacy did *not* want to risk being left behind.

The door opened again and Catcalls entered. They'd initially always come in pairs, one with a gun at the ready, but with Onions dead, Catcalls would probably come alone from now on. I got the feeling it was beneath Pockmarks to be delivering us food. It would work to our advantage. Disable whoever brought us lunch, and we'd only have the other to deal with if we got caught sneaking out.

Unless it was the demon woman who caught us trying to escape. I remembered her words from last night. Although she seemed to have some general sympathy for our plight, it was clear that she'd look out for her own interests first—and those interests included bringing us to auction. She wouldn't help us escape. And if she caught us trying, she'd bring us back in. We couldn't rely on her. As much as I wanted to think of her as a sympathetic character, she was just as much our enemy as these two men.

Although Catcalls didn't appear all that menacing right now. Instead of the usual broom handle, this time he carried a plastic shopping bag.

"Here." Catcalls pulled a box out of the bag and tossed it to me. Hair dye. With everything that happened last night, I'd forgotten about my red hair. This dye was a dark brown which I was pretty sure would look hideous with my complexion. I secretly hoped I had the same results with this one as the one before.

Another box flew through the air, and Tasha caught it just before it hit her in the face. She stared wide-eyed at the blonde model on the cover and looked up at the guard in confusion. "Me? I am to dye my hair?"

"That's the plan." He left and Tasha and I exchanged resigned glances.

Pockmarks had said he wanted four blondes, and since it was quite obvious that my hair wasn't going to cooperate with that demand, Tasha was about to become blonde. She could always dye it back once we got out of here. If we got out of here.

No, *once* we got out of here. We were going to do it. I wasn't going to give up until these girls were free. Maybe then I'd be able to forgive myself for whatever haunted me from my past. Maybe I'd die, but I'd die knowing I attempted to wash those sins away. But in the meantime, we had hair to color and an escape to plan.

"Come on." I put an arm around Tasha's shoulder and led her into the bathroom. We slathered the stuff on our hair, then sat and talked as Pillow, Pistol, and I had done yesterday. It gave me a weird feeling, a strange sense of camaraderie, like we were two sisters having a makeover party.

"We are not sure you were to come back last night," Tasha confessed as we sat on the floor next to each other. "I know they sell us, and they want the money, but they said there was an extra? They had an extra, and were not so worried if one of us die." She reached out to touch my shoulder. "I am worried you were the extra, the one who would not come back."

I hadn't really believed I was going to die in that room. It had been a horrible, degrading, and painful experience, but I hadn't thought Onions would actually kill me. "I think they want the money more than they want to beat one of us to death," I told her. "Rough sex. Bruises and minor cuts. That's as far as I think they'll go."

She shivered. "I don't know. The one who brings food, he likes to hurt women, I think. He looks at me and I think he would like to hit me with that pole. I think he would like to hit that demon woman with the pole also."

"She said she's forbidden from hurting them," I told Tasha. "Otherwise I'm pretty sure all three of those guys would have been eviscerated before we even got off the truck. Catcalls might want to hit her with the pole, but he won't. He's scared of her. They both are scared of her. I think the only one who isn't scared of her is this boss they talk about."

Tasha laughed. "I am scared of her as well. She is beautiful and deadly like a snake. I think she could make slave of us all, wrap around and squeeze the breathing from us as we smile. She is a bad woman who takes and gives nothing. She will leave us empty."

The demon woman scared me too. Or was it more respect than fear I felt toward her? I was well aware of her charm, of her powers to enchant others. And I had no doubt she could be absolutely deadly. But unlike Tasha, I saw the demon woman as a caged animal, pacing the bars, unable to reach her captors, or those who stood watching outside our cage.

What would happen if she were free? Pockmarks, Catcalls, and no doubt this boss would be dead—of that much I was sure. But what about us? Would a deadly serpent see us as prey? As lesser beings worthy of sympathy? Would she spare her hand and walk away, leaving us alive, or would the police arrive to find our bodies alongside those of the two men? I honestly wasn't sure.

"Art history," Tasha suddenly announced with a smile and a laugh.

"*Art history?*" Had I misheard her? Her English was pretty good, but with her thick accent, she might have actually said something else.

"Art history. That is what I like at home in school. I hope to get summer job at museum, but how can I say no for chance to work in America? I waitress. I spend my no-work time on beach or talk to cute American boys. My English gets better. My mother tells me I am only a young girl once, and to do it. So I do it. They kiss me goodbye at airport and wave, happy for my chance."

And she ended up here. "What's it like back home? Your family, I mean."

"We are like others. My mother works in office. My father works in office. I have little brother and little sister." Her eyes suddenly glistened with tears. "These things do not happen to people. You understand? We think we are safe because we have mother and father who work in office, and little brother and sister. We think we are safe because we all eat at table every night, and are warm, and have school, and summer trip to beach, and car. You understand?"

I did understand. Things like this happened to runaways, kids from the projects, addicts, and prostitutes. They didn't happen to nice middle-class girls with a loving nuclear family. Tasha had thought she was coming over on a work-abroad visa, and like Pistol, she'd gotten snagged in this horrible net. Unlike Pistol, her parents were in another country, not likely to have the kind of clout to find her in time. And unlike Pistol, she was a foreigner in this country without any of her identification. I thought once more about Baa and Lacy and how lucky it was that Tasha at least spoke English well enough to ask for help if she got out of here.

"You'll see them again," I promised—a promise I wasn't

sure I could keep. "You'll see them again, study art history, eat dinner with your family. We're going to get out of here."

The girl's smile held an ocean of doubt. "Yes. We will get out of here," she agreed, both of us committing to the lie, as if somehow voicing it, giving it substance, would make it true.

Tasha's hair turned out more of a light golden brown than blonde, but it would have to do. I wiped a strand of mine off and grimaced to see the bright red under the dye. I'd probably end up bald, but I was going to leave it on another twenty minutes or so, just to try to make this color stick. The alternative was a whole lot of pain at the demon woman's hands, and after seeing what the others had gone through, I really didn't want to face that.

Tasha headed out with the others while I sat inside the bathroom by myself, savoring some time alone. Then I counted, rinsing my hair when I figured I'd reached another twenty minutes. It was still red, absolutely unchanged from before.

The bathroom door swung open. Mess peeked in. "It's almost lunch time by my reckoning. Are we good to go?"

"Yeah. Here." I handed her the lid to one of the toilet tanks. The thing felt like it weighed thirty pounds. Not easy to swing, but definitely a decent weapon. Mess's muscles in her arms stood out as she took it and I realized the woman was stronger than I'd thought. She hefted it, testing its weight, then looked up at me, caught sight of my hair, and laughed.

"Did you even try to dye it, or are you just flushing that stuff down the toilet?"

I shrugged. "Doesn't matter. Make sure you're off to the side with the lid so the guard doesn't see you. I'll be out in a minute."

That was our plan. Whack Catcalls in the head with the toilet lid, then make a run for it and hope we could get out of the warehouse before Pockmarks or the demon woman caught us. We were armed with broken plastic cups, screws, a few sharpened wires, and a thin chain from the toilet tank that might serve as a garrote. Other than that, we were weaponless. Our biggest problem was going to be reach. If we had a confrontation with Pockmarks, he'd be able to hit us with his broom pole before we could get close enough to do anything with our makeshift weapons. And we'd be totally screwed against the demon, of that I was sure.

Escape. Run for it. And each of us had instructions not to wait for any of the others. If a chance presented itself, get the heck out, get to safety, and send help back for the rest of us. If just one of us could get out, today would be a success.

"Got it. Pray for us, Red. We'll need that guardian angel of yours." Mess was just turning to leave when we both heard voices. This wasn't the normal, quiet conversation of the other women, one was clearly a man's voice. Were they bringing lunch in early? Mess could hardly walk out of the bathroom and across the space between this door and the guard carrying a toilet tank lid and hope to go undetected. She looked over at me, and I could see she'd come to the same conclusion. With a quick motion she propped the toilet lid against the wall and cracked the door open to listen.

One guard and the soft clear voice of the demon woman. I hesitated, not liking my options one bit. My best case scenario had been us sneaking out of here without ever encountering the demon woman. I hadn't wanted to think about fighting her, about her fighting us. But here she was, throwing a big wrench in the middle of our escape plans.

It didn't matter how I felt. What mattered was that eight women relied on me to do what I needed to do to get out of here. The demon woman had picked her side.

Strange, elusive memories hung just out of reach. Choosing between those I loved. *I just need time to convince them they're wrong*, I had argued. *It's too late for that*, he'd replied. *They've made their choice, and now you must make yours.*

I'd made the wrong one, because I'd thought there was all the time in the world to change someone's mind. I wouldn't make that mistake again.

"He's leaving," Mess said softly. "She's still here. What do we do? He'll probably come back with the lunch, but what if she doesn't leave?"

"You go out there," I whispered. "If she doesn't leave in a few minutes, then send her in here. Tell her she needs to check on my hair or something. When she comes in, I'll take care of her, bring the toilet lid out to you, then come back in to make sure she doesn't come around and screw everything up. Then when the guard delivers lunch, you can take him down."

"Then we get out of here." There was a hint of a question in Mess's statement.

"Yeah," I told her with far more confidence than I felt. "Then we get out of here."

CHAPTER 10

*M*ess slid through the doorway. I picked up the toilet lid and stepped to where I wouldn't be seen by anyone entering the bathroom, yet not be hit by the swinging door. And then I waited, feeling sick to my stomach over what I was about to do.

Go away, I thought. If she would go out with the guard, get in her car and leave, or fly away on her broomstick, or whatever mode of transportation demon women favored, we could still keep to our escape plan. It was one thing to whack a guard across the head with the lid from a toilet tank, another entirely to hit *her.* Yeah, she was a demon. Yeah, she'd told me straight up she wouldn't help us, that she'd bring us back if we tried to escape. She was the enemy. The enemy. Just as much of an enemy as those guards. And maybe if I kept repeating it to myself, I'd believe it.

I'm not your salvation, she'd said. But she'd untied me when I'd asked. She hadn't punished me when I'd slapped her. She was just as trapped here as we were, but she was standing in the way of my girls and their freedom. It was her or them. I needed to make a choice, and that choice was clear.

Didn't make it any easier to do this. I'd slapped her, but this seemed so…excessive. I was about to hit her as hard as I could in the head with a heavy chunk of ceramic. I needed to knock her out—make sure she was really knocked out so we'd have time to escape before she came to. Which meant what I was about to do might kill her. She was a demon and I didn't know how much force to use, so I was going to give it everything I had. I couldn't risk her just being stunned. I couldn't risk her stopping us.

Could someone kill a demon with a toilet tank lid? I was probably about to find out.

I heard the high-heeled footsteps across the floor. Darn it all, why hadn't she just left? Why hadn't she just checked Tasha's hair and walked away?

The door opened, and I didn't think any more, I just swung. The demon woman wasn't very tall, so I made sure to put an upward arc into the toilet tank lid trajectory. It hit with a sickening thunk, and the woman flew backward, slamming against the wall. Everything slowed. There was a spray of red. It painted the floor and the heavy lid, hit my face in warm droplets and splatters. As she slid down the wall I saw another streak of red. *I think I killed her. Oh my God, I killed her.*

She lay crumpled in front of me, her beautiful face unrecognizable—a mess of crushed bone and torn flesh. Blood seeped onto her clothing, oozing from the back of her head and along the long black tresses. I remembered how her hair had felt in my hand, how silky and smooth it had been, how incredibly gorgeous she'd been, how sultry.

"I'm not your salvation." Bile burned in my throat. I hadn't wanted this. I hadn't wanted this at all. I'd been forced to make a choice. If I'd just had more time, I could have convinced her to change her mind, to be on our side. If I'd just had more time.

But I didn't have time. The last time had resulted in the death of those I loved. This time… I hoped that this time I'd made the right choice.

I'd killed her. I was pretty sure she was either dead now or soon would be. I stood there in shock, staring at the crushed, bloody face. Then I took a breath, got a better grip on the toilet tank lid, and went out into the main warehouse room to find the other women staring anxiously at me.

I killed her. I killed her. What if I could have changed her mind, talked her into helping us? What if I could have saved her?

What if she could have saved me?

Kitten gasped, and clasped a hand over her mouth.

"I did it. I did it. We just have to take down the guard, and get out of here and you'll all be safe." The words were flat and emotionless. My hands were shaking. I was covered in blood that reminded me in a darkly humorous way of the color of my hair.

"Damn, girl," Sugar said. I wasn't sure if that weird note in her voice was admiration or apprehension.

"Are you okay?" Pillow asked taking a step toward me. She raised a hand to touch my shoulder, only to lower it with a grimace.

I killed her. Maybe I could have convinced her to help us, to come with us. Why did my decisions always end in death? Why?

I nodded at Pillow. "We need to get ready. Get ready for the guard. When he comes…then we'll leave and you'll all be safe. I need to make sure you're safe."

They slowly surrounded me. Mess reached out a hand for the toilet tank lid. "I got this."

"No. I got this." I took a step back, clutching the lid to my chest. "Me. I got it. I'll…I'll do it."

"No, you won't." Her voice was soft, kind. Her image blurred. I started to shake so hard I nearly dropped the lid.

"We agreed that I'd do it. And you're in no condition to be hitting someone else upside the head right now."

"I killed her. Her face…her head. I killed her and I don't want you to have to do that. I've already got blood on my hands."

I had more than blood on my hands. So many had died. *They'd* died. *Let me be the one who sins and leave them clean. Let it all rest on my soul, so they can be safe and free.*

"No." Mess reached out and took the lid from my hands. "It's my turn, Red. It's my turn to be strong. That's how we do it. Sometimes you're the strong one. Sometimes it's me. Right now, it's me."

I nodded, looking down at my hands. Blood. Her blood. I rubbed my palms down my sweat pants, trying to get it off.

"Go clean up and change," she told me. "Hurry, before he gets here. I don't want you to see."

I looked over at the bathroom door, feeling a surge of panic. "I can't go back in there."

"Here." Pillow held out a towel. "It's damp from my shower. And I put a change of clothes over on your cot."

I followed her over, changing and kicking the bloody clothing under the cot, wiping my face and hands as best I could with the damp towel. Then I sat on the mattress. Kitten sat on one side of me. Tasha and Pillow sat on the other, blocking our view. Sugar and Pistol stood at the end of the cot, Baa and Lacy across from us.

We heard the squawk of the door opening. Kitten hid her face in my shoulder. I shut my eyes tight.

A sickening thud. The clang of a platter hitting the floor. I took a deep breath, opened my eyes and stood, edging past Sugar and Pistol to see.

Catcalls was on the floor next to a spilled tray of sandwiches, a pool of blood spreading from his head. He had been knocked out, but it was instantly clear to me that Mess hadn't used near the level of force that I had. She stood over him, toilet tank lid poised and ready for another strike if the guard so much as stirred.

"He's down," I told her. This time it was me taking the lid from her hand and setting it on the floor.

"Did I… Is he…"…?"

"No. You didn't kill him." I wasn't sure how I knew that, but I did.

"I should have. You heard. He killed one of the other girls. He deserves to die."

"So let Red finish him off and let's get out of here," Sugar said, eyeing the open door. I knew what she was thinking—we were all thinking the same thing. There was still one more guard, and if we didn't get out of here, there was a good chance Pockmarks was going to catch us.

I looked over at the other girls, all staring at me, waiting for me to tell them what to do—hopeful, expectant. "We need to go. Now. Remember the plan. If just one of us can get out and bring help, we win."

"But we need to stick together, to help each other," Kitten protested. "We're family."

I nodded. "We're family, and we're all going to get out of here, but if something bad happens, and any one of you has a chance to get free, then go—go and send help."

Everyone nodded, and we cautiously made our way out the door of what had been our prison for the last three days.

CHAPTER 11

*E*veryone lined up behind me, clutching their makeshift weapons. I realized I'd left the toilet lid behind. Didn't matter that it left me without any sort of weapon. I didn't think I could use that toilet lid again, didn't think I could swing it into someone's face even if I was fighting for my life. As it was I'd forever see the spray of red, the crushed bones of her beautiful face. *I could have saved her. She could have saved me.*

We padded barefoot through the warehouse. The cold of the cement floor seemed to crawl right up the bones of my legs as I moved. It was a huge, open space, the offices to my left, the bay doors straight ahead. I glanced around looking for a smaller exit off to the side—one that wouldn't set off a fire alarm. A light was on in one of the offices with a window —Pockmarks enjoying some private time, I assumed. I couldn't see him through the window, which hopefully meant he couldn't see me.

We made it to the bay doors without incident. I looked in vain for some less noisy way out, then grimaced as I punched the button with the up arrow in white on a green background.

The sound was deafening. It was like a dozen bulldozers roared into the warehouse. Sound echoed off the walls. The office door with the light flung open, and Pockmarks ran out with a shout, brandishing his broom handle. He slapped a switch on the wall and the lights went out, plunging us into darkness. Worse, the bay door froze about eight inches off the ground. The girls screamed.

"Go. Go." I pushed Kitten and Lacy toward the door. They were the smallest. If both of them could get out while I tried to hold the guard off, they could go get help.

The two girls tried to wedge themselves under the door, but couldn't manage to get through the space. Tasha and Mess grabbed the door, trying to lift it by hand while Sugar and Pistol searched the walls for a manual override. Pillow and Baa turned their backs to the bay door, brandishing their sharpened cot springs. Pockmarks was almost upon us, cranking the broomstick back to swing once he was within range. Pillow and Baa didn't stand a chance. None of them stood a chance. So I took a few steps forward, putting myself between them and the guard.

The stick hit me on the upper arm, just below my shoulder. I braced for it, but Pockmarks was a big guy and the impact knocked me to the side. I managed to turn with the blow, swinging my right arm around to grab the stick and move with the momentum. With the broom handle tucked under my arm, Pockmarks wasn't able to land another blow. He yanked and cursed, trying to get his weapon free, while I shouted for the girls to get the door open. We were trapped here, and although I had our one opponent engaged, I feared I wouldn't be able to hold him for long.

Baa darted past the two of us vanishing into the darkness of the warehouse. I knew what she was doing. This guard was going to get the best of me, but if I could hold him off, keep his attention on me for just a few seconds more, Baa could hit the power switch.

We just needed the bay door to lift a few more inches, and the girls could slide under to freedom. I struggled with Pockmarks, trying to wrest the broom handle from him. If I could just get his weapon, I'd turn it on him with all the force I'd used to brain the demon. And I wouldn't have any regret at all about killing him.

A few pulls back and forth and it was clear that I was losing the tug-of-war with the guard. "Hurry," I shouted to Baa, wishing I knew the word in Spanish. Pillow jumped forward to help me, stabbing Pockmarks with her sharpened wire. It didn't do more than puncture the skin, but the man yelped. He twisted, still keeping one hand firmly on the broom handle while he punched Pillow in the face with the other. Her head rocked backward, blood flying from her nose. Then he yanked and the pole slid from under my arm. I grabbed at it with my hands, but he was too quick, swinging it out of my reach, then bringing it in a broad sweep down to hit Pillow across the chest. She gasped, doubled over, and I sprang forward, taking the next hit meant for her against my shoulder.

The lights went on. The bay door roared as it resumed its slow upward process. Just a few seconds. I only needed to hold Pockmarks off for a few seconds. The stick came down again and again. I blocked as many blows as I could with my arm, but a solid blow impacted my head and I staggered. It was enough for Pockmarks to lunge past me, grabbing Lacy by her long hair and kicking Kitten away from the door. The other girls jumped him, stabbing him with wires and jagged bits of plastic while he kicked out and swung with the pole, keeping a tight hold on Lacy's hair the whole time. Kitten crawled toward the bay door, but a well-placed kick had her rolling on the ground clutching her stomach.

Baa screamed, and I looked over to see that Catcalls had recovered from Mess's blow and had grabbed her, slamming her face-first into the wall. She crumpled to the ground and the guard reached forward to hit the button once more. The sudden darkness blinded me and I felt two more blows of the pole that drove me to my knees. I heard the cries of the other girls, the frustrated shriek as Lacy and Kitten were pulled away from under the bay door.

"Get under the door," I shouted. "Somebody, anybody get under the door." There were nine of us and only two guards. If just one of us could get out and run for it, if just one of us could make it out, we'd all be saved. I crawled forward, realizing the Catcalls had joined the party from the noise of more than one stick hitting human flesh. I reached forward, feeling the edge of the bay door. I didn't want to leave the girls behind, but one of us had to get free and go for help.

A foot smashed down on my hand, then kicked me so hard I was launched backward several feet. The lights came on, and I saw that the two guards had managed to bunch us together and knock us back away from the bay door. Pockmarks was standing over us, breathing heavy and bleeding from cuts, scratches and small puncture wounds. Catcalls jogged back from where the switch was to join him, landing a few hard kicks to Pistol's back when he arrived.

We were lying on the ground, most of us curled into a fetal position. I heard crying, a soft moan, a sob. Rolling over I tried to rise to my knees, quickly counting.

Nine. No one had made it. Not even one of us had managed to get out, and now we were all battered and bleeding. I was pretty sure a few of us had broken bones and concussions. Come morning we'd be covered in bruises. And there was no demon to fix us. It was a strange sort of satisfaction to realize that we wouldn't be perfect for their sale, that the buyers would show up to find us severely beaten and, no doubt, worthless. So much for all the money they thought they were going to make. I hoped their boss was pissed at them. I hoped he killed them.

He'd probably kill us too.

"Get up." The end of a pole jabbed me in the lower back. "Get up now and walk, or we'll drag you."

I staggered to my feet, helping the others rise. Then using the poles, both men managed to gather us together and herd us back into our room. Pistol could barely walk, gasping with every step, blood streaking her newly blonde hair. I half-carried Kitten as we shuffled forward, easing her down on the nearest cot. Pillow sat beside her, still clutching her waist, her face gray as she took small shallow breaths.

We'd lost. And with the condition we were in, it was unlikely we'd be able to attempt it again.

"Where the fuck is the demon?" Pockmarks roared. I flinched, but kept silent. They wouldn't kill us, would they? They wouldn't risk the wrath of their boss and the loss of their cut of the profits for the satisfaction of beating us to death, would they?

But we wouldn't be worth anything battered. Maybe they *would* kill us. Or maybe they'd just kill one of us to vent their rage and set an example. I remembered that they had an "extra" and caught my breath. An extra. If they found out I'd killed the demon, that extra would be me. And this time I was pretty sure there would be no guardian angel to save me.

The broomstick swung, this time hitting Tasha hard enough that it made a splintering noise. "Where is that damned demon?"

A door opened and everyone froze, even the guards.

"Stop yelling, you idiot. I'm right here. And I'd like to know who hit me with a toilet." A feminine voice demanded.

"This was one of my favorite shirts, and it is ruined. And I'm going to have to re-do all of my makeup."

Fear spiked through me. I turned slowly, expecting to see a zombie, a dead woman with half her head smashed in. Instead I saw the demon woman, wiping blood from her still-gorgeous, perfect face with the corner of a wet towel. Kitten bit back a scream and scooted behind me. Baa crossed herself and whispered what were surely prayers in Spanish.

"Who. Hit. Me." The repeated words were less a question and more a demand. Her eyes searched the room and landed on Mess.

No. I couldn't let anyone else take the blame for this. If someone was going to die for attacking her, it would be me.

"I hit you." I stood and stepped forward, putting out a hand to silence Kitten's soft "no."

I was oddly relieved that I hadn't killed her. It was a mixed blessing. She could now fix our injuries, although that process would most likely be just as painful as the injuries themselves. Healed, we could try to escape again.

But healed, we'd be sold at an auction in two days. And we were back to having three barriers to our escape—one of them a demon who bounced back unhurt from a crushed skull. If a heavy toilet tank lid across the face didn't keep her down for more than a few minutes, I wasn't sure what would.

I only hoped that I'd survive whatever she had in store for me.

Pockmarks laughed. "Some kind of demon you are, taken down by a little slip of girl. Wait until the boss hears this one."

The air suddenly felt charged. The demon woman looked over at Catcalls with a raised eyebrow. "Looks like I wasn't the only one. It won't happen again."

"No, it won't," he agreed. "You go ahead and punish her,

then fix all of their injuries. No more food for them. I'd chain them to the cots, but I don't want to have to clean up their shit and pee. Next time you girls try something like this, one of you is going to die. Understood?"

No one responded.

"Maybe I'll go ahead and kill one of you anyway. Or better yet, beat you just to the edge of death, then have this demon woman bring you back. And do it over and over again all night long. I want you quiet and obedient. If we say line up, you line up. If we say bend over so we can screw you in the ass, you bend over and say 'thank you' and 'please.' Understood?"?" Pockmarks slapped his palm with the broom handle for emphasis.

This time we all whispered a chorus of frightened yeses.

Catcalls reached up to touch the side of his head. "I want the one who did this. If the demon gets some revenge, I get some too."

"Later," Pockmarks told him. "Tonight you can have your pick. Let the demon woman fix them up first."

The two guards left, locking the door behind them. The demon woman tossed the bloodied towel on a cot and stalked toward me. There was murder in her eyes, and I scampered to put one of the other cots between us, thinking that I'd rather be raped and beaten to death by one of the guards than let this woman get her hands on me.

"Come here," she hissed.

"Why aren't you dead?" My voice sounded tiny and far away. "I saw you. I saw what I did to you. Why aren't you dead?"

She stood on the other side of the cot across from me. "Because I'm a demon, you little fool. I was going to let you keep your hair that ridiculous color, but now I'm not. I'm going to fix it myself. Then maybe I'll do a few other things to you just to teach you a lesson. Now come here."

I tensed, ready to dart the opposite way whenever she made a move. Yes, I was just delaying the inevitable. There was nowhere I could go to hide, and I couldn't escape this room. She'd eventually catch me, but I was too scared to go easy and suffer whatever she had in mind for me. I remembered the screams of the other girls, the agony on Pistol's face when the demon had subjected her to those cosmetic enhancements. I really, really didn't want her doing that to me.

Out of the corner of my eye I saw Mess creep forward, toilet lid in hand. The demon woman must have seen her too, because she flung out a hand and grabbed the other woman's wrist. Mess cried out, and the toilet lid fell, breaking in half as it hit the ground with a huge crash. That wasn't the only thing that broke. Mess's hand dangled at an odd angle, and she dropped to the floor with a scream as the woman shoved her. When the demon turned toward me I saw her eyes completely black with no pupil or white at all. Gold scales sprang from her skin and a narrow forked tongue licked her lower lip. Perfectly manicured nails thickened and lengthened into claws.

I felt the sharp bite of adrenaline spiking through my fear. I needed to get out of here. We all needed to get out of here. Suddenly the danger wasn't the men with their sticks or the threat of being sold into sexual slavery, it was this monster that snapped wrists with a gentle twist of her fingers, that healed from what should have been a fatal head wound in seconds. That looked anything but human right now.

"Come here." This time the hiss sounded truly reptilian.

I started to shake, knowing what was coming. Still, I couldn't make my feet move. I couldn't make myself walk willingly to slaughter.

"Come here." Her eyes locked with mine and I felt my muscles screaming to move. She tilted her head, regarding me curiously like a snake about to devour a mouse. "Interesting. You are resistant to compulsion. Let's try this instead. Come. Here."

The pull on my muscles vanished and I stumbled from the release. The room felt heavy and thick with something blue and sweet. Every nerve inside me came alive and I felt a sweet seductive beckoning. She was so beautiful. In her arms I would know ecstasy. In her arms I would feel pleasure greater than I ever imagined.

But I wanted more than pleasure. Even though my body melted at the thought, my mind rebelled, knowing that the love she offered me was a hollow, empty thing. The other women stared at her, transfixed, but she only had eyes for me. I felt the warmth, the seduction increase and my knees wobbled. One of the other women whimpered.

Then with a frustrated hiss, the heaviness was gone. I sucked in a breath, disoriented from the change and unable to move quick enough as she jumped across the cot to grab me. She twisted one of my arms behind my back, wrapping my hair around her other fist. Then she shoved me ahead of her toward the bathroom. I heard Kitten crying softly. Now would have been the time for the others to jump her, but everyone was so injured.

"Don't." Mess stood in front of us, her words muffled from the swelling in her face. "I won't let you hurt her."

The demon hissed. "Move, foolish girl."

"I'll be okay," I lied. "Guardian angel, remember? I'll be okay."

I felt the demon stiffen, her hand twisting my hair tighter. "What did you say?"

"She has a guardian angel." Mess lifted her chin. "And I hope he explodes you on the inside, like he did the guard that raped her. I hope he leaves you dead on the floor with smoking black holes for eyes."

There was a moment where the demon didn't seem to breathe, then she laughed. "Angels don't do that. They don't protect humans. They don't care in the least about you and your friends."

"Then what happened to the guard?" Mess asked defiantly.

I felt the demon shrug. "One of the other guys probably poisoned him, or something. It wasn't an angel. No angel is going to save you."

Mess narrowed her eyes and planted her feet, her chin lifting with a stubborn tilt. "It's okay," I told her. "I'll be okay. Don't interfere. I don't want you hurt any more than you already are."

The girl hesitated. "Come back, okay? We need you. Promise you'll come back."

The demon woman muttered something under her breath about stupid idiot humans. I ignored her. "Promise."

"Move, or you'll be next," the demon snapped. Mess hesitated a fraction of a second, then stepped aside. The demon woman kicked open the bathroom door and shoved me forward, closing it behind her. She put her hands on the handle and I heard the grind of metal, the smell of something hot, and I realized that she had locked it in some supernatural fashion—locking me in here with her.

I scrambled to my feet, putting my back against the wall and eyeing her. There was nothing at hand I could possibly use as a weapon, and I knew my strength couldn't match a demon who broke wrists so easily.

"I'm going to have to fix her wrist once I'm done with you, and all the other injuries as well." Her voice was calm, but those eyes were anything but reassuring. "I am furious with you. First you assault me—not once but twice. You were obviously the one who organized the escape attempt with those other girls. You've caused the men to hurt the merchandise—injuries I'll need to spend energy repairing. You are a problem, and I find myself wondering how much trouble I would be in if I killed you." She took a step toward me. "It's an ideal solution. Kill you and throw your battered body out there. All the other girls would fall in line. It would be so enjoyable, torturing you for hours until your flesh could take no more. And just before you died, I'd take your soul and keep it for my own. What fun I could have with your soul for all of eternity."

I curled my hands into fists. I might get killed. I might die for this. But I was going to die fighting. My only regret was that I would go back on my promise to Mess. I wouldn't be here to help the other women. Maybe they'd escape without me. It wasn't like I was all that special. I wasn't any kind of hero. I was just a junkie from the streets who couldn't remember more than shadows of her past. A junkie with weird, bright-red hair that didn't seem to take any kind of dye.

"I'm not allowed to kill you." The demon's voice was tinged with regret. "The terms of my summoning don't allow me to harm any of the guards or the boss, and I can't kill the merchandise. I can *hurt* the merchandise, though. As long as I fix it afterward." Her long claws combed through my hair, her golden-scaled skin catching on the strands. "And fixing will cause you just as much pain as killing you."

I swung, punching her as hard as I could in the jaw. She laughed, so I did the same with my other fist, then kicked her in the legs. She stepped in to me, maneuvering her body so I was trapped against the wall. I fought like a wild animal, punching and kicking, grabbing her hair and trying to gouge those frightening eyes out. It was like fighting a piece of clay. Every scratch and bruise healed before my eyes. She just stood there in front of me, amused at every blow I landed until I was spent and shaking.

"Are you done, little red bird?" she asked. Then she slapped me and my head rocked to the side. Warm liquid filled my mouth and dripped from my nose. Everything dimmed with a second blow, and I felt myself start to slide down the wall. She caught me, claws digging into the skin over my ribs as she held me upright. Then her mouth met mine. The kiss was a strange mix of passion and pain…and desperation. With her lips on mine, her tongue licking and tasting, I *felt* her—knew with complete certainty that she was a trapped animal, desperate and lashing out at everything that entered its tiny cage.

The kiss ended and I saw my blood on her lips as she smiled. Her scaled body pressed against mine, holding me in place as her clawed fingers moved from my waist to grip my hair.

"And now the fun begins," she whispered with a wicked smile.

Something sharp and hot slid through me, through my hair and into my scalp. I gasped and would have dropped to the floor if she hadn't been pressing me against the wall. It felt like she was stripping layers from my skin, sanding and slicing her way down to the bone.

"Isn't this enjoyable?" She nuzzled my neck and chuckled as I panted and tried to keep from screaming. Pain and pleasure merged together. Then the feeling of being sliced abruptly stopped. She hesitated, then I felt her push as if she were trying to shove past a blockage.

Nothing. A harder push. Pain bloomed up in me, searing through my mind, but I got the impression it was *her* pain, not mine.

Her dark eyes peered into mine and she frowned. "Don't fight me, pretty red bird. It will only hurt worse."

I thought hurt was what she wanted. Again there was that sensation of her pushing in through my skin, like she was stabbing me with a thousand tiny knives, sanding the layers from me. The pressure increased until I couldn't breathe, then something snapped. There was a roaring sound. Pain. A scream that tore through me. Everything went white, and when the world swam into focus I realized I was lying in a heap on the cold tile floor, my bright-red hair covering my eyes. I pushed it away with a shaking hand and saw the demon woman clear across the room from me. Her skin no longer had scales. Her claws were back to beautifully mani-cured nails. Dark human eyes stared at me. She was breathing hard, as if she'd been running for her life. Some-thing like fear flickered in the back of her eyes and I realized that the scream I'd heard hadn't come from my lips—it had come from hers.

"What…" Her voice trembled and she swallowed hard. "What are you?

CHAPTER 12

What did she mean? I tried to sit upright and failed, my body cold and trembling. I wanted to throw up. I wanted to curl into a ball and drift into nothingness. Everything hurt and I couldn't get warm. Was this some kind of delayed detox? This body, this flesh felt like a betrayal, like a horrible weakness that I needed to shed if only I knew how.

"What are you?" she asked again, this time with a hint of firmness. Had I imagined that fear in her eyes? Because it was nowhere to be found right now.

"I—I don't know." I wrapped my arms around my knees and held on tight, trying to keep from shaking myself apart. "I don't remember much of anything. I woke up on the truck with the other women. I had track marks on my arms, so I think I was a junkie they grabbed off the streets."

She looked at my arms and shook her head. "They beat you, just as they beat the other girls out there, but you are now uninjured. Every bruise has faded and vanished. There's not a scar on you. Not a mole or a freckle. Not a wrinkle or blemish. Your skin…and your hair…"

I had figured that my flawless skin was why the men had taken me. I doubted a passed-out junkie was their ideal candidate for this sex slave ring. None of the other girls were users, although with the exception of Pistol and Kitten, they were all girls who wouldn't be missed or whose families would have difficulties in finding and/or rescuing them.

"You fixed your injuries." Her voice was full of wonder. "The dead man had beaten you. The other two beat you. I've done nothing to repair your injuries. You've done it yourself. Are you part demon? If so, you must be more than a half-demon hybrid."

"I don't know." I *did* know that the thought of being part demon made me shiver with revulsion. I couldn't be a demon, could I? If so, why was my memory gone? If so, then why couldn't I kill those two guards and whisk us all to safety? It made less sense than Mess's guardian angel theory.

The woman crawled closer, looking to be in just as much pain as I was. "You are the most stunningly perfect human I've ever seen, and I've seen the most beautiful nature can provide. You resist compulsion. You fight against me with the force and power of a demon hybrid. No matter what I do, I can't change your red hair. And any pain I inflict on you rebounds to me three-fold. What are you? Was your sire a powerful ancient and your mother a werewolf or Nephilim, perhaps?"

"I don't know," I insisted.

The pain she'd tried to inflict on me rebounded three-fold? How could that be? I had no idea how she'd survived it if that was the truth because I never could have made it through three times what she'd just done to me.

"Tell me what you *do* remember." She stopped just in front of me, once more eyeing my red hair.

"I like to listen to old-school rap, and I can't resist French fries with extra salt." I hesitated, probing my memories. "I love the smell of the earth after a warm summer rain, the feel of dirt sifting through my fingers, the way boulders jut up from the ground up in the mountains, their surface colored with lichen and pitted from thousands of years of rain. I feel…I feel like there are two of me. There's a part that feels like a book I once read, that's fading away before my eyes. And there's a part…a part that I don't want to remember, that I want to go away."

Why was I telling this demon these things? She'd hurt my girls. She'd tried to hurt me. She'd threatened to kill me. But in spite of all this, there was a weird feeling of kinship whenever she was around—kinship and an embarrassing attraction.

"You're mentally ill?" The woman tilted her head and regarded me. "Split personality?"

Maybe. Probably. Heck if I knew. "I think I had a family once." I frowned in thought, struggling to remember. "I think they died. It was my fault. I should have been stronger, I should have done something. I could have stood by their sides, made a stand. Instead I was a coward, and now I need to atone."

The demon's laugh was short and bitter. "Humans and their guilt. Trust me, little red bird, whatever killed your family would have killed you too if you'd made a stand. Better to flee and live than to fight and die."

"No, it's not better to flee." I managed to sit more upright, pushing back a wave of nausea. "Because now I have to live with their loss on my soul. I have to live with the constant remembrance of what I didn't do. I'd rather have died by their side than live with this."

She shook her head, scooting herself around to sit beside me against the wall. "Then beat yourself with a birch rod, throw on a hair shirt, and suffer. Isn't that what you humans do for redemption?"

There. The memory was there, hovering tantalizingly out of reach. "That's what I'm doing. This is my hair shirt. I need to atone."

"Well, in my opinion, getting picked up by a group of human traffickers and sold as a sex slave is a bit excessive as a penance. This kind of suffering does your dead family no good. It just wastes your life." She shrugged. "But it's too late to back out now. I only hope you die quickly and with as little pain as possible."

That's not what she'd wanted a few moments ago. I remembered the sensation when she'd first touched me, the feeling that she was an animal trapped, lashing out in desperation.

"Maybe you *should* have stayed and helped your family." Her laugh this time carried actual humor. "If you can hold your own against a demon, you probably could have taken out that gang or whatever killed your people. But then again, I'm not particularly strong compared to other demons. Succubi and incubi have their own special skills, but we're not the heavyweights of Hel."

She truly *was* a demon. I don't know why, but I'd seemed to accept that without any sort of internal panicking. It felt right to me. Maybe she was right and I was part demon, because sitting next to her like this was like sitting next to a peer, an equal.

"I do believe that you must have a demon or Nephilim parent, because no human should have been able to resist me like that." Her dark eyes peered at me, and her smile this time was downright charming. "Of course, immunity to my compulsion and fighting me off doesn't mean you'll survive whoever buys you at the auction, if you make it that long. Those men are furious. I wouldn't be surprised if they kill one of you just to prove a point. I recommend you give up your plans of escape until after you are sold. Your chances would be better one-on-one with whoever buys you, especially once he lets his guard down."

"It's not me I need to save," I told her. "The other women —their lives are what's important. I need to save them, even if I die in the process."

She shook her head, still smiling. "There's that silly need for penance again. You think sacrificing yourself for others will buy you forgiveness? Pretty red bird, there is no forgiveness. All that will buy you is death."

"The forgiveness isn't in the sacrifice," I argued. "It's not being a martyr that will bring me redemption. It's me being strong and standing up for what's right, for what I believe to be true. It's about helping others. And there *is* forgiveness, but it comes from within, not from outside of me."

"Humans." She sighed then extended her hand toward me. "Shall we start again, my red bird? My name is Leethu. I'm a succubus who has been summoned from Hel in the service of these disgusting vermin."

I shook her hand. What a surreal experience this was. "I don't know my name. The other girls call me Ariel, like the mermaid. Or Red."

She peered at me. "No, not a mermaid. You're a little red bird who sings in a cage and pecks fiercely at whoever reaches in to stroke her feathers."

How odd for her to say that. "You too. You're also in a cage, pacing along the bars, slowly losing yourself to madness the longer you're confined. Soon all that will be left of you is anger and hate, and the driving need to destroy every living thing that comes within your reach. If you can't get away, you'll die inside."

She sucked in a breath and pulled back. "How…?"

I shook my head. "I don't know. When you first touched me, tried to change my hair color, I felt you. I felt your desperation, your prison."

She laughed and turned her head, but I caught her expression and it surprised me. I didn't know anything about demons, but she didn't seem quite the evil being she'd appeared to be when she'd dragged me in here.

"I *am* trapped. The human who summoned me made sure that there is no way I can escape. I cannot harm him or those who work for him. I cannot seduce them, have sex with them, steal their souls. I must do everything the summoner tells me to do. And the only way I will be released from my prison is if the one who summoned me dies."

"The boss is your summoner?"

She nodded. "Yes. He has brought me here before to help him with specific tasks, but the last time he summoned me, it was for a different purpose."

"To fix girls up for sale?" I asked.

"Yes. To aid the others and to provide ambiance at the sale. He wants money. He wants to build a loyal client base, a reputation for getting the best girls and providing a risk-free venue for the purchase. I need to make sure customers can buy without fear of being caught by human authorities, and that the boss does not come under legal scrutiny as well."

I rolled my eyes. "Turn water into wine, and all that as well? He's asking a lot from a succubus—a lot that I wouldn't think would be a specialty of a sex demon."

"It's not, but I have to do whatever he commands. I am a succubus, and one of the most respected sex demons in Hel, not a beautician, party planner, and security guard." There was a hint of pride and scorn in her voice that brought a smile to my face.

"Well, from what I seem to remember, those who live a life of crime tend to not live long," I commented dryly. "One of his customers or competitors, or one of the guards will take him out sooner or later."

She shrugged. "Probably. And compared to a demon's

virtual immortality, a human's normal lifespan is not so long. Even if he lives until ninety, it will only be a moment of *my* life. Still, it chafes that I must serve him. And the longer he controls me, the more I feel myself slip away. By the time he dies, I worry I will no longer be the Leethu I once was."

"Help us and we'll help you," I offered. "You can escape with us. I'll find a way to break your contract, or kill this boss or something, if you help get us out of here and to safety."

She laughed. "I told you yesterday that I can't help you. I cannot help you escape. It would violate the terms of my summoning to do so. As far as you helping me, I am incredibly doubtful that a group of runaways, prostitutes, and a junkie can track down the boss and kill him, or negate my summoning vows."

I went to argue and decided against it. She was right. Most of the women in the other room would run as far away as possible if we got out of here, not try to sneak back and kill a man who, even if he didn't have guards surrounding him, would be able to easily overcome us. We weren't trained assassins. Which meant I had nothing to offer Leethu in exchange for either help, or not hindering us in further escape attempts.

And that bothered me. I *wanted* to help her. I had a horrible twisting feeling deep in my stomach that leaving her behind wasn't an option.

"What happens if you leave with us? Can we get you somewhere safe? Is there someone who can send you back to Hel?"

Her head tilted and she wrinkled her nose. "It would take someone very powerful to break my summoning. I'm not sure with the way it's worded even a sorcerer could break it."

"But when I was in that room, and the one guard died,

you were calling to someone. Other demons? Could they maybe break the summoning?"

"Yes, by killing the summoner. But they'd need to find me first. I can't contact them to ask for help, and it could be decades before they are able to locate me." She shrugged and gave me a sad smile. "And they are busy. Ni-Ni and Dar… they have their own troubles. I doubt they will be able to devote much time to locating me and setting me free."

My heart hurt at the loneliness in her voice. She had friends, but no one who put her first, no one that made her a priority. "There must be *someone* who can help you," I insisted, thinking of Aladdin rubbing a lamp. "Or maybe…is there a Devil? Satan or someone? I'll get out of here and contact them, tell them where you are so they can come and rescue you."

I shivered at the thought of bringing the actual Satan here. He'd probably kill all of us as well as this summoner. I got the impression that if there was a real Satan, he was rather indiscriminate when it came to slaughter.

"The Ha-Satan. That's Ni-Ni." Leethu tapped her bottom lip with a fingernail. "She has a lot of responsibilities right now, but if she knew where I was, I'm sure she would come to help. And she does like to kill things. I can't directly ask her to kill the summoner, but perhaps someone else could do it for me."

There was a thinly veiled question there, but I wasn't about to go track down Satan and ask him, or her, to murder the summoner. Maybe I could e-mail Satan, or send her a letter or something.

"But even then, I can't help you," Leethu told me. "I can't help any of you escape. I've been given very specific instructions to keep all of you here and to prepare you for the sale."

So much for winning this demon over to our side.

"I won't tell you anything about our plans then. But just

in case we manage to get out of here, let me know how I can get in touch with someone, and I'll let them know you're stuck here and need some help."

Her head whipped around and she stared at me. "Why?"

"Why what?"

"Why would you help me? I can't help you in return."

"I know. I just…you need help. You're as much a victim as we are. They're forcing you to do these things to us. You don't have any choice."

"You do realize that I'm a demon? Yes, I'm trapped here and I need to do as they command, but I've done worse in my lifetime. Under any other circumstance, I'd seduce you, tie you to me for the rest of your life, then take your soul for my own. They aren't asking me to do anything I would normally find objectionable. It's the fact that they are ordering me around that angers me, not what they want me to do."

I kept thinking of her as a sympathetic character, forgetting what her being a demon actually entailed. What was I thinking? Why in the world did I have sympathy for this creature that wouldn't blink an eye about seducing me and taking my soul. Wait—seducing me? She had said she was a succubus, but seduction wasn't the sort of thing I associated with demons. Tearing me limb-from-limb, yes. Flaying the skin off my back then dipping me in boiling oil, yes. Seducing me, and whatever kinky stuff "tying" was, no.

"Why…why would you seduce *me*?" Suddenly the room seemed heavy and warm. I wanted to touch to this demon, feel her hands on my skin.

"Because I'm a succubus. That's what sex demons do. We seduce humans, fulfill their fantasies, then siphon their sexual energy." Her dark eyes were full of promise as they met mine. "I tie my prey to me so they supply me with that energy for the rest of their lives. Every time they have sex, they think of me. Every time they masturbate, they think of me. And each time, I feed once more."

I shivered, wanting to scoot away and put some distance between us, but unable to move. I was trapped. And I got the feeling that if she kissed me, I'd be lost—just another among the thousands who lived only for her touch.

A surprisingly sweet smile curled her lips. "Do not worry, Red Bird. Right now I cannot use my succubus skills of enchantment on you, take your sexual energy, tie you to me, or Own your soul. Sex with me would be just that—only sex. You are safe from me." She reached out and touched my hair. "For now. Maybe if you survive your new owner long enough for me to escape, I'll come for you. You're very beautiful. I think your energy would be sweeter than any I've had in the last century."

My future wasn't looking too good. Death at the hands of the guards trying to escape. Death at the hands of whoever bought me at this auction. Death by this succubus. At least with the succubus I'd know pleasure, although I got the impression her sort of pleasure would tip me into insanity.

Abruptly she rose, then reached out a hand to me. I took it and let her help me up, noticing again that all my wounds had healed. My hair was still bright red, my skin still unblemished and unmarked.

"Do not try to escape, Red Bird," she told me. "The guards will kill you, and I would be very sad if you died."

"I'm going to die anyway," I replied. "Does it matter whether it's by them or by some sicko who likes to use a knife while he's raping me?"

She thought a moment then chuckled. "I guess not. Such a waste. Such a shame. Too bad you cannot be mine, Red Bird. Too bad."

She left to go repair the other girls' injuries and I slid back down the wall to sit on the cold tile once more, my legs shaking as I clasped my hands around my knees. I *did* feel sorry for her, just as I would feel sorry for a murderous tiger pacing the bars of her cage. But releasing the tiger would most likely mean my death at her claws and fangs. As much as I wanted to save her, to save the others, I didn't want to die.

But I was going to die anyway. And if I had to pick a way to go out, a demon was probably no worse than a bullet to the head or a knife at my throat.

I stayed in the bathroom, covering my ears when the screams began. Pockmarks had ordered the demon woman to fix our injuries, and that's what she was doing. I could feel the sharp bite of her energy as she repaired bruised and damaged flesh, mended broken bones, all at a cost.

But not me. I wasn't sure if what she'd been trying to do to my hair had fixed my own injuries, succeeding there where it failed when it came to my stubborn red locks, or if there was something inside me that super-charged my healing. She'd thought I was part demon. Maybe I was, but it didn't seem to do me a whole lot of good. I could hold my own against the demon woman in a fight, but didn't seem to have any advantage over human men. I could heal my own injuries but couldn't do a thing to help the others. Whatever supernatural skills I had, they weren't any use in getting us out of here.

There was another long scream, ending in a whimper. I pressed my hands over my ears wanting it all to go away. Why was this happening to me? What horrible thing had I done that I needed to suffer this? And what about the others? They were innocents, victims of a cruel fate that didn't care if they were raped and tortured. Every one of those girls out there deserved a better future, especially given some of their lives to date. They all deserved better.

So did that demon woman.

Leethu. It was a beautiful name, silky and seductive with a deadly bite, just like she was. Deceptively small and frail. Strong and loyal. And lonely. So very lonely.

I stood, pushing off the wall as I walked out into the room. Leethu had her hands on Pillow's ribs. The girl was gasping and crying, begging as the silvery glow suffused her flesh. When the demon was done, she slumped, panting to the floor. Then Leethu turned to Mess.

"No." Mess backed away, cradling her broken wrist. "Don't. Leave me alone."

"I'm sorry I lost my temper and hurt you." The warm blue aura enveloped them both, so soft, so comforting. "I do not normally do such things. In self-defense, yes, but I had no reason to fear you or to hurt you. I give pleasure, not pain. It sorrows me that this is who I am becoming. Please let me fix your wrist. I will be as gentle as possible."

A sleepy, drugged expression came over the girl's face. "I don't want you to hurt me. No more hurting. No more."

Leethu reached out and took the girl's arm, holding it gently. Then the light came from her fingers and Mess began to scream. When the demon was done, the girl's wrist was fixed and all her bruises and cuts were healed, but there was a hollow, desperate look in her eyes as she scurried away. Leethu watched her, shoulders drooped.

Lonely. Trapped. No one cared enough to come help her. Eventually they would, but there wasn't anyone who loved her enough to be frantic with worry over her absence, who would turn the world inside-out to find her. No one who would come with feathered wings to her rescue.

"Don't let her do that to me again," Mess said to me, her voice raw and ragged. "No more. No more men profiting off my body. No more being told who to have sex with, where to sleep, what to eat. I want to be in charge of me. For once, I want to be the one who decides what happens to me, not some man. And not some demon."

I wrapped my arms around her, hugging her tight, promising her things I would never be able to deliver. "Soon. Soon that will all stop, and you'll be free."

"Free." She buried her face in my shoulder. "I can't do this anymore. I can't be strong anymore. It's my turn. From now on *I'm* the one who gets to decide what happens to me. Promise me, Red. Promise me that I get to decide from now on."

I couldn't promise that, not with the sale two days away and our chance of escape dwindling to zero. I couldn't promise that, but I could hold her and tell her that soon she'd be free—we'd all be free. Then nothing would ever touch them again. I could lie.

The demon woman looked around, checking to make sure we were all perfect and injury free, without a cut or bruise on us to mar our beauty, then with a sad smile my way, she left, locking the door behind her. It wasn't the first time I'd seen her do this, lock and unlock the door without using a key. I remembered her welding the bathroom door shut behind us, then reversing the magic as she went to leave. Clearly her skills did stretch beyond seduction and the ability to alter human physical appearance. Clearly there was more to this demon woman that met the eye.

We slowly made our way to the cots, everyone huddling together on Mess's and Sugar's with a few of us sitting nearby on the ground. There was a heavy sense of desperation in the air. We knew our chances for escape were pretty close to zero, that in just over a day we'd be sold at auction, split up. Even if one or two of us managed to escape, we'd never be able to find the others after they sold us.

If. I doubted street pimps were going to be paying high dollar for girls at an elite auction with the sort of buffers against police interference Leethu had said she was providing. These were serial killers looking for a victim, or people who wanted a sex slave, or private clubs who wanted their own personal girl to take turns with. There would be no sting operation to save us, no undercover officer answering an internet ad and showing up at a sleazy hotel room to arrest us, no lazy pimp to escape when his back was turned. These clients would have us locked and chained, and probably kept in some cabin in the middle of nowhere. Once we were sold, there would be no hope. We had tonight and tomorrow to figure out what to do, and judging from the look on a few of the girls' faces, many of them would rather die trying to escape than meet whatever fate held for them at the hands of their buyer.

"We thought she'd murdered you," Kitten whispered, putting out a tentative hand to touch my shoulder. "When she dragged you in there, and we heard the screaming, we thought she was killing you."

"And having sex with your corpse," Sugar added. She laughed as the others turned their shocked gazes her way. "What? There was a bunch of screaming, then silence, then a weird sexy-time vibe. Don't tell me I'm the only one who figured demon-lady was screwing Red's dead body in there."

"You're disgusting," Pistol told her.

"What *did* happen in there?" Mess asked. "The door was welded shut. We couldn't come to help you."

"The woman is a demon. It's not like we *could* have helped her," Pillow pointed out.

"She tried to change my hair color." I picked up a lock and showed it to them. "Obviously it didn't work."

"But she tried." Pistol shivered. "I heard you screaming. I know how much agony you were in."

A few of the others nodded in sympathy. It had been agonizing, one of the most painful experiences of my life. I might not remember my past, but I was positive I'd never felt pain like that before.

"She screamed too," I told them. "I think it hurt her just as much as it hurt me."

"Good." Sugar's eyes narrowed. "Too bad it didn't kill her."

"But what was…" Kitten blushed. "What was the other thing?"

"Yeah," Pillow added. "It got all quiet, then suddenly it was like I was rolling on Molly or something. Everyone felt it."

Yeah, I'd felt it too. "She's a succubus. A sex demon. She screws humans and takes their sexual energy to feed on."

Kitten's eyes were huge. Every one of the women stared at me.

"Did she…did she…?" Kitten stuttered.

"Did you guys seal the deal?" Sugar asked. "Lesbo sex with a demon? I guess not if you're still standing and not dead on the bathroom floor."

I snorted. "Uh, no. We did not 'seal the deal.' She didn't rape me. And I don't think she necessarily kills people when she has sex with them. Besides, she told me she can't kill us. There's a clause or something in her summoning contract that says she can't use her succubus mojo on us, take our sexual energy, take our souls, or kill us." I looked around at the others. "Or help us escape."

"Damn." Sugar grinned. "I was kinda hoping you'd seduced *her* and she was going to whisk us away to safety. Although since she's a demon, she'd probably be just as likely to whisk us away to some lava pit in hell."

"Do you trust her?" Pistol asked, eyeing me like she wasn't sure if I wasn't secretly a demon also.

"I trust her to be her. She's a demon, and according to her she's under the thumb of the boss—the man who summoned her. I don't think she'd be completely on our side even if she wasn't, though. I do believe she'd help us escape if she could, just to stick it to these guards." I thought for a second. "Although she might just steal their souls, then do the same to us."

"Doesn't matter." Sugar waved a hand. "She's under a summoning. She can't or won't help us. And seems like bashing her brains in with a toilet lid again isn't going to do more than knock her out for five or ten minutes."

"How hard *did* you hit her?" Mess grimaced. "I'll admit I probably held back when I hit that guard. It's one thing to punch someone, but I just couldn't crush his skull or deal with the thought of brains splattered across the room."

"I broke her skull," I admitted. "I put everything into it. She was a demon, and I wasn't sure what it would take to stop her. Guess it takes more than a blow to the head."

"I doubt a bullet to the head would stop her," Sugar commented. "We're just going to have to try to sneak out when she's not here. Or when she's sleeping or something."

"How would we know when that is?" Kitten asked. "We can't hear what they're doing out there, and they said they're not going to feed us anymore. What if they don't open the door again until they come to take us out to the sale?"

"Then we try to figure out a way to get the door open ourselves," Pistol said. "Maybe use parts from the cots to take the hinges off or something. And if that doesn't work, we try to get out when they come to move us for the sale."

"There's a stage out there in the warehouse," I reminded her. "And stacks of folding chairs. I think they hold the auction here, which won't give us any time to escape during transportation."

"Can we get the door off the hinges, you think?" Kitten asked. "If we wait for the auction, we'll be out of this room, but then we'd need to fight off a whole bunch of buyers in addition to the guards and the demon. I think our chances are better if we can get out before then."

Pistol stood up and went to look at the door. Sugar climbed up on the counter and looked at the air return ducts.

"None of us are going to fit through these," she announced. "Not even Lacy, and she's built like a ten-year-old."

"These are pretty industrial sized hinges," Pistol said. "We can try to get them off, though."

"Then let's each take turns trying to unscrew the hinges," I said. "Pistol can start first. The rest of us cover every inch of the walls in the space, tapping and poking holes with wires to see if we can maybe break through the drywall into the warehouse or another room that isn't locked. Sugar, check the air returns in the bathroom and see if they're any bigger. We need to find a way out of here, and we need to do it fast."

Super fast. We had tonight, tomorrow and tomorrow night, then we'd be out of options.

The guards did return that night, not to bring us food but to examine the demon's work in fixing us up, and to choose a new play toy for the evening.

"Your pick," Pockmarks told Catcalls. "How about the Russian girl? She looks like fun."

Tasha caught her breath. I moved to stand in front of Kitten and Pistol while Mess did the same to Sugar and Baa. Pillow and Lacy sat wide-eyed on their cots, frozen with fear.

"No, I want the bitch that hit me," Catcalls said, glaring at Mess. The girl sucked in a sharp breath, but set her jaw and lifted her chin. I stayed where I was, feeling as if I were in a giant chess game. Protect the pawns. Advance when my opponent's intent is clear.

Pockmarks gave the other guard a sharp look. "Think you might take it a bit far with that one. Screw that Mexican chick instead. She looks sturdy enough for what you like to do."

I wasn't sure which "Mexican" chick he was referring to. Baa stood rigid behind Mess, unable to follow the conversation. I shifted to the side, trying to block Pillow and hoping Pistol could protect Kitten if needed.

"She'll just lay there and cry," Catcalls complained. "I like one that's got a little game, you know what I mean? There's no fun in punching some unresponsive bag of meat. I like one that's gonna give me some cause to land a few blows."

"Well, I don't," Pockmarks told him. "I don't want to have to fight some chick to get my rocks off. Nice and quiet. Please and thank you. That's what I want."

Would they take two of us tonight? A feisty girl like Pistol or Sugar or Mess for Catcalls to beat around and screw, and Lacy or Kitten or Tasha for Pockmarks? I hated the thought of any of my girls being subjected to these men, but with two out of this room, maybe there would be a better chance of one escaping. We just needed one to escape and bring help. Just one.

"How about I take the bitch that hit me and you take that one?" Catcalls jutted his chin at Kitten. I caught my breath, knowing that of everyone here she was the one most in need of protection. She wasn't street-hardened as most of us were. She was an innocent and probably a virgin. And she was only thirteen. I wouldn't let them take her. I'd fight to the death if I had to, but I wouldn't let them take her.

"I'm no damned pedo." Pockmarks sneered and I took a relieved breath. "Besides, the underage innocent ones bring the most money. I'm thinking the Russian over there, or the Chinese girl."

Tasha's eyes grew wide. Lacy must have gleaned something from the men's gestures, because she scooted back on her cot, putting her rear against the wall.

"Thought you weren't no pedo," Catcalls laughed. "That Chinese girl looks younger than the other one."

"They all look young. You go first, then when you're done with your girl, I'll take whichever one I like."

Catcalls smiled and took a step toward Mess. She shrank back and I moved to stand in front of her.

"Take me instead. I'm the one who organized the whole thing. It was me."

He hesitated, looking between me and Mess. "She's the one who hit me."

"No, it was me. I'm the one that brained your demon and planned the escape attempt. I'm the one who hit you."

"Don't you remember who knocked you upside the head?" Pockmarks asked.

He frowned. "Nah, she hit me from behind. Pretty sure Red was over with the other girls. She's the only one that wasn't there. Had to be the black chick."

"It was me," I insisted. He couldn't have seen me. I'd had my face buried in my hands, the girls all around me, so I didn't have to see a repeat of what I'd done in the bathroom.

His eyes narrowed. "I saw your red hair. Not like anybody could miss that from a mile away. You were over with the other girls. She was the one who wasn't there. She was behind me. She was the one who hit me."

Cursed bright red hair. "I'm the one who told her to hit you. I hit the demon. I plotted the escape. Take me instead."

"That red-haired one's prettier." Pockmarks grinned. "She's the best looking one of the bunch. Imagine the bruises on that pretty skin of hers."

"She's not the one that hit me, though."

"I'll fight," I told him, desperate to keep the other girls safe. "You'll need to drag me off, beat the crap out of me, tie me up, even gag me. I'll give you plenty of reasons to hit me."

I took a step forward and he reached out to grab my arm. Lightning fast he pulled out a pocket knife and cut a shallow line across my arm. It burned, pain radiating outward. Blood welled up, bright red in contrast to my pale, porcelain skin.

"Bruises don't show as well on dark skin," he muttered.

I seized on my chance to convince him. "None of it would have happened without me. Take me instead. Punish me instead. And you…" I took a deep breath. "You can do whatever you want. Anything. Anal. Anything. Force me at knifepoint to give you a blow job. You can be as rough with me as you want. Punish me as much as you want. The demon can always fix me afterward. And if not… Well, you do have an extra, don't you?"

Kitten began to cry softly in the background. I saw Mess standing very still, hardly daring to breathe, her expression a mixture of fear and sorrow.

"She's worth a lot of money," Pockmarks warned. "Yeah, we got an extra, but if you kill her, it's coming out of your share of the profits. Every last dime."

The guard's fingers tightened painfully on my arm. The blood had streaked across my skin and was falling to the floor in crimson drips.

I was afraid. I was so afraid. But better me than them. This guy was…he was going to be brutal. I couldn't let that happen to any of my girls.

Catcalls looked over toward Pockmarks. The other man shrugged. "Your pick. I don't care which one you take."

"Last guy that fucked her ended up dead with his eyes all burned out of their sockets," Catcalls said. "Not sure I want to take the chance of that happening to me. Sure is pretty though, with that skin. Even the weird red hair is kinda cool."

"That had nothing to do with me," I assured him. "I was tied to the bed."

He hesitated, eyeing the streaks of blood on my arm. "Nah. Not gonna take the chance. I'll fuck the other one instead."

Mess let out a cry, and I tried to block Catcalls from her. "I'll do anything you want. Anything."

He shoved me out of the way. "Next time, Red."

Something snapped. I jumped on his back and grabbed his head, trying to break his neck. All the strength I'd had when fighting the demon vanished and all I could do was pull his hair and scratch his face.

"Get her off me!"

Pockmarks hooted and laughed as Catcalls spun around, grabbing and trying to yank me off his back. "I'm thinking you should take this little firecracker instead. Or is this too much fight for you? You too much of a pussy to handle her?"

Catcalls launched himself backward, slamming me into the concrete wall. It knocked the breath out of me and loosened my grip on his hair enough that he was able to yank me off and throw me to the ground. A foot stomped down on my stomach, then another kicked me in the side. I grabbed at his leg, fighting to get my breath against the waves of pain.

Another kick launched me across the floor and into one of the cots.

Catcalls grabbed Mess by the arm and half dragged her out of the room while Pockmarks held the rest of the girls back with the threat of the broom handle. Then he backed out the door, locking it solidly behind him.

"Are you okay?" Pillow and Tasha bent over me, smoothing my hair away to check my face. I straightened on the floor, taking tiny breaths. My arm stung where he'd cut me. My stomach and back felt like someone had worked me over with an iron pipe. Carefully the girls helped me sit up as I eased my way into taking full breaths.

And then it was gone. The pain washed away and I inhaled deeply. Looking down, I saw my arm was unmarked aside from the streaks of blood.

"I'm fine." I told the girls, hoping I didn't have to somehow explain my miraculous recovery.

They helped me to my feet, fussing over me a bit. Then we all stood and stared at the door, miserable and not sure what to do. He'd taken Mess. He'd taken one of my girls. And I was terrified for her.

It should have been me. Why wasn't it me? All I wanted was to keep my girls safe, and I'd failed. Mess was out there on her own with that monster, and I couldn't help her. I could only pray that the guardian angel she'd teased me about was real, that he would swoop in and save her.

But I was pretty sure there was no guardian angel. None for me, and probably none for Mess either. Instead I closed my eyes tight and prayed for the demon to save her. *Leethu, wherever you are, help my girl. Don't let him hurt her. Don't let him kill her.*

"Is Mess going to be okay?" Kitten asked. "I'm scared. I'm scared for her. I don't want them to hurt her." I noticed Sugar didn't have a smart-ass statement in reply. In fact, the sassy blonde was unusually silent, chewing her fingernail, her brow furrowed with worry.

Then Sugar reached out and put her arm around Kitten's shoulder. "You can survive a lot when you have to. Just let yourself go to a secret place inside, away from your body. Hide there, and no one can harm you. They can rape you, they can bruise and cut you, but they'll never hurt you. You'll always be safe there."

She was teaching the younger girl how to endure rape and torture. I was listening to a seventeen-year-old girl tell a thirteen-year-old girl how to emotionally deal with being sexually and physical assaulted. The idea that Sugar knew this from personal experience made me sick to my stomach.

"Mess has a secret place inside her just like that. She'll be safe there, no matter what happens," Sugar told the girl.

"I couldn't save her," I said, more to myself than the others. "I tried. I tried to take her place."

"She'll be okay," Sugar repeated. "It's not like we both

haven't had a john beat on us before, or have some guy fuck us in the ass, or shove crap up inside us. She'll be fine."

"They hurt Red," Kitten reminded her. "They hurt Pistol and Tasha. What if she's not fine?"

"He's just going to punch her around a few times, have sex, then bring her back. We're merchandise. He's not going to do anything that might limit their profits. And she has her safe space to hide in so he can't reach her, remember? She'll be okay."

I heard the worry and doubt in her reassurances. I was worried too. They had an extra. They'd been expecting eight and now they had nine. And Catcalls might be pissed off enough to think one less girl to make money off of was worth getting his revenge. He might think it was worth it to blow all his profits on killing one of us.

Tasha reached out to stroke Kitten's hair. "She will be okay. The other man will not let him go too far. They want money, and dead means less money. And you hear? Other man say he make him pay for dead girl. He will not want to lose all his money just to kill."

"But she's already been through so much," Kitten whispered, her eyes tearing up. "She told me about how the neighbor kids when she was little, how they used to rape her and how her mom just disappeared one day when they were living under a bridge. She hasn't been safe once in her life, not once. And now this."

"Her safe space," Pillow echoed. "She'll go to her safe space and survive this. We all will survive this."

It was an unpleasant reminder of what our future held, where surviving would be our primary goal, where even a safe space deep inside might not be enough.

"Well we all better get used to it," Sugar said, suddenly reverting to the crude pessimist we all knew and loved. "This is going to be our life from here on out—and the only blessing is it will probably be a short life. Those guys won't be the most pleasant dudes I've ever banged, and they'll probably beat the crap out of us or cut us, but they won't be anything compared to whoever buys us. Better to die here, trying to escape, than suffer whatever the buyers have in mind for us."

"Not now. We don't need that kind of talk right now," I told her firmly. She was right, and I'd been thinking the same thing, but we couldn't dwell on a worst-case scenario. Such a line of thinking wouldn't do us any good.

"We don't know for sure what the buyers will do to us," Pillow said. "Could be whoever buys us just want someone to clean his house and give him blow jobs. Maybe they're really ugly, or old, or lonely, and need to pay for sex, but want something more than a town prostitute. Maybe it won't be that bad. Nothing we haven't done before."

"I haven't done that before," Pistol protested, angrily wiping a tear from her cheek. "I was a college student, not a prostitute."

"Well la-dee-da," Sugar sneered. "Miss high and mighty here thinks she's better than us. Well, let me tell you, college girl, you can survive a whole lot of shit when you need to. So get used to spreading your legs, sucking dick, and pretending you're having the time of your life because it's better than starving to death, and it's a whole lot better than dying."

"Cut it out, all of you. We're a family. We need to support each other." I stood and glared down at Sugar. "Guessing about what these buyers are like isn't going to do us any good. We need to get out of here, and that needs to be our focus. Let's get back to work on the door hinges and the drywall and hopefully by the time they bring Mess back, we'll be in a position to escape."

Hopefully. I was worried that Mess might not be in any condition to run for it when they brought her back. And what if they didn't? Or what if when they brought Mess back, they took one of the other girls? Would we halt our escape plans if one of us wasn't here to make a run for it with us? Would we leave one of our own behind?

I knew the answer to that. I couldn't jeopardize the other girls' chance at freedom waiting. If we broke through, or got the door open, we'd need to go, whether we left one behind or not. The good of the many outweighed the good of one.

If we could, we'd escape—no, they'd escape. I'd stay behind, because as scared as I was, there was no way I would ever leave until I was certain that every one of us was able to get away to freedom. And that meant Leethu as well.

Hours later the door opened and Catcalls half carried Mess into the room. She was barely recognizable, her face battered and bloody, her lip and cheek split open. One eye was swollen shut, and from the way she was hunched over, I was guessing a few of her ribs had been broken. We all jumped to our feet. I and ran forward, reaching out to take her from the guard.

"See what happens when you try to escape? When you hit me?" He pushed her.

"Your angel didn't come to save me," Mess whispered as she fell into my arms.

No. No, he clearly hadn't. I wished he had. I wished Pockmarks and Catcalls had suffered the same fate as Onions. I wished the same for the boss, for anyone else who'd been involved in taking these girls off the street like they were inanimate objects to be sold. Right now, seeing Mess this way, I even wished the same for the demon woman. If she couldn't help us, if she wouldn't help us, then I wanted her to suffer the same fate, to explode on the inside, her eyes nothing but smoking black holes in a corpse on the floor. I couldn't keep making excuses for her. I couldn't keep thinking I could win her over to our side. She needed to make a decision and make it now.

And so did I. Emotionally I was back to where I'd been in the bathroom, holding the toilet tank lid. I was going to save these girls no matter what it took. I'd save her too, but she needed to do something, anything to show she was on our side. Otherwise I was going to make sure she suffered the same fate that these guards did.

Pockmarks walked in, the demon woman last through the doorway. I held Mess gently, letting her weight rest on me as I eyed all three of them, waiting for the demon to do something, anything that would put her on the right side of all this.

"You. My turn, and I'm picking you. Come with me," Pockmarks commanded pointing at Lacy. The girl might not have known any English, but she understood well enough to shrink back, shaking her head and pleading in a foreign language.

"She's begging you not to hurt her. She doesn't want to die. She says she will do anything you say, just please don't hurt her," Leethu translated.

Pockmarks turned to her in surprise. "You speak Chinese?"

The demon woman's lip curled. "She's not Chinese, you idiot, she's from Laos. And I speak over forty human languages. Laotian is one of them."

Pockmarks looked impressed. Briefly. Then the scowl returned. "Tell her that if she doesn't fight me, and doesn't try to escape, she won't wind up like this other one."

Leethu spoke to the girl, who nodded vigorously as she replied. "She's terrified," the demon told the guard. "And she weighs all of a hundred pounds soaking wet. Just look at her. You won't have any trouble. She'll do exactly as you say."

"Good. That's what I want. Nice and compliant." As if she understood, Lacy walked over toward him, eyes lowered, the perfect picture of submission.

"Fix her so this other one doesn't die on us." Pockmarks gestured toward Mess. "I've waited long enough. It's my turn to have some fun."

The demon woman stopped abruptly, staring for the first time at the battered girl in my arms then turned to Catcalls in anger. "What did you do to her? You are not supposed to beat them like this. They're merchandise. It's two days until the sale, and look at her."

Catcalls shrugged. "You're a demon. Fix her up. Not my fault if I got a bit carried away. Bitch deserved it."

"No," Mess moaned, clinging to me. Her voice was wet and reedy, blood bubbling from her mouth. "No, don't let her. Hurts too much. Don't want to hurt more. Just let me be."

"She's dying," Leethu snapped. "Look at her face. Her nose is broken, and so is her orbital socket. Her brain is swelling from head trauma. She's bleeding internally. I'm guessing a fractured rib punctured a lung. This isn't just 'a little carried away.' Do this crap to your own woman, not one we're supposed to be selling in two days."

"So? I had fun. Don't tell me you haven't thought about doing the same thing to the redhead bitch that hit you in the head."

The demon shot me a quick look. "Not like that. Not kill her."

"Liar." Catcalls laughed. "She's still breathing. Fix her up and we can still sell her."

"No, we can't." Leethu glared at the guard. "I can't fix this. I'm a sex demon. I don't heal, and I don't resurrect people from the dead. Fixing bruises and a broken bone or two is one thing. This is beyond my ability."

"She's not dead yet," Pockmarks told her. "Fix her the best you can, and we'll sell her at a discount. Might as well make some money off her."

"She won't make it," Leethu argued. "She'd dying and there's nothing I can do to prevent that."

"All she needs to do is make it to the sale. Maybe we'll give her to Miller as a bonus. Bundle her in with one of the others. Just patch her up so she lives a few more days."

"I'm not a fucking angel," the demon muttered under her breath.

"Fix her, or I'll tell the boss you refused," Pockmarks said. Then he and Catcalls left.

Leethu shook her head, muttering something else that sounded like "fucking pigs," then she took a step toward us. Mess shrank against me, repeating "no, no" as if it were a mantra. I turned, blocking the demon with my body.

"Leave her alone," I told Leethu. "She's been through enough. Just let her be."

The demon hesitated. "She'll die. Tonight or in a few days, she'll die. They've really hurt her. It looks like he used one of those wooden poles on her, and I'm thinking in her as well. She has internal bleeding and a fractured skull."

"Then you should have stopped him," I snapped. "You're a demon. You could have done something to keep him from beating her like this."

"I can't," she snapped back. "I told you I'm forbidden from hurting the guards. And I can't help any of you escape."

"You could have protected her," I argued. "You should have done something. Do you even care? Doesn't it bother you that one of those men raped her and beat her to death? You could have done something to help her."

"I couldn't." Her voice rose. "I thought he was just having rough sex with her. I thought maybe he hit her a few times. I didn't know he had done *this*." Her eyes met mine. "I'm a sex demon. I'm limited in my skills, and the man who summoned me made sure I can't use my strength or my enchantment abilities on them."

"You could have done something else. Locked the guard out of the room, put them both to sleep. Made yourself look like her and taken her place. You should have done something. You should have done *something* to help her."

I was shouting at this point. It wasn't just Leethu I was angry at, it was me. I'd let them take Mess. Yes, I'd begged and pleaded and fought and tried to take her place, but I should have done more. I should have fought harder. *I* should have done something to keep Mess from them. Anything. And now they'd taken Lacy. Fear surged through me at the thought that she might return with similar injuries, no matter what Pockmarks had said, no matter how much she complied willingly with his requests.

Leethu stared at me as if she was reading my thoughts, then she reached out for Mess. "I can fix her, but I can't heal her. And with her injuries, what I do will only help her for a few days. I can fix her long enough to get through the auction, but that's the limit of my abilities."

Get her through the auction. What kind of blessing would that be? Fix her up only to have her suffer more beatings and rape at the hands of whoever bought her, then die in a few days. It would only prolong her torture. Leethu was a demon, a powerful demon. She needed to do something. She needed to prove to me that she was on my side. She needed to heal my girl.

I eyed her in disbelief. "You healed bruises and broken bones before. This can't be too different. Heal her. Make her okay again. I don't want her to die. She can't die."

"This is more than a breast increase, bruises, or broken bones. She's bleeding internally. She has swelling inside her skull. She's too badly injured for me to help her." Leethu gestured helplessly. "I want to heal her—to do this for you. But anything I do will be only temporary. She's beyond my ability."

"What are you saying?" I demanded. "Are you saying she's going to die? She can't die. She can't."

Her eyes met mine. "I can fix her, and maybe it will last a few hours, maybe it will last a few days, but soon what I do will give way. The swelling and the bleeding will start again, and she'll die."

"Then we need to get her to a hospital," I argued. "Please."

The demon shook her head. "They don't care. They just want her to survive the auction, then whatever happens afterward they can say it was something the client did. There is no way they would ever allow her to go to the hospital. None of you all are leaving here unless it's with a client that bought you."

Or in a body bag, I thought.

"I'll fix her," Leethu told me. "Then maybe she'll be okay. Maybe the client will let her see a doctor or take her to the hospital once she leaves here."

I knew a lie when I heard it, and so did Mess.

"Please," the girl whispered against me. "I don't want to hurt anymore. I just want peace. I want to decide what happens to me. For once in my life, *I* want to decide."

I suddenly realized that both of them were relying on me. The injured woman in my arms wanted me to support her decision. She didn't want to go through any more than she already had, but what if she didn't make it through the night? What if she died? She couldn't die. I couldn't lose one of my girls. I couldn't. Leethu had to fix her, to make her better.

Although from what the demon said, she'd only be delaying the inevitable.

Leethu... She could have shoved me out of the way and fixed Mess against her will. But she waited, looking for me to make the call, looking for me to tell her whether she should honor this woman's request or not. I knew she was under the compulsion of some sort of summoning, but still she found the strength to defy the guards and defer to my decision.

"Please," Mess begged. *Death isn't so bad. Sometimes it's a relief. Sometimes it's the happy ending of a tragic life. And I'd rather it be now than continue on for days of additional suffering, only to meet the same fate. Let me go, Red. It's your turn to take care of the girls. It's your turn to take care of me.*

Tears stung my eyes, but who was I to question or judge another's decision? She'd had a hard, hard life. Maybe it was time to put all that behind her, to find peace at last. I'd be with her every moment. I'd hold her in my arms as long as it took—whether it ended with her last breath, or a painful recovery. I would be there. And no auction, no buyer, no being human or otherwise would have the power to tear me from her side.

"Do not fix her," I commanded. "Leave her in my care."

Leethu did something between a nod and a bow, and turned to go, hesitating as she reached the door. "The other girl, Lai, if I can somehow help her…"

I waited for her to finish, puzzled. Was she going to ask me for a favor in return for protecting the girl?

The demon shook her head and gave me a sheepish smile. "Never mind."

Then she left, locking the door behind her.

I was a bit stunned by her easy acceptance of my decision. She'd pay for it if Mess died or wasn't perfect for the auction. Pockmarks, and the even more intimidating boss, would blame her. She'd suffer, perhaps far longer than any human could imagine. *She* was the brave one—she and Mess. Mess had been our protector from day one, shielding the other girls and comforting them. She was the glue that bound us together as a family. She was far more brave than I was. More brave even than any of us.

And Leethu… The demon had the most to lose, and yet she let Mess have this final dignity, she let the woman have her autonomy, her choice, her decision regarding her future.

"Come on," I told Mess, carefully lifting her into my arms. "Let's get you into bed."

"Deena," she gasped. "That's my name. That's my real name."

I understood. She wasn't One Hot Mess anymore, she was a scared girl with an uncaring, abusive mother. She was a homeless girl on the streets. She was someone who had been selling her body for almost a decade, just to survive. She was a soul in need of an angel.

It didn't matter that her blood was staining the sheets, that she was naked as I held her on the cot. Pistol pulled out one of the blankets and draped it over us. I held it inches from Deena's battered body, cradling her with gentle soothing hands. She slept, her pain receding into a far hori-zon. Her body relaxed against mine, and as the night stretched on, I whispered all the things she should have heard in her life. She was beautiful. She was clever and smart. She was precious. She was loved. The memories of her life streamed into me, weighing down my soul, becoming my burden as they lightened hers. And when I finally carried all of her pain, all of her sorrow, all the agony of her heart. When her burden had fully become mine, she was free. It was then that Deena Lucille Hayworth flew away from her mortal shell into the arms of the Creator.

CHAPTER 16

The next morning the door flew open, Pockmarks and Catcalls running in, a sense of immediacy and alarm about their sudden appearance. They hadn't brought Lacy back last night, and I was scared for her. The fact that she wasn't with them now scared me even more. Had they killed her? Were they prolonging her torture? We'd reverently wrapped Deena in a sheet, trying to give some respect in the treatment of her body that the disposal surely wouldn't have. We were all disheartened over her loss, the energy and enthusiasm for our escape attempts dulled by the death of one among us. If they'd killed Lacy, all of our hope would die with her.

The two guards looked around, counting and visibly relieved by our presence. I wasn't sure why they thought we'd be gone. We hadn't been able to make any progress on getting the hinges off the door, and all the drywall backed into cement block that would take us months to chip our way through.

"Get the demon," Pockmarks snarled. Catcalls scurried out of sight while the other guard counted again, somehow not noticing that one of us was dead and not sleeping. He grabbed the nearest one of us, which happened to be Pistol, and started shaking her. "Where is she? Where?"

"Where is who?" Pistol asked.

Pockmarks backhanded her across the face then shoved her back down onto the cot. "The Chinese girl. Where is she?"

I stood, putting myself between him and the other girls. "How should we know? You two took her out of here."

Was Lacy gone? How had she managed to escape? A tiny ember of hope flamed to life inside me at the thought she might have made it out of the building and be bringing help to us right now.

"She's gone." He grabbed my arm, his fingers digging painfully into the skin. "Where is she?"

"The door is locked. It's not like any of us could get out," I told him. "And if we could, don't you think we'd be gone too? We'd hardly let her escape then come back here and lock ourselves back in."

The logic seemed to sink into his tiny brain and he hesitated before yelling once more for the demon. When Catcalls and Leethu came in through the door, he let go of my arm and turned on her.

"Where is she? What have you done?"

The guard was practically frothing at the mouth, while the demon regarded him with a sort of tolerant calm, like she was watching a toddler having a tantrum.

"Have you lost one of the girls? Is that what you are screaming about?"

"I didn't lose her," he shouted. "I locked her in the room and went out for a smoke, and now she's gone."

Leethu lifted an eyebrow. "And what do you expect me to do about it?"

"You let her escape. You helped her escape," he snarled.

Her dark eyes were expressionless as she stared him down. "You know very well that part of my summoning forbids me from either harming the merchandise, or assisting any in escaping the building. Perhaps you forgot to lock the door behind you when you went out for your smoke."

He took a menacing step toward her, but the demon held her ground. "I locked the door. And when I went out, the girl was on the inside, sitting all nice and obedient on the bed, awaiting my return."

A bored expression slowly seeped into Leethu's eyes. "Then perhaps she was not as nice and obedient as she pretended to be. Perhaps she knows how to pick locks. Either way, a valuable piece of merchandise has slipped away on your watch. That's something *you'll* need to account for with the boss, not me."

"He's gonna be pissed if we have to move the sale and the girls." Catcalls had drops of sweat on his forehead. "What if that Chinese girl goes to the police? We need to get everyone out of here. We'll need to reschedule the sale, let everyone know we're holding it in an alternate location."

"No." The word cracked as sharp as a whip. "We'll lose client trust if we delay and move the sale at this late a date." Pockmarks rubbed a hand through his hair. "She doesn't speak any English. She's got no idea where to go, and no one who would understand her even if she tried to tell them. We'll be fine for the next twenty-four hours, then all the girls will be sold and we can close up shop here and find a different spot for the next sale."

"At least we still have eight," Catcalls said.

Uh, no they didn't. As if sensing my thoughts the two guards turned toward the cot with Mess's body. Pockmarks swore, then walked over to check her. Then he swore some more and paced the floor. "I told you to fix her. Why the hell didn't you fix her?" he snarled at Leethu.

"Because, as I told you, there is a limit to my skills. I'm a demon. I'm not an angel. You beat one of them that severely, and this is what happens."

"I'm not taking the blame for that." Pockmarks pointed at the body. "That is not my fault."

"No, it's his fault. The Laotian girl escaping is your fault." Leethu inspected her fingernails. "I hope the boss hires some reasonably competent humans after he kills the two of you, because this sort of thing is inexcusable. You're both beyond incompetent."

Pockmarks snarled, taking a menacing step toward the demon. His hand balled into a fist, then he must have realized what he was about to do, because instead of hitting her, he turned around and flipped a cot over.

"Very mature." Leethu shook her head. "I hate working with humans. Such idiots."

"We only have seven girls," Catcalls said, his voice high with panic. "We posted nine on the sale website. We were supposed to have eight at least. And now we only have seven."

"Basic math. Nice. I'm impressed." Leethu's tone was dry and sarcastic. It was a side of the demon I'd never seen before. She wasn't an animal pacing the bars of her cage, slowly losing herself anymore. She was powerful, intelligent, and very much in control. The cage of her summoning might still restrict her, but she was getting obvious pleasure from the things she *could* do in the space between the bars.

"Shut up," Pockmarks roared, giving the cot a quick kick. "Shut up and let me think. Do we have time to go get another girl? One that looks like either the dead one or the one that got away? The boss is expecting eight. We need to have eight."

"We can't grab a girl from this city, it's too risky. And we don't have time to bring another down from New York," Catcalls said. "The sale is tomorrow morning. There's no time."

Pockmarks paced a few more times, then kicked at the overturned cot while we all tried to stay out of his way and remain silent and unnoticed.

"It's your fault." Catcalls jabbed a finger at Leethu. "You were supposed to fix her."

"I'm here to make them look pretty and sex everyone up, not clean up the messes you jackasses make," she retorted. "You can't keep your fists off the girls, that's your problem, not mine."

"We ordered you to fix her." Pockmarks stalked over toward the demon. "You were supposed to fix her enough to get through the auction."

"I did fix her," Leethu lied. "She died anyway. I told you there were limits to my skills. Maybe you should have thought of that before you beat the crap out of our merchandise."

"You screwed up," Pockmarks continued. "You did it on purpose. You let her die on purpose to get us in trouble. Well, it's *you* that's going to get in trouble. I'll tell the boss that you refused to fix her, and that you let the other one escape. He'll put you in a box for thousands of years."

"A lot of good I'd do him in a box for a thousand years," she scoffed, folding her arms across her chest. "Demons aren't easy to summon and hold. He needs me. I'm the valuable one here. You two, on the other hand, are completely replaceable."

"We're fucked." Catcalls began to pace. "We're so fucked."

"You get rid of the body," Pockmarks told the other guard, then he turned to Leethu. "And you go track down the girl that ran away. Find her and bring her back."

"I'm not a bloodhound." She shrugged. "And I really think you should have me take care of the body. You're in enough trouble without the police finding a corpse in a nearby dumpster. I'm sure they're already sniffing around. All that runaway girl had to do was draw them some stick-figure pictures of what was going on, and lead them right back here."

"We're fucked. We're fucked. We need to move the girls and move the sale." Catcalls was tipping over the edge into panic.

"We're not moving the sale," Pockmarks snapped. "The demon will make sure the police don't come too close to the building. That's part of her deal with the boss, right?"

Leethu examined her nails. "Yes. I believe it is."

I bit back a smile as bits and pieces of her thoughts bloomed in my mind. Uniformed police, yes. Those not in uniform…well, all these human men look the same. How was she to tell if someone was a client or a law enforcement official not in uniform? And a female officer…the sorcerer had been carelessly specific about gender when he'd made the contract with her.

She was on our side. I still didn't completely trust her, but she was on our side. She'd somehow managed to help Lacy escape. She was riling up these guards. She'd find a loophole in her contract and help us when she could, regardless of what that might mean for her future. At this moment I could have run over and kissed her.

Pockmarks ran a hand through his hair, then turned to Leethu. "You fix these girls up. Any little detail. I want them perfect. I want them to be every man's fantasy. Then you get rid of the body. I'll go look for the girl myself."

The two men left, leaving us alone with the demon. She smiled at us, a shimmer of gold scales on her skin. There was a power about her, a confidence, a defiance that was more seductive than any of her succubus skills. Her eyes met mine and I felt something snap in place, some sort of connection between us.

She tilted her head as she regarded me, then inclined her chin toward the bathroom door. "Would you all mind terribly if I had a word alone with my Red Bird?"

CHAPTER 17

The others stared silently at the demon, then watched as the two of us crossed the room, entering the bath area and closing the door firmly behind us.

"What are you going to do with Deena?" I asked the moment we were inside.

"The dead girl? Incinerate her, most likely. Is that an acceptable form of body removal for humans?" Her dark eyes searched mine. "I am not very good at digging large holes in the ground. I could bury her ashes if you like."

Was she asking me? She wanted my approval on how to handle my friend's body? Why did she care what I thought or felt?

"I thought you would just throw her in a dumpster or out in the woods."

"That's what the men would have done." Leethu wrinkled her nose. "I knew that would disturb you, that you wouldn't think that a respectful way to handle human remains. I don't really understand these human customs of honoring decaying corporeal forms, but I will honor them."

I thought for a second. "Cremation is acceptable. But the

ashes should be buried somewhere. And there needs to be a marker with her name—a big marker. A monument."

It seemed kind of silly to ask for this. None of us could afford a huge stone gravestone. And it was unlikely any of us would be in a position to go visit Deena's grave. Even if we got out of here, we'd all scatter back to our homes. Go back to the lives we had prior to being taken. We'd never see each other again. Sugar would find a new pimp. Baa and Lacy and Tasha would be flown back to their countries. Pillow would return to Cleveland to wait for her father's release from prison. Pistol and Kitten would be reunited into the loving arms of their families. Me… I looked down at my arms, at the clear, perfect skin. I guess I'd go back to shooting up.

None of that was acceptable. The happy family reunions, yes, but the rest of it, no. And I didn't like the idea of us never seeing each other again. We had a bond. We were sisters. We were family.

"I can do that with her body." Leethu's expression was intent. "Would that please you? Such a thing would ease your sad heart?"

She was doing this for me? She cared about my grief and wanted to please me? This had to be the most surreal conversation I'd ever had. A demon wanted to please me.

"You helped her, didn't you?" I asked, realizing that the guards were right. "You helped Lacy escape."

"Her name is Lai." Leethu stepped closer to me then reached out to run a finger down my cheek and along the edge of my jaw. "And she is a very smart girl. I am forbidden by the terms of my contract from helping any of you to escape, but there was nothing prohibiting me from being otherwise occupied while the girl left an unlocked room and snuck out as those fools were off smoking or sleeping."

"So you didn't help her?"

"I am forbidden to help any of you escape."

It was a lie couched in a truth. "But you did. Somehow you found a loophole and helped her escape."

Leethu smiled, that enigmatic smile that made her seem otherworldly. "Of course not. I merely went into the room to retrieve something and forgot to lock the door upon leaving. These things happen, you know. I have been known to occasionally leave other doors unlocked and even ajar. It's a failing I readily admit to."

"Why?"

The demon tilted her head, regarding me with those dark eyes, her fingers lightly caressing the side of my face. "Why what?"

"Why did you do it? You didn't help Deena, the other girl. You didn't help anyone else. Why her?"

"It had nothing to do with her." Leethu's thumb brushed across my bottom lip and slid down to gently pinch my chin. "There are ways to creatively interpret every contract. Humans aren't as smart as they like to think they are, and even this summoner wasn't as thorough as he should have been."

"And there were no loopholes to keep you from helping me when that guard was raping me? Or when they beat Pillow, or Deena?"

Her eyes searched mine. "I did not try very hard to take advantage of loopholes then, I was too busy feeling angry and sorry for myself to bother about any of you."

"Then why Lai?"

"You were angry about the other girl. You want to protect them all, to keep them safe. I can't help you with all of them, but I thought if maybe I helped with one, you might forgive me all I must do to the rest of you."

"But you said you would help us when you could." My words were breathy, her fingers against my skin, the nearness of her making it hard to think, let alone speak.

"I will do all that I am able to do." She sighed, her thumb once more brushing against my lips. "I wish things were different, Red Bird. I wish the summoner were dead, and I could have you for my own—my own human toy for as long as you live. I would cherish you, pretty Red Bird. I would save the lives of all these girls just to see you smile. But I cannot. I am trapped, and you will be sold to some human tomorrow morning. And then I will never see you again."

I didn't want to be her toy. I wanted to be more than a toy. As seductive as she made it all sound, I got the impression what she was envisioning wasn't too far off from what whoever bought me tomorrow would have in mind. It would be a gilded cage of pleasure, but a cage nonetheless.

But here, in this building where we had seen pain and fear and death, this seemed to be a lifeline. It wasn't, but how bad would it be to have a moment of joy, to indulge in desire before everything went to crap, before I most likely died trying to get these girls to freedom?

She leaned forward, her body so very close to mine. "Humans are so difficult. It's rare that I find one I truly enjoy being with instead of just seducing them for their sexual energy. I would enjoy being with you, Red Bird. I would love more about you than just the sexual energy you gave me. There would be more with you than the usual seduction."

I was entranced, and the realization didn't particularly bother me. The heroin might have held me tightly in its grip, but I got the feeling no matter powerful this succubus, she lacked that ability. I was stronger now, different than I'd been before. But what this demon couldn't do with her sexual wiles, she could do with her heart. I knew right then if she ever offered me more than just sex, I'd be lost. Because it was my heart that was weak, my heart that was desperate for a partner to salve the ache, to fill that gnawing hole of need.

Her lips brushed my cheek, then hovered tantalizingly

over my own. I waited for her to close the distance, to kiss me, but she hesitated.

I didn't hesitate. Leaning that fraction of an inch closer, I felt the softness of her mouth against mine. It was a chaste kiss, gentle and lingering with a shared breath, but it lit me up inside. I drew in a shaky gasp, missing her lips the moment they pulled away, wanting again to close the tiny distance between her mouth and mine.

"Human energy is so sweet," she whispered. "And they can be quite a lot of fun. Such creative sexual fantasies. Such enthusiasm. But afterward, I am done with them. I seldom want to repeat the experience once I have tied them to me." Her voice was soft against my cheek as she leaned closer. "It's a rarity that I meet a human I want to do more than have sex with, one I want to have with me all the time, to be my own special toy."

"I wouldn't want to be your toy, or your special plaything," I told her. "I can't do that. I need more."

She pulled back and eyed me. "But you are attracted to me. With you it's different than the other humans. You want more than just the fulfillment of your fantasies. You want *me*. It draws me like nothing has ever done. I've never had someone truly want me. I've never known someone outside of my foster siblings who wanted more than sex or favors. Am I wrong? You do want me?"

I squirmed, growing uncomfortable with the conversation. "I do, but that doesn't mean I want to be a demon's toy."

"You would enjoy it," she said confidently. "Humans always do."

"How many human toys have you had?" I asked, oddly stung that I wasn't the only one she'd made this proposition to.

"Two." She smiled. "I'm not very old—just over a thousand years. And as I said, I do not often find a human I want to be mine."

"But you have relationships with demons, right?" The idea made me feel a bit hostile. "Humans are prey or toys, and any partnership-type relationship, where you treat the other as an equal, is with another demon?"

She took a step back, breaking the spell between us. "Some demons do that. There are difficulties. We are very much alike, and long-term demon romantic partnerships often end in the death of one of the partners. Instead we form short-term alliances that are sometimes based on a breeding contract, and are sometimes based on the strategic necessity of combining households. My household is part of the Iblis's, the Ha-Satan's, right now, not because of any romantic interest but because I needed her to shelter me when I ran into some trouble with the elven high lords." She shot me a mischievous glance. "Elves do not like to have intimate associations with us. Not only did I do so, but I formed an elven/demon hybrid with one of their royalty."

I thought my eyes were about to fall out of my head. "You had a baby with an elf? You seduced an elf, fed off her sexual energy, and impregnated one against her will?" Suddenly I had a whole lot less sympathy for this demon. I wanted her, but I should never forget that she was a demon, with a completely different idea of morality than what I and the other girls held.

"Oh no, it was not against her will at all. She came to me and asked me to sire a child. Some elves have great difficulty in becoming pregnant, and demons can bypass these problems. I was thrilled to sample elven sexual energy, although our agreement did not allow for me to tie her to me or take more than she gave in that one instance. Oh, but it was quite the experience. Elves are far more passionate than I ever would have expected. And there was a bit of fear to our encounter that made it all the more tantalizing."

Why was I suddenly so angry? She was a demon. Of course she did this sort of thing. Did I have some stupid, foolish idea of how noble and good she was underneath? Was that why this story upset me so? Or was I…was I jealous?

"It wasn't long before rumors spread," she continued. "The elven woman was put to death. I would have been put to death as well, but the Iblis sheltered me. And the child is protected by one I trust, one who loves her. She is here, hiding as a human in the human world. Even the elves would not be able to find her among seven billion humans."

My anger faded, only to be replaced by sorrow. She didn't care about that elven woman. She didn't have any romantic interest in the head of her household, this Satan character. She had only had two human toys in over a thousand years. Was she lonely? Did she just lack the ability to form a long-term meaningful romantic connection with any other being?

Why did I even care?

"Have you met your daughter? Do you see her often?"

Her shoulders slumped. "No. It wouldn't be safe. The elves know that I sired a half-breed. Now that they are here among us, I'm sure there are those who watch me. I do get reports from Irix on her, and sometimes will carefully be nearby to just look at her."

This time it was me that moved closer to her. "Your own daughter. Does she even know what you look like?"

The demon shook her head. "She thought she was human until a few years ago when her powers began to reveal themselves. It was too dangerous for either me or her elven mother to meet her. Someday I would like to get to know her better." The demon smiled, admiration and affection written across her face. "I hear she is a remarkable being. She is everything I hoped her to be, the best of the elves and the best of us demons."

I reached out to touch her shoulder. "Thank you. Thank you for helping Lacy, and for offering to bury Deena." I wanted to thank her for so much more. She wasn't just some monstrous demon. There was a complexity to her that attracted me like no other had.

"You are very welcome, Red Bird." She stepped into me, enfolding my body against hers. Then she kissed me.

It was soft and gentle, like the other but far from chaste. Her lips were soft and tantalizing against mine, her tongue exploring with a sweetness I hadn't expected. The kiss was lingering, her mouth clinging for a brief second before it left mine. We froze, sharing a breath as we came to terms with what had just happened, as *I* came to terms with the heat roaring through me.

"May I have you, Red Bird?" she asked softly. "Will you be mine, if only for this moment in our lives?"

There was only one answer I could give to that question. And the answer was "yes."

CHAPTER 18

I nearly ran into Pillow and Sugar as I exited the bathroom. The others were there too, only a little farther back away from the door. Kitten blushed bright red when she saw me. Tasha grinned and fanned her face. Baa quickly smothered a giggle with her hand while Pistol openly laughed.

"Busted," Pistol said.

"Who, me, or all of you?" I teased.

"Both. Damn, girl, that takes sleeping with the enemy to a whole new level," Sugar replied. Then they all fell silent as Leethu walked out behind me. It was awkward. I knew they weren't sure how to treat the demon. Was she a comrade and no longer the "enemy"? Or was she just the female equivalent of the guards, getting action using her succubus magic instead of dragging us away and forcing us?

"We'll talk later," I told the girls. "Right now, Leethu is going to bury Deena."

"Bury her how?" Sugar asked. "Dig a hole in the concrete floor?"

"No. I will find a human cemetery and mark the spot with an appropriate stone," the demon told her.

It was very clear by the expression on Sugar's face that she didn't believe Leethu. "How do we know you aren't lying? She was one of us. Deena was family. I've been friends with her for years. I don't want her body tossed in a dumpster or out in the woods somewhere."

"Me either, but I don't really want to spend the next twenty-four hours in the same room with decomposing remains," Pistol said. Everyone eyed the sheet-wrapped body warily, no doubt imagining that experience.

"I've given my vow," Leethu told them. "And I will cremate the body before transporting it."

"No," Pistol took a step back, her hands raised. "Oh my God, no. You'll burn the place down. And…I don't want to be graphic, but there's a reason those crematoriums are out in the middle of nowhere. You can't do that here."

"I'm not truly burning it. I convert the molecules. I break them down and reassemble them into something else all in a fraction of a second. It's a skill that demons have. That's how we can change our form, and alter physical items. That's how I 'fix' your injuries. I'm taking the damaged flesh and recreating it using the existing molecules as a pattern."

It wasn't truly creation, making something from nothing, it was change. It was the formation of something new from something destroyed. And I had no idea how I knew these things.

"Turning water into wine," Sugar mused. "Or lead into gold."

"Those are both far more complicated than they sound," Leethu told her. "Actually lead into gold would be easier than water into wine. I'm a succubus, so my skills in this area are limited. And it all requires energy—energy that is in somewhat limited supply here in this world."

"But it's magic," Kitten commented. "Can you magic the door so it doesn't lock? Magic the guards' poles so they turn into streamers or something? Magic the guards' feet to stick to the floor?"

"She can't harm or kill the guards," I told them. "And she can't actively help us to escape."

"But she can passively help us to escape?" Pistol's eyes lit up with hope.

"I have promised to do everything within my ability, as long as it doesn't go against the vow I took upon my summoning, to help you all to freedom," Leethu replied.

"Damn, Red. You must be one hell of a good lay. Well, except for exploding that one guy, that is." Sugar reached out to cuff me on the arm.

"So with Deena…" Pillow glanced over again at the sheet-wrapped body. "It will only take a second? And she will be ashes? And it won't set the room on fire with us trapped in here?"

"It will be instantaneous from your perspective. And no, the building will not be on fire. And I will ensure there is no unpleasantness in terms of odor or what you see."

Tasha took a step toward the demon. "But you say these things take energy, and energy here is not much. This will make you tired, no? It will make it so you have less energy to help us when you are not-helping us?"

"It will deplete my energy, yes," Leethu replied. "But this is important to you humans, and it is important to my Red Bird, so I will do it. Plus, the things I am limited to in passively assisting your escape aren't likely to require much energy."

I looked around at them all. "Are we agreed? Is it okay for her to use her demon skills to reduce Deena's body to ash, then bury her remains in a marked grave?"

One by one the girls agreed. We all followed the demon,

forming a circle around the cot. Each one of us said our goodbyes, then I nodded to Leethu and we all stepped back.

It was rather anticlimactic. One second there was a body wrapped in a sheet. One later it was gone, the sheet collapsing around a lump of ash. I stepped forward and carefully pulled the bottom sheet from the cot, tying it into a knot around the ashes, then handing it to Leethu.

"Promise you won't just ditch it in some alleyway," Sugar said, her voice choked with tears. "Promise me."

"I vow on all the souls I Own that I will bury these ashes with respect in accordance with human customs, and provide a marker to identify the location of the remains."

It sounded solemn, formal, and binding. The words satisfied Sugar, who took a step back.

Leethu picked up the bundle easily, giving me a quick backward look as she headed for the door. "I would wait on any attempts to escape if I were you. The one guard has returned, and they are both in the main warehouse area. They'll see you if you try to leave this room."

"Thank you," I told her. And I meant for a whole lot more than the warning. She was on our side. And having a demon on our side meant everything to me. Having *this* demon on our side meant everything to me.

I liked her. I more than liked her, although I wasn't sure how much of that was due to circumstances and our physical encounter. Only time would tell. And I hoped that we both had lots of time to explore this thing between us. I hoped we had a lifetime to do so.

* * *

As soon as Leethu left, Pistol went over to the door and tried it. It appeared to be locked, but as she turned the handle, the door edged open.

"Don't," Sugar hissed. "They'll see."

Pistol eased the door shut and practically skipped back to us. "It's unlocked! I'm so tempted to make a run for it. We're going to get out of here. We're going to be free. We'll make it."

"And we owe it all to Red," Pillow said, all admiration.

"What, for fucking the demon?" Sugar snorted. "Hell, if I had known throwing some pussy that way would get us out of here, I would have been screwing her since day one."

I felt my face heat up. Was that my contribution in her eyes? I screwed a demon, and that was what was going to save them?

But would we have been able to escape without Leethu's help? We'd had one failed attempt already. The only one of us who'd managed to get free was Lacy, and she'd had the demon's help getting out of here. I wasn't sure how that made me feel that my worth was in doing it with a demon and evidently being good enough at sex that she wanted to help us.

"No, dumbass," Pillow retorted. "Red would have gotten us out of here without the demon. She's our leader. She's the strong one, the one who isn't afraid to face those guys. When we were trying to get out the door the other day, she's the one who took on Pockmarks to buy us some time."

"You attacked the guard too," Kitten reminded her. "So did Baa. And she ran to turn the power back on. You both risked being trapped here so that we could get out."

"Yeah, yeah, we're all heroes." Sugar grinned. "Well, except for me, anyway. So what's the plan? How are we to know when a good time to escape is? Is the demon woman going to give us a heads-up? Five-minute warning before she takes the guards in a back room, turns on some loud music, and serves them pizza or gives them blow jobs?"

"That bay door is really loud and echoes all through the

building," Pistol commented. "No loud music is going to drown out that sound."

Her words made me realize something. "There has to be another door somewhere. Lacy couldn't have gone out the bay door. Catcalls would have heard her opening it and come to see what she was doing."

"But where?" Pillow asked. "I didn't see another door."

"In one of the offices?" Tasha asked.

"Not in the one I was in," I told them. This wasn't good. The time it would take for us to search the other offices, would greatly increase our chance of getting caught. Seven women couldn't exactly sneak around the warehouse looking for another door either. "We'll have to try the bay door again. I'll stand there by the power switch and make sure it stays open, fighting whoever I need to fight. I'll need one or two of you to volunteer to take on either guard who heads for you all so that the others can escape."

"Maybe we should split up," Pistol said. "It would increase our chances. There are only two of them, and seven of us, especially if the demon makes sure she's busy elsewhere when we're trying to escape. Two or three of us can look through offices and other places in the warehouse for another door. Red can guard the power switch. The three others can be trying to get under the bay door before one of the guards stops them."

Sugar nodded. "Worst case scenario, Red gets beaten to a pulp, and we lose one or two of the girls trying to get under the bay door. At least one of them has to be able to get away. And, if we're lucky, the other three looking through the offices can get away as well."

"That's if there's another door or two in the offices," I warned. "If not, then those three girls are going to be trapped in those offices with no other way out."

Everyone fell silent at my words. I knew they were calculating their chances, wondering who would be the most likely to get out and get help. Once I was beaten to a pulp, that guard would move to either help his buddy, or go for the girls in the offices. And what if there was only one office with a door to the outside in it? The other two girls would be out of luck. Actually all three might be out of luck if we picked the wrong offices to search and got caught before we could check them all.

"At least one can get away," Kitten said. "One under the bay door if she can squeeze through in time. And maybe one through an office door if there is one."

Which meant the rest of us would be in trouble. The guards might decide they had to move us and postpone the sale, and the one who escaped might not have enough time to bring help before they loaded us up and took us away.

"It's been at least twelve hours since Lacy escaped," Pillow said somberly. "Do you think Pockmarks caught her and killed her?"

Sugar shook her head. "Nah, he'd bring her back. You saw how freaked out they were at only having seven of us."

But we were all worried. There should have been SWAT teams swarming the warehouse by now. Had she gotten lost? Had someone just as bad as the guards grabbed her off the streets? Was she dead in an alleyway right now? Or locked in jail for being without identification and unable to speak any English to communicate what was going on?

"One," I said firmly. "We only need one of us to get out of here. And we need to decide right now who that's going to be. Whoever has the best chance of getting under that door, running fast barefoot, and finding and convincing the authorities to come help before the rest of us are moved. Everyone else needs to promise that we'll do all we can to get that one person out—whether it's fighting off the guards, or distracting them. I'm going to guard the power switch and make sure the door gets up, no matter what they do to me. Three of you can search the offices. I need two to ensure our chosen one gets under the door—protecting her with everything you've got, no matter what happens."

"Kitten. She's the smallest, and people are going to believe her when she tells them what's happening. I mean, look at those big brown eyes. How can you not believe that sweet face?" Sugar reached out and pinched Kitten's cheeks, as if she were an affectionate grandmother greeting a child. It made us all smile.

Kitten looked relieved at the suggestion. "I'll run really fast. And I'll send help right away—I promise."

"I'll help with the bay door." Sugar's voice turned serious. "I'll make sure the kid gets out."

Pillow had been translating for Baa, and at that time the girl raised her hand. "Baa says she'll help at the bay door too."

I nodded admiringly at the Guatemalan girl. She'd repeatedly stepped up, a badass eager member of our family.

"That leaves Pistol, Tasha, and me to search the rooms," Pillow continued.

"There are six rooms," I told them. "The one closest to the stage is where Onions took me. There's no way out of there, so don't bother with that one."

"I will look in the first room next to here," Tasha said. "This used to be a food place, no? I think there would be door near where people go to eat lunch."

"I'll take the next one," Pistol said.

"I'll take room four," Pillow replied. "Pistol, when you're done, search the next one down the line—room three. I'll move on to room five. Tasha, when you and Pistol finish, if you haven't found anything, meet me in room five. If you find a door, then go. Get your asses out that door and run like crazy. If there's time, the other two of us will backtrack and escape as well."

I was proud of these girls—proud of their bravery and their ability to tactically plan. This was our best chance at escape, better than our prior attempt. Hope bloomed up, filling me with warmth. We were going to get out of here. We were going to be okay.

But some of us probably weren't. I felt a cold dread that the two at the door might not live to see rescue. If Kitten and others escaped, would the guards kill the remaining girls and take off before the police showed up, leaving our bodies where they fell? Even if they moved us immediately, hauled us far away, we would all be made to pay for the loss of the others.

The boss would be furious. And the guards would put all the blame on us. Even Leethu wouldn't be able to save us from their wrath. I didn't just want to save two or three girls, I wanted to save our whole family—every one of them including the demon.

And me. I wanted to live. It had been a long time since I'd wanted to live. Redemption was at hand. I felt it just within my grasp. I just hoped I lived to see it.

CHAPTER 19

_L_eethu returned right about the time when we should have gotten dinner had they not decided to starve us. She told us the guards were unnerved by Lacy's escape and didn't want to leave the building, so they were sending the demon out for beer and food.

"They don't trust me," she said with a wry smile. "They'll come by and check the door after I leave. It's locked on the outside, but not from the inside, so they won't think there's anything amiss. Wait another half an hour, then go and go fast. They're on high alert. Any noise, any sound at all, and they'll be on you."

I tried to look confident, even though my hands were sweating and my heart was pounding. This was our chance. It was our last chance before the sale tomorrow. We had to make this work.

"I hope you're not here when I get back," Leethu told me. Then she leaned forward and kissed me. "I'll find you, Red Bird. As soon as I can get away from the one who summoned me, I'll find you."

"Or I'll find you," I told her. "We won't be apart for long."

"Knock it off, love birds." Sugar rolled her eyes. "Save the kissy-kissy for when we're out of here and safe."

Leethu grinned at me, the smile making her look completely different then the scary, stern woman she'd appeared to be that first day.

"See you on the outside," I told her.

We watched her leave and waited, trying to appear defeated and resigned to our fate when Catcalls came to count us and make sure the door was locked. We all silently marked the time, then I stood and motioned for them to follow.

Baa, Sugar, and Kitten were right behind me, as they'd have the farthest to run and needed to be at the bay door all the way on the other side of the warehouse. Tasha, Pillow, and Pistol brought up the rear. I held my breath and gently turned the handle, then eased the door open just wide enough for me to look out.

There was some noise coming from office number two that sounded like a television. I couldn't see or hear anything else. Carefully, I closed the door and turned toward the girls.

"They're in the second office from us, which changes the plan a bit. Pistol, you skip that one and take the next office down. Tasha, when you're done with the first office, you search the second one. They'll both run out the minute I start up the bay door, and you can sneak in after them."

I figured that was probably where the door was. It made sense the two guards, paranoid as they now were, would set up shop in the room with the only non-noisy escape route.

The girls nodded, and I opened the door again, practically crippled with the adrenaline racing through my body. This was it. This was probably our last chance. We couldn't screw up. Slowly I edged out the doorway, pausing to make sure no alarms went off with my exit of the room. Then I hunched down and ran, silent on bare feet, toward the power switch.

The others burst from the room, everyone as stealthy and purposeful as if we were some well-trained military team.

I watch the others run for the bay door, held my breath hearing the faint scurry of bare feet. I had to be ready. Once they hit the switch, the guards would come running while they stood waiting for the thing to inch it's way upward enough to squeeze through.

My hands were sweaty. I wiped them on my pants, wincing when the roar of the bay door sounded. Then I spun around to intercept the guards.

They ran from the office with a shout. I planted my feet, determined to guard the switch. It took them a fraction of a second to eye the scene, then Pockmarks took off for the bay door, while Catcalls came at me.

He swung the pole and I turned to take the blow in the stomach, folding myself around it and trying to dissipate the force as much as I could. The wind was knocked out of me, but I managed to pivot and get the pole under my left arm, both hands gripping it. He yanked, and I let myself stumble forward, knowing I couldn't stand firm against his superior strength. Somehow I kept to my feet, the pole burning my palms as it slid a few inches away. I heard a shrill scream, and glanced over to see Baa on Pockmark's back trying to garrote him with the chain from the toilet tank. Blood droplets flew from her hair as the guard spun around, trying to dislodge her and beat Pillow with the stick. I couldn't see Kitten, but prayed she was already out the bay door, running as fast as she could.

The pole twisted in my hands as Catcalls shook me back and forth, trying to break my hold on the pole. I gripped harder and dove forward, hoping to throw Catcalls off balance with the unexpected thrust.

Unlike me, he was able to plant his feet, immovable. Then he mirrored my move, pushing forward with a rush. I scrambled backward, frantic to keep my grip on the pole and not wind up on my ass. We edged closer to the power switch and I started to panic. There was a sickening thud from across the room, but I couldn't take the time to look. I had to keep the bay door opening.

A motion to the left caught Catcalls' attention—Tasha scurrying into the room the guards had just vacated. I took the opportunity to turn, pushing my weight against the pole and bringing me close enough to twist my hips and kick out. I was barefoot, and the blow landed a bit higher than I'd intended, smacking him in the thigh as opposed to taking out his knee.

Imagine my surprise when Catcalls abruptly let go of the broom handle, throwing me off balance. As I teetered backward, he grabbed my leg at the ankle and twisted. I screamed, trying to turn into the motion and wound up on the ground, my head smacking painfully on the concrete. The stick clattered, but I managed to keep hold, swinging it upward as I quickly evaluated the situation.

Not good. I wasn't sure what was happening over at the bay door, but from the sounds I was imagining Baa and Pillow being beaten to death. A memory of Deena's broken face and body swam up and my chest hurt thinking that I might lose two more of my girls tonight.

Catcalls had retained his hold on my leg. He twisted the already broken ankle and I nearly passed out. Somehow I managed to land a blow with the stick and evade his attempts to grab it, but I couldn't evade the kick that slammed into my hip, rolling me partially onto my side.

The next one landed right in the kidneys. I gasped and ineffectively swung the stick, unable to land any further blows from my weird position twisted on the floor. This time he managed to grab it and yank, pulling me up off the ground. I scrambled to stand, biting back a scream as the foot with the broken ankle hit the floor and twisted again.

"Stop the damned door," Pockmarks screamed.

Catcalls snarled. "Tryin' to." He yanked on the pole, and I couldn't manage to hold my balance with only one leg. I fell forward, trying to grip the pole to my chest and use the weight of my fall to pull it from his hands. The thing wasn't all that effective as a weapon with me on the floor, but at least Catcalls wouldn't have it to beat me with.

As I fell forward, the guard raised his knee and rammed it into my face. I heard a crunch, felt blood pour from my nose. My hands, wet with sweat and blood slipped from the pole. As I hit the ground, I heard the grind of the bay door halt, and reverse. Then the blows rained down on my face and body until everything faded to black.

CHAPTER 20

I regained consciousness as I was dragged by my hair across the concrete floor. It felt like my scalp was being ripped off, but that was hardly the only pain I was experiencing. Abruptly, whoever was dragging me let go, and I lay on the floor, dizzy, nauseous, and trying to open eyes that seemed to be swollen and glued shut.

Someone was crying. More than one person was crying. Girls crying. Afraid. Hurt. A wave of heat swept over me, burning, cleansing...healing. I shuddered, feeling my ankle snap into place, bones grind and reposition, damaged flesh replaced. My eyes blinked open and I saw blood-stained bare feet, huddled close together.

"Get up." A pole hit my backside, hard enough to sting but not to bruise. I staggered to my feet and counted, my heart dropping. Five of my girls were clustered together against the wall, Catcalls standing in front of them with his stick at the ready. Only one got away. Only one of them.

Pockmarks grabbed my shoulder and shoved me in to the group, kicking my rear as I scuttled forward.

"Can I have her?" Catcalls growled. "I want the red-haired

one tonight, and she ain't gonna leave my room in one piece, either."

"No." Pockmarks swung his stick. "Back in the room. All of you. Now."

We were herded into the room, me intentionally bringing up the rear so I could take any punishment these guys felt like dealing out on the way. I'd somehow healed from my injuries, but the other girls were hurt. Baa was bleeding from her head, her hair wet and sticky, red staining her shirt. Pillow's face was so swollen one eye was shut. Tasha was limping. Pistol and Sugar were bruised.

"Sit," Catcalls ordered. "One on each cot." We obeyed, walking as slowly as we could without risking a beating. Every second was one additional second that Kitten had to get to safety—and get help.

"Keep them here," Pockmarks told Catcalls. Then he pulled a pistol from his pocket and handed it to the other guard. "Here. One of them so much as looks at you wrong, shoot them."

I caught my breath at the significance of the weapon. They'd always used their fists and sticks on us because, I assumed, Leethu wouldn't be able to repair the more serious gunshot wounds. The introduction of the pistol meant they were done fooling around with us.

Catcalls eyed the pistol. "What about the sale? I shoot one, that demon can't fix her."

"If I can't find the girl that snuck under the door, then there won't be any auction. The boss might be willing to forgive us for being one short, but two? And one of them the teenage girl that's racking up all the online bids?"

Catcalls scowled. "He'll kill us."

"I'm going for the girl. If I can't find her in the next half hour, we're going to shoot them all, take what we've made so far and get out."

"What about the demon?" Catcalls asked.

"She gets back before I do, send her out to look for the girl. Next time she returns all she'll find is dead bodies and us gone. Let her try to explain what happened to the boss. Let him take it out on her."

With that, Pockmarks spun around and stalked purposefully out of the room, not even bothering to close the door. His footsteps echoed as he broke into a run. He slid through the half-open bay door, and into the darkness. He'd left both doors open, tempting us, calling us to freedom. One glance at Catcalls' face told me why. It didn't matter anymore. If one of us tried to run for it, he'd shoot them down. They were guys with nothing left to lose. Death, or sold into slavery. I knew which option I'd choose, but I still held out hope that my girls wouldn't face either.

If I couldn't free them now, I'd do it later. If I couldn't get them out of here before the sale, I'd do it later. I'd kill whoever bought me, track down every one of them and release them. They were family. And family didn't give up on each other. Family didn't turn their back on someone they'd pledged themselves to. Family didn't divide itself, didn't make someone choose sides, didn't tear their bonds apart over stupid, senseless matters and arrogant pride.

"You'd find her faster if two of you were looking," Sugar commented. I shook my head at her in warning, knowing exactly what she was thinking. If both guards were gone, we could escape. They couldn't track us all down once we were out of this building.

But I knew there was a horrible price to pay in that plan. My stomach knotted up at the thought of both men out there, hunting down Kitten. She was just a teenager, just a kid. She was probably scared and crying, running barefoot through whatever was outside those bay doors. I didn't want her to get caught, and her chances were better if she didn't have two men after her. But there were five girls here in this room with me that deserved freedom as well, and I knew that's what Sugar was thinking. The good of many over the good of one.

No. Never again. Unless that sacrifice was me, I would never do that again. I would never turn my back on someone I loved even for a moment. Never again.

"You got out of a locked room, and I'm thinking you'll do it again." The guard sneered. "That demon's helping you, isn't she? She let that girl die, helped the other one escape, and is trying to help you escape too. The bitch is setting us up to take the fall. Well, fuck her. It's her that's gonna take the blame for this. Her."

Kill us all, and let the boss blame the demon. Or if they found Kitten… I held my breath and eyed the gun, wondering if they would shoot Leethu. Could a demon recover from a gunshot wound? Weren't they afraid the boss would be just as mad over the loss of his succubus as the loss of nine, now seven, pieces of valuable merchandise?

"You must be really pissed at her," Sugar continued. "You're going to lose everything—all the money from our sale, all the money that you would have made helping with future sales. And the boss…he'll hunt you down and kill you for this. He might take his wrath out on the demon, but he'll know she didn't put bullets into our heads. He'll know. He'll hunt you down and kill you both."

"Shut up." Catcalls pointed the gun at her.

"But if you find Kitten, the kid, then it's all good, right?" Sugar's voice crackled as she stared at his gun. "You can blame the demon for the other two, and the boss will be okay with seven at the sale. Hell, Red and the girl alone will make him a fortune. You can tell him how you both screwed up the demon's plan and kept us from escaping."

"Shut up," he snarled.

"It will all be okay if you just find the girl. Lock us in here. Check the door and make sure it's locked, then go help find her. It's the only way you're going to get out of this mess alive."

The gun wavered. Indecision flitted across the guard's face—indecision and fear. Then a muscle twitched in his jaw and the gun roared.

Everyone screamed and huddled on their cots, covering their heads—everyone except me and Sugar. The blonde girl sat as if frozen. I panicked for a second, then saw the chunk out of the concrete wall behind her, about two feet above her head.

"Shut. Up." Catcall's voice was soft and even. "Or the next one is going between your eyes."

I saw Sugar's chest rise with a tiny inhalation, and she nodded. We all obeyed, silent and afraid to move. I kept looking through the open doorway, across the warehouse floor, through the space under the bay door into the dark night. I could smell the cool damp air, feel the sharp jab of broken pavement under my feet. Freedom, so close. So close but completely out of reach.

Something shimmered just outside the bay door. Movement. A man hunched down to squeeze under the half-opened door, pushing someone ahead of him. Tears stung my eyes as he straightened and I saw Pockmarks, holding Kitten tightly in front of him, one hand tight on her forearm, the other twisted into her hair. He marched her across the warehouse floor while I held back a sob, then shoved her through the door and ordered her to one of the empty cots.

Catcalls let out his breath in a whoosh. "Damn, I'm glad you found her. Wasn't looking forward to being on the run the rest of my life."

"Yeah me too," Pockmarks agreed, his eyes hard as he looked us over, counting, making sure we were all present and accounted for. "This shit can't happen again. Give me the gun, then go get that rope and the chains."

We all eyed each other, knowing what was coming. Sure enough, Catcalls returned and began to tie our hands behind our backs, chaining each one of us to the metal frame of a cot. When he came to me, he tied my hands, yanking the rope tighter than with the others, then pulled me to my feet.

"You can't kill her," Pockmarks told him. "We can't lose any more girls."

"She's the ringleader of this little rebellion," Catcalls replied. "I'm not leaving her in here with the rest of them. Who knows what they'll do next with her around?"

I glanced behind me at the girls as Catcalls hauled me to the door, silently promising them that I'd rescue them. Maybe not tonight. Maybe not tomorrow or this week, but I'd come for them. I wouldn't rest until they were safe and free.

They took me to the room where Onions had stayed, where he'd tied me to the bed and raped me. There were still bloodstains on the floor. The sheets were stiff and crusted brown with the man's blood, a perfect outline of white where my body had lain. Pushing me to sit on the bed, Catcalls yanked my one leg onto the mattress and chained it to the frame. I could lie down to sleep, but the chain was too short to put that foot onto the floor.

"Stay here, Red," Pockmarks warned. He'd kept the pistol aimed at me the whole time, and was now shoving it into my face. "If you run away, every one of those girls dies. Every last one of them. You run, and you're killing them."

He jabbed the barrel of the gun against my forehead for emphasis and I nodded, knowing that he meant it. When he left, he turned the lights off, swinging the door closed and locking it.

"I failed." It was as if something inside me had curled up and died. "I failed."

You tried. A voice inside me said. *You didn't give up. You won't give up. Until your dying breath, you'll be doing everything you can to find these girls and free them. Them and Leethu.*

But would my determination be enough? Sometimes someone did all the right things, fought with everything they had and still lost in the end. Sometimes the good guy didn't win. I'd suffered for my sins. I'd done my penance. But would it be enough? Would I be able to save these girls who'd become my family, or would I fail and be plunged into the depths of heartbreak and regret once more?

That night I'd heard loud voices in argument. I'd heard the screams of the girls as Leethu fixed them. She hadn't come to me. She would have known I had been already healed even if the guards hadn't told her, and it was better if we kept some distance between the both of us right now. The guards knew she had something to do with our escape attempt, and they'd quickly notice whatever the succubus and I had going on between us and use it for leverage against her. I slept fitfully, hearing every step, every clink of a beer bottle discarded through the door. I assumed it was morning when they came for me, leaving my hands tied as they escorted me back into the room with the others. My entrance was greeted with relieved smiles, but we had little to celebrate. Today was the sale.

One at a time we showered, one of the guards watching and "helping" while the other stood guard. Clean, we sat on the edge of our individual cots and waited. Leethu was out in the warehouse, and from the voices and sounds of metal chairs being unloaded and set up, she wasn't alone. It wasn't just about escaping two guards now, one with a gun. Were there two, three more out there? Our chances were slipping away, approaching slim to none.

Leethu slid into the room, her eyes briefly meeting mine before edging away. "The boss has arrived."

Pockmarks tensed, holstering the pistol and folding his arms across his chest, a studied expression of cool disinterest settling on his face. I bit back a smile. He would have seemed weak, needing a gun to hold a bunch of girls at bay. Catcalls made no attempt to hide his unease, swiping a hand across his forehead and shifting from foot to foot, the pole clasped tightly in his other hand.

They moved respectfully aside as the boss walked into our room. He was older than I'd expected—a man in his sixties with slicked-back silver hair and a wispy mustache. He was tan with lighter circles of skin around his eyes from sunglasses. A tan from the golf course? No, he looked more like the yacht type, with his open-collar button-down shirt and an expensive suit tailored for his fleshy body. He was clearly a man who liked to indulge—a man who wouldn't allow anyone to get in the way of what he wanted, whether that was a snifter of brandy or an empire of wealth built on human sex trafficking.

"Line up," Pockmarks ordered.

We stood and did as he said, partly because we were thrown off balance by the appearance of this new man in our room, and partly because the new man had a pistol in a shoulder holster clearly visible under his open suit jacket. I doubted he'd shoot us, not with the sale today, but I was pretty sure if any of us so much as sneezed, Catcalls wouldn't hesitate to hit us with the pole. Neither of the guards would want to appear weak or lacking in control in front of this guy, especially when he was about to realize he was missing some of his merchandise.

"Strip," Pockmarks ordered. We complied, and stood while the boss eyed us dispassionately.

"Leethu, do your thing," the boss commanded.

Suddenly the room was thick with sexual energy. Our pupils dilated, breath coming short and shallow. Every girl in the room felt like they were on the edge of an orgasm. The guards weren't unaffected either.

"Enough."

The atmosphere fell with the word and we all gasped. So that's what Leethu was to do at the auction. We'd be turned on, climax hovering teasingly just out of reach. And the clients would feel it too, wanting us and paying more than they probably would have under normal conditions. We'd all be drunk on sexual energy, to maximize profits.

"A nice batch," the boss commented. "Have King get more young girls next time. Ten to fourteen years old. That one has racked up some serious online bids already. Eight her age or a little younger. We can do a specialized sale."

"Will do boss," Pockmarks agreed quickly.

He moved down the line. "I like the Russian girl. Nice. Very nice. This Mexican girl has a great ass." He jabbed a finger at Baa. "And this one's a pretty blonde, although she looks a bit used up. No more hookers or junkies, okay? They're just not worth as much."

"Got it," Pockmarks replied.

"This…" He paused and stared at me. "Why is her hair that color? Her skin is amazing. It's like alabaster, but that hair is very unnatural."

"It wouldn't take the dye," Leethu explained. "We tried three different boxes, and they just washed right off."

"And you didn't think to use your demon abilities?" The boss's voice held a recrimination. "You can enhance breasts, but you can't change someone's hair color?"

"I tried, but I wasn't able to do so."

There was a staring match between the demon and the boss. "And why was that?" he finally asked.

Leethu shifted ever so slightly. "I believe she may have a tiny bit of demon in her background. Possibly a few generations ago."

"I see." He moved on down the line, then paused. "Didn't we have an Asian girl? And a black girl? King was bragging about the diversity of this bunch. I think I remember him saying something about a Russian, two Mexicans, an Asian, and a black girl."

I felt the tension in the room. Catcalls swiped his brow again. Leethu bit her lip, the eyes briefly meeting mine full of amusement.

"No, these are the only girls we have," Catcalls said, sweat dripping down his face.

"Leethu?" The boss turned to look at the succubus.

"There were nine. King sent us an extra this time. These girls are a feisty bunch and there were several escape attempts. The black girl died. The Asian girl escaped."

The air was so thick that I struggled to drag air into my lungs.

"The Asian girl escaped," the boss commented, his tone indicating nothing beyond mild curiosity. It frightened me more than any overt anger could.

"I had her behind a locked door," Pockmarks explained. "You told us we were allowed to sample. I didn't harm the merchandise. I left her behind a locked door with no windows, no means of escape. She was gone when I returned."

"And you didn't think to tell me?" The boss made a clucking noise with his tongue and shook his head.

"It was yesterday. She doesn't speak any English. No one is going to understand her. We'll move locations for the next sale." Pockmarks remained calm and collected, but I saw the edge of his eye twitch.

"Her value will be deducted from your take," the boss told him. "What happened to the black girl? I liked her picture. She was generating a lot interest online."

"She was punished." The look Pockmarks gave Catcalls was pure calculation. The boss followed his gaze and raised an eyebrow.

"The bitch hit me with a toilet lid," the guard explained. "Knocked me out and damned near escaped. I taught her a lesson. Not my fault if the demon refused to heal her."

I held my breath, praying that Leethu wouldn't take the blame for honoring my, and Deena's, decision.

"Isn't this the second girl that has died from your overzealous punishment?" the boss asked Catcalls.

The man looked as if he'd suddenly been turned to stone. "The first. I just got carried a bit away. This one, she deserved the beating. She hit me, could have killed me. And the demon should have fixed her. She refused to do it. She's trying to set me up—set both of us up. She helped the Chinese girl to get away. She's been helping them in their attempts to escape. She's refused to follow orders. We told her to heal the black girl, and she didn't."

The boss turned to her, waiting.

"She was beaten to death," the demon calmly explained. "Even if I had been able to fix her injuries, she would have died within a few days. They took the discipline too far. There is a limit to my abilities when it comes to repairing human injuries. As for the others, you know I am forbidden by my summoning contract to help any of these girls escape."

"The demon refused to fix the black girl and she died," Catcalls protested. "She didn't even try."

"I did all I could," Leethu lied. "I've repeatedly told them that I can only make cosmetic adjustments, repair minor broken bones, bruises, and abrasions. Internal bleeding, ruptured spleen, punctured lungs, perforated bowel, and swelling of the brain are beyond my skills."

"There seems to be a lot of things you can't do lately," the boss commented. "Hair color. Fixing the injuries of one of our product."

The demon didn't even flinch as she met his eyes with a steady gaze. "When you summon a succubus, you get a sex demon. If you want someone to heal mortal wounds, I'd suggest next time you call upon an angel."

I held my breath, worried she'd taken it too far. There was a moment of silence, then the boss chuckled. "True. So very true. I've no desire to summon an angel, though. In the future, my staff will just need to ensure they don't beat the merchandise to death. What do you imagine the worth of that dead girl to be?"

Catcalls relaxed. "Three grand maybe. She was one of the hookers, and older. She wouldn't get as much as the kid or the others."

"Still, she was very pretty from the picture." The boss shook his head, the corners of his mouth curving downward. "She had a very exotic look about her. I'm thinking she might have brought closer to six."

Catcalls swallowed hard. "Then take six out of my take for the sale. If that's more than my share, I'll pay the difference."

The boss smiled and nodded, the tension in the room dropping noticeably. "I appreciate your willingness to make financial restitution."

Then with a smooth motion, so fast that no one had time to react, he pulled the pistol from its holster and shot Catcalls in the chest. The man crumpled to his knees, hands pressing against the wound as blood poured between his fingers.

"Two girls have died because you don't know when enough is enough," the boss told him. "Two. I'm tired of losing valuable merchandise due to your inability to control yourself. It's embarrassing to tell clients that an advertised product has been pulled from the sale. It makes them think we're doing deals on the side, that we don't value their patronage. I'm tired of making excuses."

"I'm sorry." Blood bubbled from Catcall's mouth. "I won't do it again."

"No you won't." And with that, the boss pressed the barrel of the gun to the guard's forehead and pulled the trigger. My stomach lurched as blood, bone, and brain matter splattered across the wall and onto the baseboard. I glanced at the others and saw that while Pockmarks had paled significantly, Leethu appeared disinterested. No doubt she'd seen worse in Hel. No doubt she'd done worse.

"I'll send two other men to work with you for the next sale," the boss told Pockmarks. "I trust there will be no more escaped or dead merchandise?"

"No, sir," Pockmarks replied, his voice hitching on the last word. "No further issues."

"Good." The boss looked down at Catcall's body. "Take care of this. Stuff it in a back room or something. Make sure there is no blood or anything to alarm our more delicate clients." Then he turned to Leethu. "Prepare the girls. Auction begins in one hour."

* * *

"ARE YOU IN TROUBLE?" I whispered to Leethu once the men had left.

She shrugged. "Probably. I won't have as much freedom as before. He'll keep me contained and only let me out to accomplish specific tasks for him. It was worth it, though. I only wish I could have freed more of you." Her eyes met mine, her palm rising to cup my cheek. "I wish I could have freed *you*."

"I'm not giving up." I leaned into her hand. "No matter what happens, as long as I'm alive, I won't give up. I'll save these girls, and I'll save you too."

Her smile was sad, indulgent, as if I were a naive child to be humored. "I know you won't give up. Just promise me you'll keep yourself safe."

"Is there *anything* you can do to help us?" Pistol asked. "Cause a distraction? Rain down a plague of locusts? Throw a burning bush into the mix?"

Leethu shook her head. "There was some leeway before, but with the boss here...he will keep a tight leash on me. He knows magic. He has amulets and spells to instantly negate pretty much anything I could do."

The girls gathered close around us. "Will they chain us for the auction?" Sugar rubbed her wrists. "Maybe we can make a break for it."

"Seven against what are probably twenty guys?" Pillow's eyes widened. "And they have guns. They'll just shoot us."

"They will only shoot you as a last resort," Leethu told her. "But if you try to run, they'll catch you and tie you up, and laugh while they're doing it. A girl who tries to break and run is seen as a little bit of sport. It's fun for them. It livens things up a little."

"But there are seven of us," Pistol insisted. "Maybe if four of us cause enough of a commotion, the other three can sneak away."

"There is no way you can sneak away," Leethu said. "There will be guards at the exits and outside, and no amount of commotion is going to be enough for you to escape. Your best opportunity will be after the sale, when you are being transported by your buyer."

"But we'll be alone then," Kitten's voice shook. "I'll be alone in the back of a truck or van. How am I supposed to get away?"

"Wait until they stop for gas, and make a commotion," Pistol suggested. "Or tell them you need to go pee, then climb through the bathroom window. Anything. If there's an opportunity, take it. Don't be scared."

"Yeah, 'cause that worked so well for you and Tasha last time," Sugar drawled.

"It's better than just sitting around and being a slave for the rest of our lives," Pistol shot back.

"Hey." I stopped the argument with a wave of my hand. "Stop. We're a family. We might be separated after today, but we're still a family. Remember that. You're never alone. Never. Be strong. Escape if you can. Survive. We'll get out of this somehow. It's not going to end this way. It's not."

"That's a lot of feel-good woo-woo there, Red," Sugar scoffed. "I'll survive, because that's the one thing I'm good at, but we're gonna be on our own from here on out. This family thing was nice, but it's over. There's no more family. There's no miracle. It's every girl for herself."

Just like it was before. I looked around at my girls and felt my heart break. I'd fight. I'd do all I could to my dying breath to save them, but Sugar was right. There was no miracle. I needed every one of them to think for themselves.

"Survive." I tried to brand the word into their minds. "Survive and never give up hope."

Leethu sighed. "And perhaps pray that Miller does not buy any of you. Your chances of survival will be greater if you are purchased by another client."

I shivered, remembering the mention of this Miller before.

"He's some kind of serial killer?" Pillow caught her

breath. "He kills the girls he buys? That's why he's at every auction?"

"Not every auction," Leethu said. "But he is our most revered client. He doesn't often buy the highest priced girl, but he's a regular customer and occasionally he will buy two. Many of the clients are one-time only. Those are the ones you want. They are willing to pay a lot for the girl they choose. I think those girls stay alive and become personal slaves. Others run high-priced prostitution rings. They don't like to spend a lot of money, but sometimes buy several girls."

"That doesn't sound too bad," Sugar commented. "No different than what I was doing out on the street. And if they're charging a lot, they're probably treating their girls better."

"No," Leethu's mouth set into a grim line. "The rings cater to those with unusual tastes. I think those girls live longer than the ones sold to Miller and clients like him, but they do die."

"So, personal slave." Pistol took a deep breath. "How do we identify those buyers, and how do we appeal to them?"

It made me sick to think my girls had been reduced to this.

"I can help with that," Leethu told her. "I'll concentrate my energy on those buyers who I believe might be looking for a personal slave. They'll want you. They'll be eager to pay more than they originally wanted. Hopefully they will outbid the others. There are no guarantees though. I don't know the clients personally, and I'm not given access to their information. What I think is a safe buyer may be a killer attending for the first time."

Pistol nodded. "Thank you. It's better than nothing. I'll take my chances and just hope I don't get some Dahmer dude."

The demon turned to each of the girls in turn going down

the line and placing a kiss on their foreheads, muttering words in a strange language. Each girl shimmered with a glow, a glamour that drew the eye and quickened the pulse. When she was finished, she came to me.

"Do I get a kiss too?" I teased her, not wanting whatever we had to end on such a desolate note.

Her hands cupped my cheeks. "You don't need my glamour, Red Bird. Your beauty needs no enhancement." Something sparked in her dark eyes. "But I will still kiss you."

Her lips met mine—soft, sweet, and full of desperation. When she broke the kiss and stepped back, I saw there were tears in her eyes. "Good luck to all of you."

She turned and fled the room, closing the door behind her. I knew without even trying that it was no longer unlocked on the inside. This wasn't a good time for escape. Later perhaps. Later when we were alone and afraid, without each other's support.

My family was about to be fractured. And something deep down inside told me this wasn't the first time I'd experienced such a tragedy as this.

CHAPTER 22

We sat for what felt like days in our room, the only sounds our breathing and the faint noises from out in the warehouse. They'd taken our clothing away, but none of us used sheets or towels to cover ourselves. Why bother?

The air was cold and thick with fear. Kitten pressed up against me, shivering. It was like waiting for our execution. Time had run out, and now one by one we'd be led up to the stage, to the scaffold. All my determination withered. I slid my hand down to lace my fingers with Kitten's, so afraid for her. Her parents were probably panicking right now that she didn't return from band camp. Her sister would be climbing into a cold, empty bed, trying to hold tight to what memories she had. They'd mourn her forever. I'd mourn her forever. All these girls, I'd mourn them all, but this young, frightened girl most of all.

I flinched as the door opened.

"Line up." Pockmarks ordered. I saw a flash of defiance in Pistol's eyes, followed by fear as she dropped her gaze. Freedom was no longer our goal, survival was. Slavery was our future, and every one of us was hoping our buyers wouldn't kill us or make us wish that they'd kill us.

Kitten stayed close as we lined up. Pockmarks rearranged us into some predetermined order, then opened the door wide. The stage was lit by two tall lamps like the kind used in photoshoots. In front was a row of chairs. It looked like there were close to two dozen men there, although I was sure a few of them were bodyguards.

The boss stepped onto the stage and welcomed the crowd before gesturing toward us. "And here is today's selection."

"Move," Pockmarks growled, poking Sugar in the ass with the broom handle.

We moved. The guard brought up the rear, keeping us going forward at an even pace, occasionally smacking his hand with the stick, reminding us the price for defiance. He lined us up on the stage, spacing us a few feet apart. The lights radiated heat and I felt a trickle of sweat pool under my breasts. The buyers moved close, staring and commenting. I kept my gaze a few feet above their heads, trying to breathe, trying not to panic.

"Turn around." Pockmarks thumped the stick on the stage and the sound echoed like thunder. We turned, and while I could still hear the buyers commenting on our backsides, at least I could no longer see them.

"Face front," Pockmarks commanded. We complied.

The boss went into an explanation of how the bidding process would commence, reminding the buyers that there were several online bidders they'd be competing with. Then he offered closer examination.

They were allowed on stage two to three at a time to run their hands over our flesh, to pinch and prod and put their fingers anywhere they wanted. They checked teeth, checked the firmness of our breasts and butts, checked how tight we were. Silent tears rolled down Pistol's cheeks, her face pink with humiliation. Baa was nearly hyperventilating, she was breathing so fast. Sugar had that dead, resigned expression in her eyes of someone who'd been through this sort of thing before. And Kitten...poor Kitten. The boss was very clear that he wouldn't tolerate any of the clients harming the highlight of the auction, but she was clearly drawing a lot of attention. Every single man fondled her, touched her, asked about guarantees of her virginity as well as her age. One man was disappointed that she was thirteen, asking the boss if he anticipated having anything under the age of twelve at the next sale.

Something flickered inside me at the boss's affirmative response, and his announcement that he intended to have several sales that were exclusively with product under the age of fourteen.

Once we'd all been felt up, the boss fielded several questions. He had a few of us turn around again for a backside view, then announced the auction would begin with the most anticipated piece of merchandise.

Kitten. He was going to sell her first. I clenched my jaw tight as Pockmarks grabbed her around the neck, squeezing as he pushed her forward.

"Internet bids are up to eight thousand on this one. Just look at her in person. Only thirteen years old and a virgin. Beautiful, young, nubile, and a blank slate to train as you want. You'll have many years of fun with this one before she even gets a hint of a stretch mark. Isn't she adorable? How about nine thousand? Do I hear nine?"

I shook with rage. We were just money to these people, just product. Deena's death hadn't mattered. A young girl died, and it didn't matter to any of them beyond the loss of money and the embarrassment of having to pull her from the auction. Catcalls beat her to the point that the bones in her face had broken, that her skull had broken, that her ribs had splintered and punctured one of her lungs. She'd been in agony. He'd raped her, beat her. He'd killed her. And none of them cared.

Would Kitten face the same thing?

"Ten thousand from Miller. Do I hear ten five?"

My breath left my lungs in a whoosh. Miller. The one who killed the girls he bought. The one who tortured and killed his girls. He couldn't buy Kitten. Let him take me instead, not Kitten. I followed the bids anxiously, my heart leaping every time Miller raised his hand. Thirteen thousand. Surely he wouldn't spend thirteen thousand dollars on a young girl just to kill her. Those crazies grabbed women off the street, they took junkies and prostitutes and girls who wouldn't be missed. They didn't spend huge sums of money buying someone just to kill them. I stared at the man, horrified as his thoughts began to spool into my mind.

He'd keep Kitten alive. She'd be special. All the other girls would die, but Kitten would be trained, coveted like an expensive crystal vase. But the things he would do to her….

"Going once. Going twice. Sold to Miller for thirteen thousand."

"No!" Kitten cried out, her hands covering her mouth. Her shoulders shook with sobs as Pockmarks grabbed the girl's arm and turned to lead her off the stage and into the hands of her owner.

"No!" I echoed, stepping forward to block them from the stairs. "He can't have her. I won't let him have her."

"Red Bird, don't," Leethu warned, her voice low with fear. "Let her go." I ignored her and stood my ground.

You can't help them if you're dead, the demon silently told me. *Let her go.*

But I couldn't. Not Kitten. And not to Miller. I raised my chin and met Pockmarks' eyes. "He can't have her."

There was laughter, a few comments of how I was feisty

and would be fun to break. Pockmarks raised his stick. "Get back in line."

I reached out and grabbed the wrist of the hand that held Kitten and held tight. "Let her go."

The stick hit me on the arm. I gritted my teeth and met his eyes. I raised my hand at the next blow, grabbing the stick in my hand.

Thunder—far off but closing in fast. The stage trembled faintly under my feet. The stick creaked in my hand. Pockmark's eyes widened then narrowed.

"Tell you what," Miller called out. "I'll throw in an extra thousand and take her as well."

"Sold," the boss replied.

A smirk curled Pockmarks' lips. "You can watch him fuck her, Red. Won't that be fun?"

I hated this man, hated him as much as I'd hated Catcalls, as much as I'd hated Onions. Fury rose from my depths, spreading outward with a silvery light. Sweat beaded on Pockmarks' skin, and he blinked in surprise. The sweat turned pink, then red—blood welling from his pores, streaming down his face and body, soaking his clothing. The blood began to smoke. The clients in the audience gasped then fell suddenly quiet.

The silence was broken by a piercing scream from the guard. Pockmarks' hand left Kitten's arm and yanked from my grasp as he pawed at eyes that were bubbling and blistering in their sockets. Smoke came from his mouth and nostrils, from the blood pouring from his skin. Then the screams ended, and hot blood flew everywhere, splattering me, the stage, the buyers seated near us. Pockmarks dropped to the ground, his eyes empty black craters.

It was just like Onions. He'd been killed just as Onions had been killed. *Was* there a guardian angel protecting me, as

Deena had thought? Or...or was it *me* that had somehow done this?

There was a gunshot that echoed around the warehouse, ringing in my ears long after the sound died. I saw Kitten slap her hands over her mouth, crumpling at the waist as she stared at me in horror. I heard a scream in the faded echoes of the gunshot. Leethu. It had been her scream, crying out in fury and fear.

Pain. Sharp and hot, radiating from my chest outward. I looked down and saw the nice round hole gushing red. My knees crumpled and hit the floor.

"Don't kill her," Leethu pleaded, tears in her voice. "I beg you, don't kill her. I'll do anything, just don't kill her. I can fix her. She'll be okay. Give her to me. I'll make sure she doesn't cause any more trouble. Please."

Two legs moved into my line of sight. I traced them upward and saw the boss standing in front of me, a pistol pointed at my head. My chest hurt. My legs felt cold. I couldn't feel my hands. A thought flitted through my mind, wondering why the boss didn't explode on the inside like the others had. It would be really nice if that happened. Why wasn't that happening?

"You want her do you?" The boss's face blurred and tilted, but I was sure he was sneering. "She's some kind of demon, isn't she? She has to be a demon, and not just a little, not someone generations ago. She's a full demon and you lied to me."

"I didn't! She might be a half-breed." Leethu's voice was closer. Shaky. Higher-pitched than normal. "She's *not* a full demon. I swear it, I swear it. I can keep her in line. Please give her to me, please."

"No."

Gunshot. Screaming. I could do nothing to catch myself as I fell to the floor. I couldn't close or move my eyes. Cold.

Static. Something touched my cheek—a hand and something wet. The pain faded and I shrank down deep inside, pulling away from flesh into something hot and bright. I hovered, rising above my body like a morning fog.

"Get over there and do your job," the boss ordered Leethu, grabbing her and yanking her away from me. She stumbled down the steps. Then the boss took Kitten by the arm and led her down to Miller who pulled her close to his side.

"The next up for sale is this lovely Mexican girl. Just look at that ass. Turn around so everyone can see how perfect your ass is. Beautiful, isn't it? Just begging to be spanked or whipped, or gripped tight as you take her from behind. Who'll bid a thousand for this one?"

I'd failed. I'd failed Kitten. I'd failed Leethu. I'd failed them all. I stared sightlessly at Baa, her back toward the buyers, her lips trembling although she had them clenched tight. I'd failed.

"You have to choose, Uri." Marax's wings snapped close to his body. We were on a beach, the surf roaring and smashing against the rocks. We could speak privately down here without fear of being overheard. And increasingly, Marax and I discussed things that should never be overheard.

"I can change his mind. Just give me some time," I pleaded, taking a few awkward steps toward him. He was more comfortable in corporeal form than I was. These legs were like moving about on foreign objects. They didn't feel like a part of me. I struggled to make them do what I wanted. Marax always told me I needed to embed myself further into the cells, drive my spirit-self into the very flesh of this form I'd created.

This is what we wanted the humans to be. Like this. It was a step in their evolution—an evolution we would carefully manage. They'd been chosen. It had been voted on. The Ruling Council had already begun to form the committees who would present the gifts of Aaru to the humans over the next three billion years. Slow and steady evolution. We had high hopes for them. We hoped they'd even surpass the elves in what they could attain.

Well, some of us had high hopes for them. Others felt we were making a terrible mistake, that we shouldn't be meddling in the evolution of these beings, or any beings at all, that we should leave their future to fate, to an increasingly chaotic universe.

"It's not me who needs to be patient, Uri, it's your brother."

Samael. It had started as a disagreement. They always disagreed, but this time the argument had taken on a life of its own. Samael had some valid points, but Michael had been increasingly intractable over the last few million years. He wouldn't budge. Now it was a matter of pride between two angels who had never managed to rid themselves of that sin.

Samael had said Michael just needed to get laid, to assume corporeal form and indulge in sensation for a glorious moment or two. I tended to agree, but was sure I was one of the only Angels of Order who would.

They told me I was corrupted by my mating, by this Angel of Chaos that stood in front of me. I felt my lips curl up as I contemplated the things Marax had talked me into doing. Being corrupted was fun, especially with someone you loved with every bit of your spirit-self.

"You need to make a choice," he repeated.

"I can't. I have family on both sides. I have you. I'll continue to try and talk sense into the pair of them. That's all I can do."

"It's war, Uri." He let the words settle around us. "Michael declared war. You need to pick a side, to make a choice."

"I'm an Angel of Order," I whispered, suddenly afraid.

"And I'm an Angel of Chaos." His eyes were dark as they met mine, the irises bleeding outward to swallow everything in a glossy black. "We're more than what they label us, Uri. Where is your heart?"

With him. Always with him, and with Haka, the child we'd created between us.

"I can't just break with Michael and the others. I'll be in a better position to stop this madness if they don't think I'm a traitor." *It wouldn't come to war. And if it did, it would all be over in a few centuries or so. Micha and Gabe had the human project to occupy them. Rafi would go along with whatever his elder brothers said. Samael had the attention span of a gnat. It would all blow over.*

"Is that really your decision, Uri?"

It sounded so final, like a life-or-death choice. It would be fine. It would all be forgotten soon enough. I'd convince them to stop arguing and it would all be fine.

"Come with me, Uri." His voice was so full of love...and a sharp edge of desperation.

"I'm an Angel of Order," I repeated. I'm a coward. I always side with Michael. *Marax would forgive me, but Micha never would.*

"I love you," he told me as he turned away. "I'll always love you."

It was the last time I'd ever hear him say that.

There was a roaring noise like a freight train was rushing by inches from my head. I felt the broken flesh that sat below me, felt the beginning stages of its decay. I grabbed hold, seizing each molecule, each atom, each particle. Light. Power. Breath. Life.

My eyes blinked. My hand stirred. My skin shimmered, alabaster white, clean, whole. Baa froze, her eyes huge as she stared at me.

I stood. The boss stopped his auctioneer routine, fumbling at the gun in a holster at his side, but my attention was elsewhere.

"Take your hand from my sister," I commanded, pointing at Miller. At the words I felt huge wings snap from my back, extending outward with the crack of thunder.

The room erupted into chaos. People dove for the floor, some ran for the door. Miller let go of Kitten and slowly edged away, his hands raised.

Shots rang out, tore into my body. I laughed, thinking it funny that the boss had finally managed to get his pistol out of the holster. I turned to him and smiled, healing wounds as the metal fell from my flesh. I stepped off the stage, hovering with my wings outstretched for a moment before slowly lowering myself to the ground.

"Kill her," the boss shouted, backing away from me. "I command you to kill her."

Leethu shook her head, squinting at me as if she were staring directly at the sun. "An angel. You expect me to kill an angel?"

"Yes, kill her," the boss screamed, stumbling against one of the metal chairs and nearly going down.

"No." There was a flicker of something in her eyes—awe, and an emotion I hadn't seen in a very long time. "No. I will not kill her."

"I command you to kill her. You have to. The summoning. You have to."

"Nothing in my summoning says I need to kill an angel." Leethu turned to look at the boss, a smile curling the edges of her lips. "Nor does it say I need to protect you from one."

He bolted.

"Leethu, can you make sure no one hurts the girls?" I followed at a more leisurely pace, knowing he'd never get that stupidly slow bay door up enough to get out before I got there.

There was a deafening clang noise at the door. An amplified voice informed us that the police were there, with a warrant, and that they were coming in. The boss was halfway across the warehouse, but quickly reversed, running back around to the stage. The buyers who hadn't already fled raced about in a state of panic, searching for an alternate exit.

I sprinted for the boss, dodging the buyers and around the chairs. Was he going to try to grab a hostage?

A door flew open and hit the rack that held the chairs, shoving it forward and knocking several onto the floor. Two humans pushed their way in, wearing protective gear and sporting some rather large firearms. The banging noise from the bay door grew louder, combined with the squawk of metal being cut and bent.

The boss reached out, but instead of grabbing one of the girls, he grabbed Leethu. The succubus wound back her fist to hit him, but her arm stopped, as if an invisible cord held it in place. The boss laughed and slapped her face. "Get the cops out of here. Do what you're supposed to do and get the police away so we can get out."

"I'm going to kill you," she snarled. "Maybe you won't die directly by my hand, but I swear on all the souls I Own that I'm going to see you dead in the next few hours. I'm going to dance on your broken body, devour your flesh, torture your soul for all of eternity."

Her eyes glowed gold. I felt the heat of her anger, but she did as he said. The banging stopped. The two guys with their rifles hesitated, lowering the guns and looking toward her.

"There's nothing here," she told them. "Nothing for you. Leave now. Don't make me harm you. Leave now."

I saw it—saw the calming blue of her words, felt her compulsion. Just as the two officers turned to leave, I reached out and sealed the door shut. The boss snarled, and pushed Leethu aside, grabbing Pillow instead. I should have had the girls run and hide, but instead I'd kept them all together, counted on Leethu to protect them. But Leethu couldn't do anything against the man who'd summoned her.

I could. And a hostage was no impediment to me.

The ground trembled underneath the warehouse. The stage shook, chairs fell over. The buyers still running around the warehouse looking for an exit screamed and cried "earthquake" as they dove for shelter.

Narrow stone monoliths shot up from the ground, blocking the back door. The boss turned to run, shoving Pillow in front of him as a shield. "I'll kill her." He pointed the gun at Pillow. "Back off and let go or I'll kill her."

"No, you won't." I teleported Pillow away from his side to the others, turned the gun in his hand to dust, then I raised my hand. Stone shot up from the ground, blocking his flight, caging him in. The only way out was toward me, and it was clear from the look on the man's face, that was a direction he didn't want to take. I flew up to the stage, cornered him with his back against the stone. Then in spite of his pleading, I reached out and wrapped my hand around his neck. He fell apart, grains of sand raining down onto the stage as his body disintegrated, setting his soul free for a judgement that wasn't mine to give.

His death liberated Leethu, and she immediately dropped the compulsion.

The bay door burst open, and dozens of armed men ran in, shouting that they were police and that everyone should be kneeling on the floor with their hands on the backs of their heads.

"Do as they say," I told the girls with a reassuring smile. Lacy's cavalry had arrived. She'd done it. Without knowing one word of English, the girl had managed to bring the police to the rescue. Even if I had died as the boss had intended, my girls would have been safe.

I looked over at Leethu. She smiled at me.

"Should I be down on my knees as well?" Her eyebrow arched with the absurdity of the suggestion. I saw her power, saw her spirit-self glowing inside her corporeal shell and felt something I hadn't felt for over two-and-a-half-million years.

"No, you should be in my arms," I told her.

She glided toward me, elegant and beautiful, my equal in every way no matter what she might think. And it was into her outstretched arms I went. My family. My new family. The family I would never fail to put first.

CHAPTER 23

"*D*amn, Red." Sugar coughed, her face gray with the dust my monoliths had stirred up from the warehouse floor. "Could you have smited that guy without a damned earthquake? For a second I thought I was going to be buried alive. And what's with this Easter Island shit here?"

Kitten walked forward, reaching out a shaking hand to touch my wings. I felt the touch of her fingers through every nerve in my body—deeper than my body, right down to my spirit-self. "Are you…are you an angel?"

It seemed presumptuous to say "yes" when I knew that her definition of the word didn't exactly match what I was.

"Yes, she's an angel." Pistol gave me a tired smile. "Even better than a mermaid."

Kitten smiled. "Yes, even better than a mermaid. Can we still call you Red? What's your real name?"

Uriel. My name was Uriel. "To you I'll always be Red."

The other girls clustered around, tentatively touching my wings and exclaiming over their softness. We all talked at once, relieved, excited, thankful that we'd be going home. Well, some of us were thankful. Sugar looked at my wings, then glanced over at Leethu before staring out the broken bay door.

"Family," I reminded her. "I'll not abandon you, Sugar. Having wings don't make me any less your sister."

A voice cleared behind us and I turned to see an officer who was not wearing a helmet, although he did have a protective vest on over his uniform.

"Excuse me. Your…holiness? We'll need everyone to come down to the station and give statements on what happened. Do we need to take anyone to the hospital? Does anyone need medical attention?" He glanced at my wings. "Probably not."

I'd take care of anything Leethu missed. "None of the girls need medical attention. I'll accompany them to the station and give a statement if you wish, but there's someone I need to find first. One of the girls who managed to escape."

He grinned. "Lai? From Laos? I was going to say that you owe your lives to her, but I guess not." He looked around, eyes lighting on the pile of sand in an alcove of tall slabs of stone. "We were hoping to take in David Brunell. The FBI has been trying to get enough on him for an arrest, but he's a slippery guy. I'm assuming that's who was heading this operation."

"If you have photos of David Brunell, we can verify that, but I'm afraid there are no remains to identify. And no living man to arrest." I felt a bit of guilt at that. These humans deserved to deliver their own justice. I'd need to remember in the future to be less quick to act, to work with these beings and not assume their laws were the same as ours.

"Who killed him?" The officer waved a quick hand. "No, I don't want to know that. There's not a prosecutor in the state that would want to bring murder charges against an angel. How could we ever find a jury of your peers? Or attempt to hold you in a human jail? I guess these sorts of things would need to be turned over to whoever handles that in heaven, or wherever you're from."

"Aaru," I told him.

"Aaru. It would be like an extradition, I guess." He looked up at me and shook his head. "Dragons and unicorns and trolls. Elves. Demon and angels. It's crazy. It's crazy, and we don't know how we're supposed to deal with all this. But I guess you know that already."

I didn't. And I felt bad about that as well. What had happened since I'd been gone? What had happened in the brief year I'd been alone in a cave, letting my guilt eat me alive? I was back, and that meant I'd need to resume my place on the Ruling Council. I'd be overwhelmed by all the stuff my brothers had, no doubt, set aside for my return.

Things would be different. I was back, but I was no longer the angel I'd been before. I'd do what was right, even if that meant facing down all of my remaining brothers. I loved them. They'd always be my family, but I had another family to think about now.

"Come on," I told my sisters. "Let's answer these questions the police have, find Lai, and then go home."

Home. Our home. Because no matter how far apart we might go, we'd always be family, and we'd always have a home. I'd make darned sure of that.

EPILOGUE

Lai's story

J'd followed the man out of the room, away from the safety of the other girls. I'd done everything that horrible guard had wanted me to do. Smiled. Been eager and obedient, even feigning enthusiasm. The whole time I'd been imagining killing him, sliding a dagger into his chest, lopping off his testicles one at a time before slowly carving his dick from his body.

I'd endure. Just like the woman with the red hair had endured. Just like the dark-skinned woman who had gone with them earlier had endured.

His attentions went on forever. He would climb on top, then when he was finished, he would play with me until he recovered. Often I was to help him recover, using my hands and my mouth. He was on top. Then I was on my knees with my face pressed against the bed, his hand firm on my neck. Each time I kept my eyes lowered, smiling and nodding, my hands calmly folded in my lap when he was done and fondling me. I thought it would never end, but finally he rose to put on his clothing, motioning for me to sit on the bed and stay.

He left, and I heard the door lock behind him. I was untied. I knew he was confident that I'd be right where he'd left me, that I wouldn't move. And he was right. How long would he be gone? I was afraid to even put my clothing on in case he returned and was displeased with me. I kept envisioning the other girl, the one who had come back barely alive. They'd beaten her almost to death. I didn't want that to happen to me. I didn't want that to happen to anyone else.

The lock clicked and the door opened. I lowered my eyes, my heart racing, thankful that I hadn't gotten dressed or shifted an inch from where he'd told me to stay. *Don't hurt me. Don't kill me. Do whatever you want with my body, just don't hurt me.*

But when I peeked up from under my lashes, I saw it wasn't one of the men, it was the evil spirit. It was bad enough spreading my legs and smiling for some guard. Would this spirit expect the same? She was in the form of a woman, but I didn't want to imagine what sorts of appendages a spirit could produce to cause me pain and humiliation.

She'd already caused great pain among the other girls. The red-haired one had been trying to win the spirit to her side, but I feared she was no witch and lacked the power to make this spirit help us, to turn her evil to good. I kept my mouth shut, holding very still and hoping she didn't notice me.

The spirit ignored me, walking over to pick up a pencil from a table, then whistling softly as she left. The door didn't lock behind her. I had listened carefully, but had never heard the sound of the bolt sliding closed. As I watched, the door even swung open a few inches.

I heard the shuffling sound of footsteps retreating and

hadn't hesitated. I slid off the bed and pulled on my clothing as quickly as possible. Carefully I eased the door open and slipped out, shutting it behind me. Hugging the wall, I looked around and saw no one—not even the spirit. But something odd caught my eye. There was a trail of flower petals on the floor.

Flower petals. The spirit had spoken to me in my language before the man had taken me away. She had said that I was to be obedient and that the flowers would lead me to freedom.

Was it a trap, or was this spirit not quite as evil after all? Perhaps the red-haired girl *was* a witch. Perhaps she'd convinced this spirit to help us. I was terrified that I'd find one of the guards at the end of this trail, that he'd beat me with the stick for not being obedient, that I'd die, but there was a greater fear in my heart. Whatever future these two men had planned for us, it was far worse than what we'd experienced so far. I was afraid, but I needed to get out of here, and I needed to help those other girls.

Picking up each petal as I walked, I eventually found myself in the rear of the building, behind where the rack of chairs had stood. There was a door, hidden from view. It was a fire door with bolts and alarms, and it was ajar. I slipped out, not daring to close the door in case it set off the alarm or made a noise. And just as I'd turned to run away, I saw a woman's hand ease the door shut, locking it tight.

Hope. It was a wonderful thing. The sweet fresh air I now breathed was full of hope. The jagged, cracked blacktop beneath my feet was full of hope. I ran, barely noticing the pain in my bare feet. I climbed a fence. I struggled through weeds and past abandoned buildings, listening for the sound of traffic. Near dawn I finally made it to a road that looked as if it might have seen some recent travel. A car came toward me and I tried to flag it down, my heart racing. What if it was the guards? What if they'd discovered I was missing and had come after me in this car? I couldn't outrun them with my bare feet.

It wasn't the guards in the car, and the vehicle didn't stop. It didn't even slow down, the man behind the wheel studiously not looking toward me as he roared past.

Which way should I go? Was it safe to stay on this road, or should I try to get farther away before I tried to flag down another car? I was well aware that time was running out. With me gone, would the guards move the other girls? I felt sick at the thought that any help I summoned might not arrive in time to save them.

I turned left on the road, trying in vain to get someone to stop for me. The sun climbed high in the sky then began to sink. My feet were so bruised and cut that I struggled to walk. I started to cry.

"Stop. Please stop," I shouted through my tears at another oncoming car. "Please, someone help me!"

I broke into sobs as the car pulled over and hobbled toward the man who got out, nearly falling into his arms. Everything poured out of me, jumbled words that told the story of how I'd been tricked into coming here, paying all the money my family and I had, thinking there was a job for me. Throughout it all, I kept repeating that the other girls needed help, that there were more girls, that I feared they would be killed if no one came to save them.

Of course, he didn't understand me. No one understood me here except for the spirit. The man peered at me in concern, saying words I couldn't comprehend. It was then I realized he was a police man, with a badge and a hat, and lights on the top of his car. I tried again to tell him, motioning to his gun, holding up eight fingers for the girls he needed to save, waving behind me and pantomiming myself being beaten.

Another vehicle arrived, also with lights but so much like the truck that had brought us to the warehouse that I began screaming and trying to get away. I clung to the police man, terrified that these people with the truck were going to take me back to the warehouse and put me back in the locked room. The guards would kill me for trying to escape them. This police man was my only hope—was the other girls' only hope as well.

The police man spoke to me in soothing tones and motioned for me to get into the back of his car. Then he followed the people with the truck down the road. I couldn't stop crying. I'd never been so frightened in my life, even when they put me in that first truck with the other girls, even when that guard led me away. Was this man a friend of the guards? Was he going to return me to them? There was a wire mesh separating us, and I couldn't open the doors. Had I made a horrible mistake? I'd trusted this man, but maybe I'd been wrong.

I nearly fainted when we pulled up to a building that was clearly a hospital. I went willingly along with the truck-people this time, but started crying again when the police man started to walk away. No! He didn't understand me. If he left without knowing what I was saying, there would be no one to help the other girls.

A kind woman helped me down a hallway and into a bed. She checked my pulse and blood pressure and spoke to me in a soft, cheerful voice as she looked at my torn feet. I kept repeating my story, somehow hoping that the words would eventually make sense to her. Then she patted me on the shoulder and left. I didn't know what to do. Was there no one in this town who spoke my language? Why did *I* have to be the only one who escaped, when no one could understand me? Why couldn't it have been one of the other girls?

I sat there forever, feeling numb, giving up hope. I was

safe now, but I felt as if I'd forsaken the others. How could I live with myself if they died because I'd been unable to save them? I called out to the spirit, hoping she could hear me, that she could unlock the door and leave flower petals for the others. Why had she let me go and not anyone else? Why not the red-haired woman who she clearly felt drawn to, the one I suspected was a witch?

It was hours later that a woman arrived, flanked on either side by two men. She had a cool confidence that let me know she was in charge, so once again I tried to tell her my story, hoping that she spoke my language. She shook her head with a sad smile, pantomiming a telephone. Then she examined my feet and the other two began to clean and bandage them.

When they came back, one of the men carrying a big box with a blue telephone and two receivers. The woman doctor handed me a card and ran her finger down the print.

It was all gibberish—words and letters in languages I didn't understand. I shook my head and she turned the page, again sweeping her finger down the text and looking at me expectantly. It was then that I saw it—words I recognized as my own. I pointed to the words, starting once again to tell my story, but she held up her hand to stop me and turned to say something to the others.

They handed me one of the receivers while the doctor took the other and dialed. A man spoke on the line, and with his words I started to cry once more. I understood him. I understood every word he was saying. My story poured out of me—everything that had happened from the moment I'd stepped foot in this country to when the police man stopped for me on the road. I told him about my rape, about the girl who had been beaten so badly, about the seven other girls— all of them still locked in the warehouse. He translated and I watched the doctor's eyes grow wide. She barked out orders to the other two and they hurried away.

The man on the phone asked where I was hurt, if they'd beaten me, or injured me in any way besides the rape. I told him that I'd not been hurt, but that many of the girls had.

The police man came back, and spoke with the doctor, then left, motioning that he was going to stand right outside. The doctors checked between my legs, taking samples and speaking to me with soothing words. The whole time I kept looking for the police man. Had he gone to rescue the others? I needed to make sure he was going to help them. I needed the blue phone back with the man who spoke my language.

When the doctors were done, they handed me my clothing. After I dressed, they brought the blue phone back, and this time it was the police man who took the other receiver. I told him my story once more, answering all his questions, impatient that he *do* something, that he rescue the others before it was too late.

He had me draw a crude map of where I'd gone when I'd run, then asked if I could point out the building if he drove me by there. I shivered in fear, but trusted him to keep me safe. He told me he was going to rescue the others, but that they had to be careful. They had to do paperwork things to make sure the bad men would go to jail, and they had to plan so that my friends, my sisters, would not be harmed during the rescue.

My sisters. I don't know if they felt the same, but these last few days had created a family. We were bound together now, no matter how far we might roam.

The blue phone was taken away, and I went with the police man. We drove through the night, and finally I was able to point out the building, recognizing the fence and the bay doors. Then he took me to a building with lots of other police officers who ran around in a flurry of activity. The police man put me in a room with a table and chairs, gave me more food than I could eat in a week and several cans of soda, then left.

Hours I sat. I knew it was morning, knew this was the day bad things were supposed to happen to us. With each sweep of the clock hand I grew more anxious and afraid. Had I been too late? What if the police man arrived to find an empty warehouse and my sisters gone?

I'd dozed off when the door finally opened and I saw her. It was the red-haired girl. Her skin glowed with a pearl-like sheen. Her eyes were black pools, shining with an inner light. And extending from her back were two enormous feathered wings. They were crimson like her hair, with gold feathers along the tips. They were folded tight as she came through the door, but expanded once she cleared the doorway.

She was *not* a witch.

I stared at her without comprehension. Had she died? Was this her spirit come to bid me goodbye? Or was she truly an angel? There had been rumors of them for the last few months, that angels and demons were walking the earth in numbers greater than ever before. We'd already seen elves and dragons and phaya naga, angels and demons weren't such a stretch of the imagination for us anymore.

"I've come for you Lai," she told me. Then she stepped aside and the others walked in. Tears filled my eyes. I felt that all I seemed to do the last few days was cry, but this time they were tears of joy. I jumped to my feet and ran to them, hugging each one and telling them I was so glad they were free, that they were alive. My heart was full. I even hugged the spirit-woman who had come in last to stand beside the angel.

"Will you send me home?" I asked the angel. Would I be given a plane ticket and sent back, or turned out on the street to fend for myself? It would be a hard life, but at least I was free. At least I was alive.

"If you wish, but you always have a home with us, Lai." The angel hugged me close, wrapping her wings around me in addition to her arms. They were soft and warm, like a childhood blanket. Instantly I felt at peace, protected and loved. "We're family, all of us. No matter where we go, there will always be a bond to hold us together. We are only a thought away from each other. Do you understand?"

I nodded against her, breathing her in. She had an earthy smell, like autumn leaves, like the damp ground in spring-time, like warm summer sun on freshly mown grass. I did understand. There was something magical that held us together—something this angel had done. We'd never be alone. Our sisters would always know where we were, if we needed their help. And with one thought we could arrive. It was a precious gift that this angel had given us.

"But you and the others who wish to remain—you and Sugar and Baa, and Pillow until her father is released—you will all have a home with me. It will be a home for all my sisters as long as they need it, a home they can return to whenever they want."

"And you?" I asked, looking into her strange, other-worldly eyes. "You will be like our mother?"

"I will be your sister, your sister and protector. From this point forward, I will be your guardian angel."

It was a miracle. All the pain of the last week faded away, replaced with the warmth of family and home. My family. Mine. I was finally coming home

Unholy Pleasures

City of Lust

* * *

<u>Imp World Novels</u>

No Man's Land

Stolen Souls

Three Wishes

Northern Lights

Far From Center

Penance

* * *

<u>Northern Wolves</u>

Juneau to Kenai

Rogue

Winter Fae

Bad Seed

ACKNOWLEDGMENTS

A huge thanks to my copyeditors Kimberly Cannon and Jennifer Cosham whose eagle eyes catch all my typos and keep my comma problem in line, and to Damonza, for cover design.

Most of all, thanks to my children, who have suffered many nights of microwaved chicken nuggets and take-out pizza so that Mommy can follow her dream.

ABOUT THE AUTHOR

Debra lives in a little house in the woods of Maryland with her sons and two slobbery bloodhounds. On a good day, she jogs and horseback rides, hopefully managing to keep the horse between herself and the ground. Her only known super power is 'Identify Roadkill'.

debradunbar.com